On This Night

by

A. D. Inman

Prologue

I sit alone staring out across the room in silence, as I usually do, night after night at the local bookstore. I sip on my third coffee trying to cheat sleep as I flip mindlessly through the pages of another book. I wonder what my life would be like if it wasn't like this one.

I'm not paying much attention to anything around me because on this night as with many before leading up to it, I am lost, lost in more ways than one. This is my last few moments alive. Death will come quick, and this life, the life that I have been forced to live will finally be over.

Chapter 1: Broken

Sitting up in the middle of my bed with a sudden jolt, I stare out into the darkness of my room feeling my heart pounding as if it will burst right out of my chest; the dream was so vivid, so shocking, and so very real. I lay back down and glance at my cell phone for the time. It is 3:35 in the morning. Slowly I shifted my gaze towards the ceiling, staring wide-eyed and alert as troubling thoughts run through my head. Forcing my eyes closed, I try to clear my mind.

The alarm sounds loud as I roll over and turn it off. It is now 6:30 a.m. and I feel as though I have been lying in my bed in a state of limbo the whole night. Not quite asleep but not awake either. The day starts as it usually does with my parents rushing around the house getting ready for work, kissing me on the forehead, and slamming the door behind them in a hurry as they leave in separate cars. I trudge into the kitchen, make some toast with butter, and pour a glass of soymilk. Slouching at the kitchen table, I eat my breakfast and then make my way into the bathroom to get ready for school. I slowly pull on the plaid uniform skirt and button up the light-yellow collared shirt. I am a senior at the private high school not far from my house and today is the last day of the school year.

As I step out onto the porch, I can see that it has rained during the night and the ground is still soggy. I feel my shoes sinking slightly into the earth beneath me as I walk around to the driver's side door of my little blue hatchback. The morning air is sticky, and it makes my clothes cling to me in an unwanted fashion. As I sit down on the seat, I look at my appearance in the mirror on the sun visor. My hair which I neatly brushed in the house, is now a frizzy mess from the humidity. I try smoothing it back into place with my hands without much success.

The drive to school only takes about ten minutes, but I am running late. The lot is nearly full when I get there, and I must park in the farthest spot from the main campus building. The bell begins to ring as I hurry past the cars stepping in a puddle of mud on my way. I brush my feet off on the mat at the front entrance and traipse into the office to get a tardy slip. The office is much warmer than it should be, and I wonder if the air conditioning isn't working properly. The day has already started all wrong.

The hallways are empty, and I feel my stomach flip at the thought of my classmates staring at me when I walk into the classroom late. I open the door as quietly as I can manage but of course, it inevitably squeaks causing everyone to turn and look in my direction. I slink across the room and hand the tardy slip to

4

the teacher. Then I sit down at my desk and stare up at the chalkboard only partly paying attention.

Time seems to go by too slowly as the day lingers. During lunch, I sit silently at the end of the cafeteria table with a group of girls from my science class. I watch my classmates hand out flyers announcing the upcoming graduation dance. It seems like the whole graduating class has been scurrying around all day making last-minute preparations for the big dance on Saturday night. I watch as they post colorful flyers around the common area and the hallways announcing the celebration. Everyone seems to be excited, I, on the other hand, am not your typical teenager and I don't care much for social gatherings of any kind. As I pick at the food on the tray in front of me and sip on a soda, the girls next to me at the end of the table giggle about who they are going with to the dance while eyeing the cutest guys as they pass by.

"Who are you going to the dance with, Abigail?" One girl asks looking directly at me, and then they all erupt in a chorus of laughter. I don't look at them. I stare directly at the tray in front of me before getting up from the table and tossing the uneaten contents into the trash can. Placing the tray in the bin next to the can, I begin to wander through the common area and down a small hallway to my next class period. I am the only one in the room until the bell rings. Fifth and sixth periods go by quickly, and I find myself in the final class of the day. The inside of the small

5

classroom is drab and dreary. The walls are a light blue, and the air is stale. I have spent the past four years of my teenage life at the old high school, and now it is finally coming to an end. The bell can't ring soon enough as I stare out the window to see that the clouds have cleared, and it has turned into a sunny day.

I feel my pulse quicken along with the sound of the bell signaling the end of this disappointment called high school and the beginning of an unknown future. I shudder at the thought. As the bell continues to ring, some of the students go running out of the different rooms throwing their papers in the air as if it is a rite of passage to their subsequent summer vacation freedom. A couple of the teachers stand in the doorways fussing about the mess only to be ignored by the students. And as quickly as it started, it is over, and the halls are quiet and barren except for the lone straggler yelling for his friends to wait. I walk out of the room as my teacher tells me goodbye and wishes me good luck for the future. I stroll down the quiet and empty hallway looking around one last time. Pushing open the double doors to the side exit of the school, I walk out into the bright sun-filled day.

The parking lot is chaotic with kids running from car to car making plans and talking about graduation. As I walk over to where my car is parked, a friend waves at me from a couple of spaces away. It is Samantha Leblanc. She has been my friend since elementary school, but we have recently drifted apart since our senior year began. She is more interested in boys, and I am mostly interested in books.

"Do you want to go to the beach tomorrow? A bunch of people from our class will be there. It should be fun!" She skips over to where I stand.

"I don't know," I say reluctantly and with a bit of surprise in my tone that she is even asking me.

"Oh, come on, it will be lots of fun. You have to say yes," Samantha pleads while smiling with exposed teeth.

"Well, since I have to say yes then I guess I don't have a choice," my tone is flat, and Samantha laughs at me.

"You're funny. Will you drive?" She giggles and stands with her hand on her hip staring at me intently.

"Uh, yeah, I guess I will unless you have a car now." My sarcasm is lost on her.

"No, not yet," she says frowning. "Be at my house around 10:00 in the morning, okay?" She starts to turn and walk away as her ride drives up and the boy in the front seat is waving for her to get in the car. It is Justin Martin, the star quarterback.

"Sure," I reply, but I am not feeling very sure about it at all as I get into my car and drive home.

The activity level at my house isn't much better. My mother is running around finalizing all the last-minute details for my 'big night' as she refers to it. I open the refrigerator, grab a soda, head for the sofa and turn on the television. I watch as a reality show about twenty people living in the same house runs across the screen. A few minutes later my father walks in from the back door and moves directly towards the hallway but not before announcing that he is home. He returns moments later having changed out of his clothes from his day at work and in jeans and a blue shirt. He has prematurely gone gray, but it makes him look distinguished and not old.

"Your father and I are going out tonight, dear." My mother is in a cheerful mood as she passes in between the television and my view. She is wearing a pink short-sleeve button-down collared shirt and a faded denim skirt with brown flats on her feet. Her light brown hair is pulled back into a ponytail, and it makes her look much younger. The smell of her perfume fills the air with a sweet floral scent that will linger long after she is gone.

"There is a frozen pizza in the freezer that you can heat for yourself," she suggests as I nod.

"We're going to the movies, we won't be too late," my father tells me, and they walk out the back door locking it behind them.

So here I sit, alone, for another late-night date with the television and a book. I lay down with my head resting on a pillow dreading my graduation on Saturday evening. On the one hand, I am happy it is almost over but then, on the other hand, I am nervous about being in front of so many people. I never like being the object of anyone's attention. Just thinking about having to walk up onto the stage in front of the entire graduating class and their families to receive my diploma is enough to make my heart skip a beat with fear. I imagine myself tripping and falling off the stage completely. Then I realize that no one will probably notice anyway, except for my parents but then again, I am not too sure about that either. I am glad that high school will soon be a distant memory, one I hope to forget.

The morning sun streams in from outside my bedroom windows. I slowly stretch and open my eyes rubbing them with my fingers until my vision is clear. Thrusting my tired body into an upright position, I lower my legs over the side of the bed placing my feet into the slippers on the floor beneath me. I stagger down the hall and into the bathroom across from my bedroom to dress in my bathing suit. I pull a white tee shirt on over my head and step into a pair of khaki shorts to cover up the suit. Running a comb through my dark blonde hair and brushing my teeth, I examine myself in the mirror for a second before grabbing a beach towel out of the linen closet and then a bottle of sunscreen out of the medicine cabinet. Leaving the bathroom, I walk into the kitchen where my father has just scrambled eggs and fried some bacon. I make myself a plate and then sit down at the table. My father pours me a glass of orange juice and hands it to me.

"Why are you up so early?" He questions as he takes a chair across from me glancing through the newspaper and drinking a cup of coffee.

"I'm going with Samantha to the beach today," I reply and roll my eyes to emphasize the displeasure that I feel.

"You don't sound too enthusiastic about it," he says with a wink and a smile. I roll my eyes again.

"Try to have some fun. I'm going for my morning jog around the lakefront. See you later." He opens the back door and is gone. I take my time eating my breakfast, savoring every small bite of egg and bacon. I sip the orange juice slowly and peer out the window at the beautiful sunny day. A gentle breeze is stirring the leaves on the trees outside, and the sky is clear of any clouds for the moment. I can see my mother in the backyard working in the flower beds. I get up from the table, dump the empty plate and glass into the kitchen sink and go outside to tell my mother goodbye. She looks up at me from under her large brim sun hat with squinting eyes.

"Where are you going this morning?" She inquires.

"To the beach with Samantha," I say as I stand and watch her plant marigolds in the fresh soil of the flower bed.

"Well, that's good. You haven't done anything with Samantha in a long time. When will you be back?" She continues to dig little holes in the dirt while placing one flower in each and covering them up firmly with the dirt again.

"I don't know, probably late," I sigh as I look out across the backyard at the fragrant magnolia trees that riddle the landscape.

"Alright, have fun. Love you." Then she blows an air kiss with her dirty gardening glove in my direction.

"I'll try. Love you, too." I smile and grab the kiss out of the air as I turn and jump into my car. I only live a few blocks away from Samantha, and the drive doesn't take very long. I arrive a few minutes too early as I park my car in front of her house in the street of course as not to block the driveway. I stroll up the sidewalk that is lined with small shrubbery and leads to the front door. I stand motionless for a moment wishing I hadn't agreed to go to the beach and thinking about being back in my comfortable bed, asleep. I ring the doorbell and can hear it stir a commotion from inside the house. Samantha's mother answers it while yelling at someone back inside.

"Hello there, Abigail. Samantha will be ready in a few minutes. Come on in." She steps back and opens the door holding it for me to enter. I walk into the little frame house and wait in the entryway as Samantha's two twin brothers run around the house chasing each other with toy swords in their hands. I can't help but feel out of place watching the noisy display as Samantha's mother yells up to her announcing that I am there. Samantha comes bouncing down the stairs a few seconds later and picks up an ice chest from the kitchen floor.

"What's in the ice chest?" I ask.

"Oh, it's packed full of bottled water and sodas for our long day at the beach. I'm so glad you decided to come today. I don't know how I would be getting to the beach if you hadn't agreed to go with me." She states.

She crosses the entryway heading towards the front door, and I know that being the one with a car can sometimes be a curse. I never really know when I'm being invited somewhere because I am truly wanted around or just because I have transportation.

"When are you getting your car?" My tone is one of slight annoyance. I open the trunk of my car and Samantha places the ice chest inside.

"My mom and dad told me that they would buy one for me this summer before I start college." She answers.

"Where are you going to college?" I shut the trunk door and make my way around to the driver's side. I scoot into my seat and place the key in the ignition starting the engine.

"I thought that I might start here at the local university then maybe I will transfer somewhere else later. How about you? What are your plans?" She asks as she pulls her hair up into a ponytail and secures it with a small band. I maneuver the car away from the curb and begin to drive down the street.

"I'm going to the university here in town too although sometimes I would like to get away from this town though," I say.

Samantha didn't seem to hear me say the last part about getting away from town, all she heard was that we would be going to the same university.

"That's great. We can sometimes carpool, especially if my parents decide at the last minute not to buy me a car," she says grinning from ear to ear.

"Yeah, that sounds great," I comment with forced excitement.

I haven't been myself lately. There is a feeling of dread deep down in my gut that something awful is going to happen. I can't quite understand why I feel this way, but it has me a little anxious and preoccupied. I try to shake it off and decide that it must be nervous jitters due to my upcoming graduation.

Samantha did most of the talking on the thirty-minute drive to the Gulf of Mexico. When we arrive at the beach, there are several kids from our graduating class already there. Samantha immediately jumps out of the car shouting and running towards them with her towel in one hand while waving the other to catch their attention. I am left sitting behind the wheel of the car, and for a moment I have the impulse to put the car in reverse and drive

13

away. I turn off the engine instead and gaze through the bug-splattered windshield at the brownish-green waves crashing onto the shore and washing up onto the beach. The sand is a warm golden color, and it looks very inviting to me.

I get out of the car, go around to the trunk, open it and pick up the ice chest with my towel and sunscreen tightly wedged in underneath my armpit. I lug the ice chest over to where Samantha has placed her towel on the beach and drop it to the sand. I then lay my towel down next to it. Plopping myself down and a little out of breath, I start applying sunscreen to my whole body. I lie back on the towel trying to catch my breath and relax. The hot sun feels good against my skin as it shines brightly in the blue sky.

There is a sturdy breeze blowing past from the gulf allowing the intense heat from the sun's rays to dissipate a little bit before I get too hot. Seagulls fly overhead balancing themselves on the strong wind currents as several clouds start to line up. The sound of the waves crashing in and then rolling back out makes a soothing noise in the distance that is calming to hear as I lie still on my beach towel. Disturbing the calm around me is a group of guys from my class running past me throwing a football back and forth in the air and inadvertently kicking up sand. I stand up and brush it off my legs and then shake the towel out. I glare at them through the dark lenses of my sunglasses although they don't see me do it, and then I lie back down to enjoy the sun once again.

"Are you going to the graduation dance tomorrow night?" Samantha asks while shifting on her beach towel trying to get comfortable and turning her head to the side to look at me.

"No, I don't think so," I reply flatly.

"You should get out more. It'll be fun!" Samantha's tone is overstated.

"I'm here, aren't I?" I sit up straight with an edge to my tone and feeling defensive suddenly.

"Yes, but it is the only thing you've been to all year long. Your whole senior year has just passed you by, Abigail." She sounds sympathetic as she turns her head and faces the sky with a pair of large brown sunglasses covering her eyes.

"Well, thanks for noticing, I guess. I'll think about it. Maybe I will." I stare out at the waves crashing against the shore, and then I start thinking that maybe I should go to the dance after all. I have never had much confidence throughout my high school years, and I wasn't asked to go to any of the dances by any of the boys in my class. Even though it had slightly annoyed me when Samantha pointed out the fact that I hadn't gone to any of the social events during the year, I knew it was only the truth. I have always felt like a wallflower. And then I begin to imagine how the dance would be for me as I stand alone against the side of the gym wall while everyone around me is having a great time dancing and laughing. The thought of it makes my insides tie up in little knots, and I decide at that very moment not to go to the dance.

I turn over and reach into the ice chest for a bottle of water. I open the top and drink in the cold liquid. It feels refreshing going down my parched throat. Someone from the class has brought a small barbeque grill. They are grilling hot dogs and hamburgers. The smell of the meat on the pit wafts through the air and is calling out to my stomach as it growls back in response.

"Abigail, I'm going to get something to eat. Do you want a hot dog?" Samantha asks hopping up quickly as if she has heard my stomach rumbling.

"Yeah, thanks," I answer. Samantha makes her way over to the pit and brings back two hot dogs with mustard and relishes on both. She hands one on a paper plate to me as I twist my body and turn over to take it from her hand. It is probably the best hot dog I have ever tasted even if it is a little crunchy because of the sand which must have blown into it as it cooked on the grill.

My body is tired of remaining in the same horizontal position, and my legs need a stretch. I decide to walk down the beach where the water meets the sand. As it laps up around my feet in a gentle motion, I look as far as I can see across the coastline. Three brown pelicans fly low hovering above the water's surface and dive down in the shallow to catch little fish. My feet and toes sink beneath me as the sand is sucked out with each wave. I pick up shells as I come across them only to toss them out into the water again. There is one shell that I decided to keep. It is a perfect sand dollar which is hard to find because they are usually broken.

Another hour passes, and the sun starts to set gradually painting the sky in a beautiful pink and orange as it spans over the horizon out past the water's edge. Some of the kids start to head home, but a few of the others start a driftwood fire on the beach. It is beautiful to watch, and I find myself entranced by the magnificent colors. They roast marshmallows and huddle around the fire swapping memories of their four years in high school together, and they all agree that it went by too fast. I nod slightly to myself and think that it is ironic that I am here with this group of peers that I have spent so much of my time with through the years but don't know them at all. Everyone wants to be done with high school, wants to grow up and be adults but when high school is finally over no one wants it to end. I sit alone on my little beach towel a few feet from the group thinking about my own life and the direction that it might take. It is the fear of the unknown that has me wrapped up in deep thought, and I wonder what the future has in store for me now that this chapter is coming to an end and a new one is just beginning.

It is getting late, and the fire is starting to go out. Everyone is slowly standing and gathering things together. I grab my towel and sunscreen. Trevor comes walking up with Samantha and carries the ice chest back to the car for us. I follow far behind them and watch as they kiss behind my car. When I approach to unlock the trunk, they break apart but still stand too close to one another as they share a longing look between them. I sit down on the driver's side seat and stare out at the night sky. Samantha and Trevor start to kiss again, and I patiently wait to adjust the rearview mirror so that I can't see them. I honk the horn. Samantha jumps into the passenger side seat beaming.

"Did you see Trevor sitting next to me by the fire?" She asks, and I shake my head up and down thinking to myself that I had just seen a lot more than that since they were making out behind my car just a couple of seconds ago.

"He is so cute and I've had my eye on him the whole year. We're going to go to the dance tomorrow night." Her face lights up like candles on a cake as she sighs to herself. I silently drive down the dark road.

"Have you decided if you are going to the dance or not?' Samantha questions me.
I don't answer her as I turn on the windshield wipers to clear some of the bug guts.

"Well...are you?" She demands.

"No, I don't think so. Dances aren't my style," I finally reply.

"Oh well. What is your style, Abigail? Sitting at home." Her tone is more sarcastic than it is joking. I ignore her and keep my eye on the road. The rest of the drive is uneventful, and Samantha did most of the talking.

About thirty minutes later, I pull the car into her driveway. I wait while she retrieves the near-empty ice chest out of the trunk and then twists her way into the house with flip-flops flipping.

It is late when I get home, and my parents are already in bed. The house smells like vanilla and sugar indicating to me that my mother has been baking a cake for my graduation. I tip-toe quietly down the hall and pass my parent's bedroom before making it to mine. I crash on top of my bed falling asleep almost immediately.

Morning comes too soon, and I awake to the smell of coffee brewing. I lay very still on top of the covers to my bed with a little blue blanket that has been placed neatly over me. My mother must have put it there at some point during the night because I don't remember doing it. As I sit up, I realize that I am dressed in my bathing suit, tee-shirt, and shorts. My hair is a knotted mess from the breeze at the beach, and it smells like saltwater. Turning to glance at my cell phone I notice that I have slept half the day away, it is 12:30 in the afternoon. I jump out of bed feeling a little guilty for sleeping so late. I grab some clean clothes out of my closet and walk across the hallway going directly into the bathroom to take a shower. The warm water runs down my tired body and wakes me up the rest of the way. After my shower, I get dressed and run a comb through my wet hair while brushing my teeth in the process. As I enter the living room, I notice that I am the only one home. There is a note stuck to the refrigerator door.

Be home soon, had to pick up something for tonight. —Mom & Dad

I reach into the pantry and take a box of cereal down from the shelf. I pour the cereal into a bowl and then cover it with milk. Sitting down on the sofa in the living room, I turn on the television. I watch while I eat. Afterward, I go outside and sit on the front porch swing and write in my journal. I pause and think about what to write down. I usually write in my journal when I have something important that I want to remember. Although I would rather forget about my time in high school, I figure my graduation day is something important enough. I sit and think but can't come up with anything. Just then a black BMW with tinted windows slows down in front of my house and then quickly drives away. I watch it as it cruises down the street. This is what I write in my journal -

May 23

As I sit on my front porch, on my graduation day, a black BMW with dark tinted windows drives down my street and slows in front of my house momentarily. I don't know anyone who owns a black BMW.

The night air smells like rain, and the clouds extend high in the sky with dark gray bottoms. Lightning streaks across the evening sky as my mother and I head out of the house to my father who is waiting for us in the car. We jump into our seats, and he puts the car in reverse backing down the driveway. Turning onto the road that runs along the lakefront, my father steers the car towards the civic center which is only a short distance from our house and where my graduation is being held. My parents drop me off at the front entrance and then park the car. The lightning rolls and thunder sound loudly through the night sky. The rain begins to fall as I make my way through the front doors. My class is in a large room off the entrance, and the teachers are lining everyone up in alphabetical order. I stand in my assigned spot with the other letter 'D" last names. After some time, "Pomp and Circumstance" begins to play, and I start to feel nervous and light-headed as I begin to pace my steps forward following the line into the auditorium filled with mostly unfamiliar faces.

The procession goes smoothly, and I file into place with my other classmates, finding my seat quickly. I scan the audience around me to see if I can find my parents amongst the sea of faces, but it is too difficult to locate them. I know they are somewhere watching me. The principal speaks and afterward, the Valedictorian gives an enthusiastic speech. Everyone cheers and the moment of truth is upon us as the first name is called out.

After a few hundred names it is my turn to be called, "Abigail Catherine Dubois," the counselor carefully and loudly announces into the microphone. I climb the steep steps of the stage and walk across it. Shaking hands with the principal, I receive my diploma and my picture is taken. Hearing my parents cheering in the back right-hand corner of the auditorium, I glide off of the stage and back to my seat. Palms sweaty and heart-pounding fast in my chest, I sit as relief floods my insides. It is finally over. We all stand as the ceremony concludes and throw our caps in the air then grab one at random for a keepsake as the recessional music begins to play. We walk back down the middle aisle not as orderly as the first time waving up to the crowd above at the sound of cheering friends and family members.

I meet my parents outside under the awning that wraps around the old civic center. They hug me tightly and with umbrellas in hand to shield us from the pouring rain we run to the car and head across town for a celebratory supper. We dine at my favorite Italian restaurant. It is the best time that I have had with my parents in a very long time. We talk, laugh and they share stories about me from when I was a little girl. At the end of the dinner, the waiter asks, "Would you care for any dessert?'

"No, thank you. We have dessert waiting for us at home," my mother says looking over at me and smiling with pride. "Are you ready to go home and eat some cake?" My mother asks.

"Yes, that sounds good," I reply and smile at her warmly.

"The check, please," my father tells the waiter. He nods and pulls the check from his smock. My father pays, and we get up from the table, leaving the restaurant. I am having a very good time with my parents, and I am savoring the moment. Lately, they have been very busy with work.

"Have you seen your advisor at the university, yet?" My father questions.

"Yes," I answer.

"What did he say?" He looks out the driver's side window of the car at the road to make sure it is clear before pulling out and turning into the lane. The rain has slowed to a drizzle now.

"He suggested that I take a light course load since it's my first semester. I will schedule most of my core classes first, of course…Oh, dad! Watch out!" I scream from the back seat as the car suddenly swerves to the right.

On this night, the last thing I see is blinding headlights coming toward us.

Chapter 2: Alone

"Where am I?" I mutter as I try to make sense of my surroundings.

"You're in the hospital, dear." One of the nurses tells me as she tapes an I.V. in place.

"Where are my parents?" I struggle and fidget in the hospital bed.

"You need to rest, dear," the nurse responds.

Feeling a rush of panic by the strange way the nurses are looking at me, I try to sit up in the bed. The nurse stands beside me gently but firmly pushing me back into a horizontal position. I rest my head on the pillow as it pounds painfully.

"The doctors think that you may have suffered a severe concussion," the nurse tells me as she checks the machines connected to me.

"What happened?" My voice is raspy and uneasy.

"You and your parents were involved in a head-on collision with another driver. Do you remember anything about it?" The nurse places her hand on my shoulder for comfort. I notice a police officer standing behind her taking notes.

"No, nothing," I reply in a confused tone. I hope that it is all just a terrible mistake. My memory of the wreck is sketchy at best, and it doesn't seem real to me.

"Where are my parents? Are they alright?" I ask again, this time pleading for an answer.

"It's alright, honey, don't get yourself too worked up," the nurse motions for another nurse that is standing beside the bed to put something in my I.V. drip.

"What is that? What are you doing?" I raise my voice in agitation.

"I have to go now. I can't stay here. There is somewhere that I need to be. My parents will be waiting for me. I must go home. There is something that I need to do."

I try to fight my way out of the bed but all the tubes that are connected to my body tug at my skin, and it is very painful. The nurse holds me down in place as the I.V. drip delivers a sedative into my veins. I feel as though I am floating above the bed as the medicine takes effect. Then everything in the room fades away. I fall into a deep sleep and begin to have confusing dreams.

It is dark, damp and a misty rain falls around me. I am lying on my back near the side of a road next to a ditch where I can see my parent's car resting upside down. Another car is on fire several yards in front of me on the deserted road. I am alone. I push myself up and begin to crawl towards the ditch, but I can't see anything anymore because both cars disappear in a thick fog. I am frightened, and I wrap my arms around my body and begin to cry. Just then a soft glow appears behind me, and I turn to see. Standing before me is an angel, my guardian angel, I presume. I murmur in a very low voice, "Am I dead?"

"No, Abigail, you are not dead. I am here to watch over you now that your parents are gone," His voice is both sweet and soothing. I reach for him, and although I can't quite make out his face, I know that I will never forget the sound of his voice. He takes my hand and helps me to my feet, and then he is gone, and all that remains in his place is the sound of clicking machines. Click, click, click. What is that sound, I think to myself as I drift between consciousness and the dream. Then suddenly I am awake staring at the ceiling of the hospital room. Click, click, click sounds the machines around me. I stay in the hospital overnight for observations, but when the doctors can't find anything else wrong with me besides a concussion, they decide to release me the following day. They consider my memory loss a result of the concussion and only temporary, but I think it is quite possibly a defense mechanism against the trauma of losing both of my parents in the car wreck.

"Not to worry," the doctors say to me, but I have heard that many times since last night. I have plenty to worry about now, now that my parents are gone. The nurses ask if they can call anyone to come to pick me up. I shake my head and say, "No, there's no one."

No one that I can remember, but there isn't anyone anyway. I don't have any brothers or sisters, and there aren't any living relatives nearby. I am on my own now at eighteen years old.

"Perhaps a friend or another family member," one of the older nurses suggests. I shake my head back and forth one more time, wondering why they don't seem to understand what I have already told them. I begin to feel overwhelmed, and my mind starts racing. I feel like the room is spinning. I wish I knew someone, anyone, that can bring me home but with my memory being blank and no emergency contact numbers in my wallet or on my cell phone other than my parents, I don't have a clue. The nurse looks at me for a moment with an expression that is both slightly confused and sad while she pats my hand for comfort.

"I overheard you calling out in your sleep last night for someone named William. Does that name ring a bell with you, dear?" The nurse looks directly at me while she waits for me to answer.

"No, I don't think so," I answer her as I wrinkle my brow in confusion. The nurse must see how upset I am, so she doesn't ask any more questions.

"Well, that's alright, sweetheart. I will make arrangements for the hospital courtesy shuttle to bring you home later this afternoon." The nurse smiles and walks out of the room.

That afternoon the shuttle brings me home to what is now an empty, lonely house. The porch light is still on, and from the outside of the home, everything appears normal. I take my keys out of my purse and unlock the door. The only clothing that I had with me at the hospital was the dress that I had been wearing the night of my graduation, and it is dirty, bloodstained, and torn. The Sisters of Charity had given me a tee-shirt, a pair of shorts and some flip-flops to wear home. I place the tattered dirty dress in a bag along with directions about how to care for the concussion and a prescription for pain medication. I wonder if the medication will be strong enough to numb the pain from the loss that I have suffered.

I step inside the dark and quiet house. I look around the living room, and everything is in the same place it had been the night that we were in a hurry to get to my graduation. The kitchen sink is full of dirty dishes, and my father's running shoes are waiting by the back door in the same place that he had left them after his morning jog. The book that my mother had been reading is on the coffee table open and upside down marking the page for her, a book that she will never finish.

On the dining room table, there is a small box wrapped in white paper with a blue bow on top of it. Next to it is a cake placed carefully on a glass-covered cake plate. I sit down at the old dining table that shows the wear and tear from countless family dinners. Holding the little box in my hands, my heart pounds, and I feel dizzy as I stare at it. I am afraid to open it. The feeling of intense grief comes crashing down on me like the weight of a thousand bricks. Slowly and methodically I peel the paper away from the tape being careful not to rip it. My mother would always wrap gifts very well. I place the paper on the table beside the box and lift the lid gently away from its bottom. Inside the little white box lying on tissue paper is a gold heart pendant with a delicate gold chain attached to it. It is the most beautiful piece of jewelry that I have ever seen and inscribed on the back of it in tiny little letters are the words, With Love, Mom and Dad. Undoing the clasp at both ends of the chain, I place it around my neck.

I turn to the crystal cake plate and take off the top to find a two-layer round cake with white frosting. On the top of the cake in blue letters is the word, Congratulations.

I don't cry at first. I just sit staring at the cake. All I can do is focus on that one word written across the top, Congratulations.

Suddenly, a steady stream of tears begins to fall from my eyes. My body shakes, and I bury my face in the palms of my hands.

Later that night, I have a second dream about my guardian angel. I am in the back seat of my parent's car, and it is upside down in the ditch after the wreck. It is dark, and I am all alone dazed and confused. I struggle to free myself from the dark confines of the twisted metal. The darkness stretches out in front of me making it seem as though I'm in a long tunnel that has no end. I cry out for help only to hear my voice echoing back at me from the darkness. Suddenly, I am being pulled from the wreckage by a man with strong muscular arms. I can't see his face, but I know who he is as he stands beside me on the deserted road. Wiping the tears from my cheeks and pausing for a moment as he looks me in the eyes, he turns his back to me and walks down the long dark tunnel. He seems different to me in this dream. He isn't glowing as he had been in the first dream. I call after him as I start to run towards him but no matter how fast I run I can't catch up to him. He vanishes into the night as I fall to my knees crying and calling for him to come back. Then from up above in the night sky, I hear his calm voice say, "Don't cry, I am watching over you."

Suddenly I sit up in the middle of my bed with sweat beading up over my forehead, soaking my hair. My heart is racing, and I am trying to catch my breath as I choke on the air. I stare out into the sullen hollow of my bedroom frightened by the dark and the quiet loneliness. I sluggishly get out of my bed and saunter down the hall to my parent's room peering in at their barren bed as I close the door behind me. I don't open it again. I move my way into the living room and lie my weary body down on the sofa, turn the television on and fall back to sleep. I stay in that same spot for what feels like forever as two days go by like time is standing still. The phone rings, but I don't answer it. A couple of times during the day there is a knock at the front door, but I don't open it. I stay in the house on the sofa with the blinds drawn.

All the final arrangements are being taken care of by the funeral home per my parent's wishes in their will, and the funeral home oversees it all. I have absolutely nothing to do but show up. It is the day of the funeral, and I finally abandon my position on the sofa, walk over to my bedroom and pick out a nice navy-blue dress to wear. Bringing the dress with me to the bathroom, I take a long hot shower. I change into the dress then brush my hair and my teeth. I put on a pair of black flats and make myself a piece of buttered toast and a cup of coffee before leaving out the door. A flower arrangement has been left on the porch by my high school administration, and the wrecker service has dropped off a package with all my parent's belongings in it. I pick them up carefully and place them inside the door on the floor. There isn't a cloud in the sky, and the sun shines as I step out onto the soft green grass. The weather doesn't match my mood, and I think it should at least match my mood. It isn't right that it's such a beautiful day when it's such a gloomy and sad one for me. Walking reluctantly across the front lawn to the driveway, I get into my little blue car and drive to the funeral home.

As I enter the viewing room filled with flower arrangements, and green potted plants all lined up along the front of the two caskets. The walls are cream, and the carpet is a deep blue clashing ever so slightly with my blue dress. The pews are brown mahogany with black velvet cushions that run the length of the seats. Everyone stands and stares at me as I walk into the room. They are whispering to one another. I can hear one of them saying in a low muffled voice, "There is Abigail. Poor child, it's a terrible shame to lose both parents at such a young age."

I pass by them as they stare, and I kneel in front of the caskets saying a silent prayer.

Several people from my father's office, my mother's co-workers, and a few of my classmates offer their condolences to me as I sit in the first row of pews. But for the most part, I don't know the people that are here. My memory hasn't come back completely because of the whole defense mechanism thing or concussion thing the doctors told me about, and that is just fine with me. They are all very pleasant and stand by me during the whole funeral asking if I am alright and if I need anything. The pastor from our church gives a very eloquent and moving eulogy describing my parents as the loving and doting type, over me, their daughter. And I know he is right; I can't remember all of it though. There isn't a dry eye in the room except for mine. I had done most of my crying the night that I had returned home after the wreck and for the past week after that. My eyes feel as though they are dried up and I will never cry again or at least not today. I sit staring at the two caskets in front of me, and I am numb.

There is a limousine waiting for me outside the funeral home that takes me to the gravesite for the burial. The limo is for family members only, and since I am the only family member at the funeral, I ride in it alone. I feel very small and out of place as I sit in the back of the massive car as it follows behind the hearse and the police escort. When we arrive at the cemetery, the chauffeur opens the door for me and nods with sympathy in his eyes. I follow the pallbearers who are holding the caskets and walking cumbersomely over to the tent next to the cemetery plots.

As the graveside ceremony ends, I sneak away not wanting to answer any questions about my future or listen to any more heartfelt regrets. I don't want to meet with people back at my house or anywhere else for that matter. I want to be left alone, and I know not to go straight home after the funeral. I will stay away from the house until I know that the coast is clear. There is one detail left for me to attend to and I want to get it over with quickly. I have an appointment with my parent's lawyer. I have the limousine driver take me back to the funeral home where I get into my little car and drive to the lawyer's old downtown office.

Early Summer is in the air. There isn't a cloud in the sky, and it is such a beautiful shade of pale blue. Everywhere I look the azaleas are in full-blown. Sitting in the drab and dusty lawyer's office is a day I know I will never forget. The air conditioner isn't working, and the heat is stifling, making it hard for me to breathe. Windows open don't make much difference. I feel as though I could die right here on the lawyer's desk and begin to think maybe it wouldn't be such a bad thing if I did. They can bury me next to my parents.

While I sit across from the lawyer at his old mahogany desk, he keeps apologizing for the heat. He then begins to read the will that leaves me the house, the car, and 'enough money to last a lifetime' as he puts it. Five and a half million dollars in life insurance money to be exact and it will be deposited into a bank account with my name on it. The money doesn't matter to me, but I am glad to have the house. It is the only house that I have ever lived in but the car, well there isn't anything left of the car. I have my car, and that is enough. It was an early graduation present. I leave the lawyer's office, drive home and fall back into bed. After today, I don't care much for sunny days.

The months go by and I haven't moved or touched a thing in the house, but eventually, I do. Deep down inside I think it made me feel a little better not to move anything because it was as if my parents weren't gone and only on vacation or something. After a while, I start to have some memories of my life before the wreck. Mainly memories jogged by family photos that I find in an old shoebox in the hall closet. But some of the memories don't always seem to be mine. I know they aren't my memories because the people in them don't look right. They look old-fashioned, and in every memory, there is a young woman who appears to be very sad and is usually crying. I don't know what else to think about it, but I know in my heart that the memories aren't mine. The dreams continue also. It is usually the same dream almost every night, tormenting me, reminding me of the loss that I have suffered. And then there is the angel, my light in the darkness, who continues to comfort me.

Chapter 3: Searching

Three years have passed since the night I woke up in the hospital after the wreck. Currently, I stand behind the counter of a small coffee shop inside a large bookstore in my hometown. I was born and have lived my whole twenty-one years of life in Lake Charles, Louisiana. It is a small city located on the southwest corner of the state and riddled with bayous that feed into several lakes and rivers. From time to time I will see someone that I graduated with, and they will pretend to be happy to see me. I can tell it is fake sincerity though. I have always been quiet and shy especially during my high school years. I never really fit into any of the standard stereotypical classifications like the popular pretty girls, the sporty type, or the dark emotional ones. I wasn't even a part of the brainy, nerdy group. I was what most people would consider a loner and still am to this very day.

I have been working at this coffee shop for about two and a half years. I don't need the money, but it gets me out of the house which is where I stayed for six months after my parents died. I usually have my nose stuck in a book when I'm not working. I am searching for answers to the questions that I have about why my life has turned out the way it has. I probably could use some therapy for sure, but I choose to read books about it instead. I am not bold enough to ask anyone for the answers and who will I ask anyway. I don't have any friends, only acquaintances at work and I don't dare to ask any of them. Since the wreck, I feel as if I am living someone else's life. I always carry around with me the sensation that something is missing deep inside my soul and so I search for it, whatever it may be. The best place, of course, to search for answers besides the internet is at a bookstore, and since I work in one, it gives me plenty of opportunities. I search through countless numbers of books, ones about overcoming loss, about dealing with depression, and about how to cope with living alone but none of them seem to help me figure out what I am feeling. There is no rhyme or reason to it.

It is just another ordinary night at the coffee shop. The other girl that is working the same shift as mine traipses up to the counter, late as usual. Her name is Jenny and she is an airhead. She loves to talk about shallow and superficial things. I will be trapped here behind the counter with her for most of the night, nodding my head and pretending to be interested. I excuse myself for a few moments since it is always slow on weeknights which gives me more time to continue my search. As I pace back and forth between the aisles looking at all the colorful covers on the books that are placed neatly in rows on tall and expansive shelves, I stumble upon a book about past lives. I have recently been reading all of the information that I can get my hands on about reincarnation because the memories that I have been experiencing have led me to believe that I have possibly lived a past life and it also allows me to free my mind of the troubles that my present life has dealt me. I pick up the book and bring it over to the little table where I usually sit and begin to scan through the pages while soaking in all the information that I can process in one glance. Usually, when I don't have time to finish looking at a book, I try to sneak it back into the coffee shop with me which is something the store manager, an older gray-haired grumpy man named Mr. Bill Ackerman, doesn't like me doing. *"This isn't a library, Abigail, go put it back or buy it"* he would always say as I would roll my eyes and put the book back where it belongs. But this night he has left early so I don't care and now I sit alone at the little table inside the large bookstore, reading, searching, and still not knowing.

After I am done scanning the pages of the book, I stand up and walk over to the computers. I look up websites about reincarnation. One website offers some useful information about the subject. I study the computer screen and read the words in front of me and I think about the possibility of having been reincarnated. Maybe that explains the unfamiliar memories, and I feel a little silly thinking about such things, but I don't know how else to explain the constant memories and dreams that I am having. I make my way back behind the coffee counter with the book in my hand. I turn and look out into the large open room watching as people casually stroll around the aisles. All of them are afflicted with the same human condition. All of them are searching for the fountain of youth, searching for never-ending happiness, searching for romance or wealth, whatever it may be in the many books that line the shelves. Everyone is searching for something. I continue to aimlessly scan the store out of boredom with being here and listening to Jenny ramble on and on about some guy that she had met the night before when to my surprise I see him. This guy appears to be in his mid-twenties and looks very familiar to me at first glance, our eyes meet briefly, and then he suddenly turns away from my gaze. Pushing past the people, he quickly exits the doors and vanishes into the night, so quickly that it blurs my vision. My eyes are wide and frozen. My heart pounds loudly in my chest. I feel as though I want to run after him. I long to follow him out the front door turning my back on this so-called life, never to return. Where is this feeling inside of me coming from and why is it directed towards a stranger. Standing here, feeling like my head is spinning, I wonder if he was even been real or just a figment of my imagination. It all happened so fast. I honestly feel as though I am starting to lose what little sanity I might have left.

I shake my head and turn to sit at one of the tables to continue looking through the book that had my attention for the last couple of hours. It is now eleven o'clock at night, and the bookstore is finally closing. Jenny is on her cell phone talking to the guy she met. I shut the book and start cleaning up from the day. I close out the register and pick up my weekly paycheck then as I wave bye to Jenny, I walk out the front door of the bookstore. The parking lot is dark and dimly lit as I trudge across to my car. I have never liked the dark much, but this night it doesn't seem to bother me. As I reach the car, I suddenly hear my name, and it startles me. I turn quickly expecting to see someone standing behind me, but there isn't anyone there. The parking lot is empty except for a few employees walking in the distance. I feel like someone is watching me, and it is unnerving. Thoughts of the guy that I had seen in the bookstore earlier flood my mind. I can't help but think that maybe he is out there somewhere lurking in the dark, but I know that I am probably just being paranoid. I breathe a heavy sigh and open the door to my car.

As I pull forward into the driveway, I notice a light on in the house. I don't remember leaving one on before I left for work and I am perplexed for a moment while I sit and stare at the light coming from the window. The thunder rumbles in the night sky as I make my way up to the front porch. Stepping up and making it under the awning just in time before the rain starts to fall from the sky. I am reluctant to go inside, but I can't stay outside in the rain either. Slowly I unlock the front door and peer inside. I walk into the living room nervously looking around and carefully listening for anything out of the ordinary. Everything seems to be in order like it was when I left. A light is on in my bedroom, and now I remember that I had forgotten to turn it off before I left for work. I cross the room to turn off the lamp on the nightstand by the side of my bed. I am more scattered-brained than usual, more preoccupied. I begin to walk out of the bedroom when suddenly from the living room I hear the front door slam shut. I scream and run back inside my bedroom to lock myself safely inside. Whoever had been watching me must have followed me home. I listen closely for footsteps. After a few minutes of waiting and listening, I don't hear anything, so I crack the door and peer out. I can see the living room from where I stand, and I see no one. I creep out of the room with the baseball bat that I keep at the side of my bed for protection and make my way cautiously to the front door to find it closed, and the only explanation would be the wind. The door must have slammed shut when I left it cracked behind me, and it was the wind that did it.

I am on pins and needles now, so I decide to take a warm bath to try and calm my nerves. The water feels good, but it doesn't help. Afterward, I make a small microwaveable dinner, open a soda and sit down to watch some television. I methodically flip through the channels before stopping on a re-run of some nineteen-eighties sitcom. I eat dinner, and my mind starts to drift back to the guy that caught my attention at work tonight. I still can't place why he looked so familiar. Even though it has been three years since the wreck, I still haven't regained all my memory, and therefore, I don't know if he is someone that I had known at one time or not. Whatever the reason, my reaction to seeing him seems bizarre. I can't imagine why I felt like chasing after him and it might have been the expression on my face that caused him to flee in the first place.

I finish my dinner and begin to settle in on the sofa to fall asleep. Somewhere between sleep and consciousness, I hear a loud thudding noise near the window outside on the front porch. I am tired and probably not thinking straight, or I don't care, but I quickly stand up and rush out the front door to see what has caused such a commotion. There is nothing once again. I notice that one of the potted plants on the porch has been knocked over. I step towards it and place the pot back in an upright position and then notice that the rain had slowed. It is a misty drizzle, and the wind is blowing the tiny droplets all around me covering my body in a delicate layer of moisture. Wiping the dampness from my arms, I turn around to step back inside the house. I am exhausted and have had a long day, so I decide that I will go to bed when out of the corner of my eye I see it in the trees. It is the most beautiful owl that I have ever seen, and it is perched on one of the branches of a large oak tree in the front yard. Its eyes are wide, round, and yellow. They blink slowly and gracefully as the bird stares directly at me. I find it odd to see an owl in the rain, but I admire its beauty for a few moments and then step inside to go to sleep.

Chapter 4: Coincidence

The early morning sun shines through my bedroom windows blinding me for a moment as it catches me in the eyes. I roll over and stare at the closet doors feeling the splitting headache that is the unwelcome start to my day. It is hard for me to drag my tired body out of bed this morning. I tossed and turned most of the night from the dreams that still plague me. I am thankful that I only work the night shift at the coffee shop because I have never been much of a morning person. After several minutes of lying flat on my back and staring up at the ceiling counting the small cracks in the plaster, I force myself out of the warm, cozy bed and wrap my robe tightly around my body while scooting my slippers onto my feet in the process.

Walking out into the short hallway and across the living room to the kitchen, I grab a pan out of the cabinet and a couple of eggs out of the refrigerator. Scrambling them up along with two pieces of toast for breakfast. I pour myself a glass of orange juice and then sit down at the little kitchen table to eat my breakfast. I will need to go to the store for a few odds and ends at some point during the day, and I figure that it will be better to do it sooner than later. I finish eating and place the dishes in the kitchen sink. I make my way to my bedroom and get dressed. I pull my hair up into a ponytail not bothering to put any makeup on except for a little bit of lip gloss. I grab my purse and head outside.

The air smells like the rain from the night before, and the ground is still soggy. I glance up at the branches of the old oak tree where the owl was last night. I get into my car and back out of the driveway and onto the street. I drive slowly to the grocery store staring out the front windshield at the cloudless sky. I look around at the inside of my car and the condition of its interior. The seats are worn and there is a large stain on the passenger's side upholstery where I had spilled coffee one afternoon on my way to work. The car had been five years old when my parents bought it for my senior year of high school and now that it's almost three years since it is showing its age. I had received enough money from the inheritance to purchase myself a brand-new car, but I never did. I know it wouldn't feel the same to drive a new car as it does to drive my old little blue foreign-made car.

The grocery store isn't busy when I get there, and I push the shopping cart down the aisle to the produce section. I pick up some apples and oranges and place them in clear plastic bags with a little green twist-tie around each one. I continue to push the cart around the store grabbing and tossing different things into the cart, half paying attention to my surroundings. I pass the meat department and pick out a small package of steaks. Then I turn the corner onto the cereal aisle, and suddenly I am face to face with that guy. My heart sinks low in my chest. It is the guy from the other night at the bookstore, the one who looks so familiar to me. He turns quickly and begins walking away, and it reminds me of all the dreams that I have dreamt only this time it is real, and the dark tunnel is now a brightly lit grocery aisle. Not knowing what comes over me at this very moment, I call out to him just like in the dreams, begging him to stop and wait. But just like the dreams, he doesn't answer me, and he keeps walking, faster now. I push the cart as fast as it will go and follow him quickly to the front of the store and out the automatic doors. The alarm starts ringing, and a bag boy comes running outside yelling after me. He stops me by grabbing the shopping cart with his hand.

"Miss, you haven't paid for your items. Please tell me you weren't trying to steal from us?" He can see the look of surprise on my face, and the tears in my eyes as the man from my dreams disappear into his car and drives away. It is a black BMW.

"N...no," I stumble on the word. "I thought I knew that guy...did you see him?" I plead. The bag boy looks at me with concern written across his face.

"Are you alright? Is there anyone I can call for you?"

"Not again! No! There isn't anyone, not one single person in this whole wide world that you can call for me!" I yell, and I am shocked by my display of raw emotion. I quietly look down at my feet as my face turns beet red. "I'm sorry. I didn't mean to yell at you." I start to push the shopping cart back into the store looking back over to my side to see the empty parking spot where the car had just been. I pay for the items and go home.

I walk into the bookstore that evening and head straight for the coffee shop to clock in for work. I am done searching in books for the answers to why my life has turned out the way that it has. I know that the answers can't be found in a book or on the internet anyway. I will try to block out the memories that I am having that don't seem to belong to me and ignore the dreams too. As far as I am concerned the memories and the man in my dreams are all just figments of my imagination. And the guy that I saw earlier at the grocery store who seems so familiar to me is only my feeble attempt to grasp at anything tangible to explain why I have been acting so irrational for the past three years. I try to convince myself that it is all just the product of my loneliness.

I start taking orders for coffee because that is my life. I am a coffee barista, and that is all. Not someone living someone else's past life and not someone who longs for the man in my dreams to save me from the depths of despair that I find myself plummeting

48

into after the death of my parents. I am just plain old ordinary Abigail, nothing special. I am an orphan with no family or friends. I am alone in the world, but despite all the obstacles, I will try to go on with my life no matter how lonely and pathetic it has become. I have decided right here and now that I will no longer worry about the things in my life that I can't control. I will just let it all go. Then it hit me, the stark realization, as I stood over the coffee machines. If I let all of it go what will I have left? I feel a twinge of panic wash over me, and my heart starts to race as my body goes numb. I try to compose myself and I am determined that I will at least have to try for the sake of my sanity.

"One medium latte, please," the customer's voice stirs something deep inside of me, almost unconsciously, but not looking up from what I am doing at the moment I notice out of my peripheral vision that this customer has cut the line that has formed, and he is standing directly to the side of me at the counter.

"Your name?" I am impatiently filling orders, and my tone is both annoyed and sharp.

"William," the man answers, and I pause for a moment because the name brings a memory back to me somewhere inside of my mind, but I can't quite place it. It is like I had known someone by that name at one time. I look up at the man standing in front of me, and I am stunned, not being able to speak. It is him. The one from the grocery store, the other night here in the bookstore, and quite possibly my dreams. I can't bear to look away, and at the same time, I am too afraid to keep staring at him. His eyes are a pale icy blue, and they seem to pierce deep into my soul. My heart is pounding hard, and I become very nervous feeling as though I will pass out behind the counter. My hands are shaking, and I know that I should put the coffee down that I am holding, but I can't move. Then I remember what the nurse said to me the night I was in the hospital after the wreck. She told me that I was calling out the name William in my sleep. My whole body begins to tremble.

"What's the matter with you?" Jenny whispers and looks at me like I am going crazy.

"Here, give that to me before you spill it," she says with a slight irritation in her tone as she takes the coffee from me.

I dart my eyes quickly down to the floor. I can feel William staring straight at me with a serious look on his face. He is so intense and very good-looking, although, I have never actually seen the angel's face in my dreams, something inside of me tells me that he is the guardian angel.

"May I speak with you for a moment?" His voice is the one that I had promised myself I would never forget. But I know that he had probably come to the shop to confront me about the incident earlier in the day on the aisle in the grocery store when I chased him out into the parking lot. I wonder if he thinks that I am certifiably insane. Just then Jenny elbows me in the ribs hard, and I manage to squeak out, "Oh, uh, is something wrong with your order, sir?" What a dumb thing to say, but it's all I can come up with at this very second. At least I hope he doesn't want to talk to me about anything other than coffee.

"No, that's not what I meant. I need to talk to you about something. When is your next break?" He asks.

Here it is, I think, he has come to confront me about what happened earlier in the day. He is just being thoughtful and is trying not to embarrass me in front of Jenny.

"Right now! She can go right now," Jenny bursts as she smiles in some matchmaking way. I give her the evil eye and between gritted teeth, I grunt, "No...we're too busy right now. I can't leave you back here by yourself."

"It's alright. Go." Jenny smiles with a gleam in her eye.

I am reluctant at first but slowly walk out from behind the counter and place my apron on the back shelf. I follow over to one of the little tables in the dining area. We sit down across from one another, and that is when I notice his eyes are so intense, and they seem to pierce through me. It feels a little intimidating to be sitting so close to him. I feel very excited though but also uncomfortable at the thought that he might be the one from my dreams. He is dressed well, wearing a light blue long-sleeve button-down collared shirt with black denim straight-leg pants and a pair of black Dr. Marten boots with a buckle on the side of each one. His hair is dark brown and medium length. His bangs hang slightly to the right of his face just above his eyes.

And then I say it, out loud, figuring that I didn't have anything to lose except maybe my dignity but at this point, I don't have much of that left either.

"I saw you today at the grocery store. Didn't you see me and why did you walk away from me when I called after you?" I blurted as he stares at me with greater intensity on his face now.

"I'm sorry, it has taken a lot of courage for me to approach you finally," he admits looking slightly nervous and very tense. It seems extremely strange that someone who appears so cool and put together on the outside could be this nervous.

"Why? And who are you?" I reply, feeling some annoyance because just thirty minutes earlier I vowed to give up on all of this, and yet here he sits across the table from me staring at me with those irresistible eyes. I feel as though I can get lost in them, never to find my way out and quite possibly never wanting to either.

"I can't tell you why. Not right now anyway. It's a long story, and you wouldn't have enough time to hear it. I don't think you would believe me even if I did tell you. My name is William," he answers the questions in the order that I asked them.

"You told me your name already, remember when you ordered coffee? I meant, who are you, as in, do I know you from somewhere? And why wouldn't I believe your story?" I am beginning to get irritated by his evasiveness, but I am also intrigued by his mysteriousness. Sitting quietly and not saying anything, I stare at him.

"Did we go to high school together? Because you seem very familiar to me." I feel like giving up on the conversation. Although I can't stop the feeling that he is the one who I have been dreaming about since the night of the wreck, I can't tell him that because I will sound crazy if I do. I can't tell him that I have lost most of the memories from before the wreck either. But at least for now, he sits across from me at this little table confirming for me that I am not completely out of touch with reality because even if he isn't the one that I have been dreaming about then at least he still exists. He isn't just some figment of my imagination like I have tried to convince myself.

"No... we didn't go to high school together." He seems aloof for a moment while he looks out into the busy bookstore as if he is thinking about what to say next.

"I just wanted to let you know that...um, well, I..." and then he stops short of what he is about to say. He sits there with a look on his face like he is in pain.

"Let me know what?" I am now frustrated with the conversation or lack thereof.

"I just wanted to apologize for earlier today." He smiles nervously at me and then looks down at his hands as he drums his fingers along the top of the table.

"Didn't I see you here the other night too?" I question him feeling a little uneasy suddenly by the thought that he might be the one following me. What if I am wrong about the dreams? What if it is all just a crazy coincidence and he is some psychopath that is stalking me? He tenses up again and stares directly at me not answering my question.

"Well, if there isn't any point to this conversation then I have to get back to work. Your apology is accepted." I push my chair away from the table, and I get up from the seat as I turn away from him and start to walk back behind the coffee shop counter.

"Wait, Abigail, I don't want it to be this way between us." He stands up suddenly and has slight desperation in his tone. I don't understand his reaction, and I feel mostly annoyed by it as I look at him skeptically. He continues to stare at me with those eyes.

"How do you know my name? I didn't tell you my name."

"It's on your name tag," he says in a flat monotone voice.

"Well, leave me alone now, I'm busy." I'm determined not to break my vow to forget about him and the memories. I walk back over and stand beside Jenny as I continue to work on the coffee orders. He won't leave me alone though because he stays at the bookstore the rest of the night pacing the aisles and watching me work as he pretends to look at the books on the shelves.

"I think he likes you," Jenny smiles as she glances over at him.

"You mean that stalker over there," I gape across the room at him but deep down inside I can't shake the feeling that he is what I have been searching for all this time. I won't find the answers to my questions in any book because the answers are in William's eyes.

William leaves the store right before it closes, and I can't help but feel disappointed. After all the chores are complete, I walk out to the parking lot and over to my car and as with all the nights before, feel like someone is watching me.

Chapter 5: Mistake

My alarm sounds loudly at nine o'clock a.m. I roll to the left side of my bed reaching and turning off the alarm with the tips of my fingers. I wake up refreshed from a dreamless sleep for a change. As I bound out of bed, I feel a more positive outlook on my day and think that it might be better than yesterday. It is also my day off from work so I decide that I will take a long walk by the lake. As I make my way over to the window, I can see that it is going to be a nice day. Nice and cloudy, the way I like it. Walking was something that I had always enjoyed during my leisure time when I was in high school, but lately, I hadn't made the time, nor had I even wanted to do it since the wreck. I have hazy memories of enjoying the outdoors with my parents, and now it will give me time to think about the things in my life that I want to change. Turning towards my dresser, I open the middle drawer. I pulled out a tee-shirt and a pair of workout shorts. Then I change out of my night clothes. Standing in front of the mirror on my dresser, I run a brush through my straight blonde hair. Walking across the living room, on my way out of the house, I stop and water the plants that I had received after my parent's funeral.

As I make my way down the sidewalk, I watch the cars driving on the street. The birds fly overhead, and the breeze blows gently, tossing my hair. I always enjoy strolling through the small park close to my house and walk quickly down the long drive that leads to the lakefront. There are families in the park along the lake flying kites and enjoying the day. I continue to walk aimlessly along as people smile and pass me. Off in the distance, I see one of my old friends from high school, Samantha. She is jogging down the concrete walkway towards me and catches up with me quickly. When Samantha sees me, she stops.

"How have you been doing? Long time no see." She smiles and gives me a quick hug.

"Oh, I'm doing alright, I guess, and how about you?" I ask, trying to be polite.

"I'm doing great," she flashes her left hand in my direction, and there is an engagement ring on her ring finger.

"Congratulations," I reply with a slightly pleasant smile.

"Thank you. We're getting married in June. I've always dreamed about being a June bride. Who says, dreams don't come true, right?" She laughs a little too loudly, and I think to myself; *I do.*

"I am so sorry about your parents. I tried calling you to talk, and I left messages, but you never returned any of them," she says suddenly in a more serious tone.

"I'm sorry about that; I was just…"

"Oh, no need to apologize, Abigail, I understand. You were going through a terrible time," she responds with an understanding tone as she wrinkles her brow.

And I still am going through a difficult time, I think to myself, but Samantha is nice, and it seems the sincerest thing that I have heard coming from anyone since the wreck had happened. Then I started to wonder why our friendship had grown stale during our senior year of high school.

After a moment of awkward silence, Samantha asked that dreaded question. "What have you been doing with yourself lately?"

I couldn't tell her about the guardian angel from my dreams. I couldn't tell her about how I am feeling like I have been living the life of someone else almost all of the time because of the memories that aren't mine or that I can't remember most of my past so I say, "Not much, just working at the coffee shop in the bookstore."

"Do you have a boyfriend?' Samantha probed further.

"Uh, no," I answer with a hint of embarrassment in my voice from the question because at that moment I felt pathetic and knew that my life had been basically at a stand-still since I had graduated almost three years earlier.

"I hate to say it, Abigail, but if you are still anything like you were in high school then it's no wonder you don't have a boyfriend yet," she giggles. And that doesn't make me feel any better.

"What are you doing tonight?" she asks me with a look on her face like she had just thought of something ingenious.

"I don't know probably rent a movie and stay home," I realize once again how much more pathetic it makes me sound.

"No, you are not. You should get out of that house and have some fun. There is a friend of Trevor's, my fiancé, who I know you would love to meet. I think you two would hit it off perfectly. We're all going out tonight to that local dance club South of town." She had a look in her eyes like she wasn't going to take no for an answer.

I hesitate while thinking and then say, "Sure, why not?" I completely surprise myself with the words that escape my mouth.

"Great, we will pick you up at 9:00. You still live in the same house, right?"

I shake my head up and down slowly, and then Samantha gives me her cell phone number to which I reciprocate by giving her mine.

"See you tonight." Samantha gives a wave and goes jogging on her way, a reddish-blonde ponytail bouncing behind her.

Later that afternoon I hurriedly straightened up around the house. It appears it has been a mess for such a long time, and I didn't want Samantha, her fiancée, and his friend to see it in such disarray. I'm not much of a housekeeper. As I am trying to figure out what I will wear on my blind date, I realize that there is a pile of laundry to do and I start to think that this "date" is becoming too much work. Work is something I have been doing too much lately, and all I have to clean is my uniform for the coffee shop. I listen to music while I clean the kitchen and mop the floor. Now and then my nerves get the best of me as I think about my impending night out with Samantha's friend. I quickly pick up my phone preparing my finger to dial Samantha's number wanting so bad to cancel my plans for that night, but something inside of me says not to chicken out.

"Stop being a chicken, Abigail, you need to do this. You need to break out of your shell," I tell myself out loud as I put down the phone.

Day turns into the night very quickly. Samantha and the others would be at my house in thirty minutes to pick me up. I frantically finish applying my makeup and feel pretty good about the way I look. I have chosen to wear a short denim skirt with a black button-down short-sleeved shirt and as I stand in front of the mirror in the bathroom getting ready, I hear a knock at the door.

Assuming they must be early, I start to get a little stressed out about meeting this new guy, and I suddenly don't feel ready at all. I reluctantly walk over and open the front door, but no one is there. I immediately think of the next-door neighbor's kids because they always play doorbell ditching. I close the door and turn to walk back to my bedroom when I see a shadow on the front porch from the living room window. I quickly open the door again and run outside to see what or who it might be but whatever it was has disappeared again. I feel suddenly spooked as a shiver runs down my spine. Just then a car pulls up in front of the house and it's Samantha with her fiancée and his friend, my date.

Samantha gets out of the car and hollers, "Are you ready?"

I answer back, "Yes, just give me one minute." I run back inside to turn off the lights and the television, take one last look in the mirror and lock the door behind me. As I walk to the car, placing my keys in my purse, I can see Samantha in the passenger seat and her fiancée sitting on the driver's side behind the wheel. In the back seat of the car, I see my date. He opens the back door of the car from the inside, scoots over on the seat to the other side, and I get in. He is a heavy-set guy with light brown hair in a very short crew cut style and spiky on top. He has brown eyes, and his teeth are slightly crooked as he smiles in my direction. He has a few freckles on his face from too much sun exposure and one little diamond stud in his right earlobe. I knew the minute I laid eyes on him that it had been a terrible mistake agreeing to go out with them.

"Hey. My name is Terry," he says in a rough-sounding voice.

"Hello, I'm Abigail," I reply with an uneasy grin.

The cologne he is wearing is too strong like he had bathed in it and I feel as though I can't breathe as soon as I shut the door to the car.

"Abigail this is Trevor, you remember him from school, right?" Samantha turns her body around in the front seat to meet my stare.

"Yes, I do. Hi, Trevor," I mutter as I turn my gaze towards him.

"Hey," he says in a flat tone without looking back at me.

Then he puts the car in reverse and backs down the driveway. We make our way across town to the nightclub. I have never been there and I'm proud to be able to say that too. The place doesn't have the sort of crowd that I like to hang around if I hung around a crowd. As we walk into the place, I can see that it is full of people. Men ogle me as I walk in the building like I am a piece of meat and they hadn't eaten in two days.

"Would you like a drink from the bar?" Terry asks me as we stand against the wall of the large room with a big dance floor in the middle of it. People are crammed on it moving their bodies to the music in unison.

"Just a soda," I respond while looking around the club at all the people dancing. He leaves and comes back after a few minutes with my drink. I took a sip of it and made a face. It's a whiskey and cola.

"Thanks." My voice has a sarcastic tone to it as I glare out across the smoky room.

"Hey, it's a bar, and we're here to have some fun. You can't have any fun drinking just soda." He steps a little too close towards me, and it gives me a very uncomfortable vibe. He has a predatory look on his face.

"Do you want to dance?" He asks as a droplet of spit flies from his mouth and lands on my arm. I wipe it away quickly trying not to gag.

"No, not really," I'm not looking at him, but he still insists, and he pulls me by my arm out onto the dance floor. He dances too close to me, moving up and down like he is trying to recreate a scene from the movie *Dirty Dancing*, only he is no Patrick Swayze. It makes me a little sick to my stomach as I keep trying to move further away from him but each time I do, he moves closer. Sweat starts to roll off his forehead, and my drink sloshes around in the cup as it spills several times onto the floor beneath us. The night continues pretty much the same as it began, horrible, for me at least. Terry seems to be having a great time dancing and making passes at me the whole night. He keeps going back to the bar and bringing back the same whiskey and cola for me to drink. I don't trust the guy, and I have heard of men putting drugs in girl's drinks to try and take advantage of them later, so I don't dare drink it. I also haven't seen Samantha and her fiancée since we arrived at the club and I am ready to leave.

"I'm not feeling well; do you think maybe we could find the others and go?" I hold my stomach and make a sour expression with my face. I try my hardest to fake being sick, but when I look at Terry, I realize that I don't need to fake that much.

"Sure, I would like a change in scenery anyway," he says as he winks at me and it makes my skin crawl. We start to walk around the crowded club until we find Samantha and Trevor in a booth near the back of the bar. It's close to two o'clock in the morning, and so, we all agree to go, and I am very happy.

As we near my street I suddenly feel extremely relieved that the night is almost over. I watch closely anticipating the car to make a right turn onto my street, but instead, Trevor keeps driving straight and heads towards the lake where he finds a place to park near the water's edge.

"Um, I'm sorry there must have been a misunderstanding because I wanted to go home. I'm tired, and it's been a long day," the words left my mouth nervously because Terry is scooting himself closer to me on the back seat with an overly excited look on his face. Samantha and Trevor were in the front seat, and they couldn't keep their hands off one another ignoring anything that I had just said. Terry looks at me in a way that makes me very aware of his intentions.

"Should we follow their lead?" He whispers as he places his hand on my thigh and it becomes obvious to me that he has had too much to drink at the club.

I look at him in complete horror knowing what he now wants from me. The mere thought repulses me. He leans in and starts to kiss me on the lips as his hand starts moving up my shirt. I push him away and open the car door and fall out landing hard onto the ground below. I jump up and start to run back towards my house. Running as fast as my legs will carry me and dropping my purse in the process, I make my way quickly through the heavily wooded park between the lake and my house. I'm not quite quick enough because he is fast approaching behind me catching up and calling out my name, toying with me from the dark.

"Wait," he yells, "Don't run from me. You know you want it too."

He catches up to me in that very instant, grabbing me by the waist and pulling me to the ground. He is on top of me now as I try to scream, but the sound seems to get stuck in my throat as he begins to kiss me too hard on the lips and starts to unbutton my blouse. I start to cry, and then all I remember next is a gust of wind and a force pulling him off me. As I lay there in the dirt sobbing, I am in shock by what has just happened to me. I look around and he is gone, nowhere in sight and then in the distance, I hear him screaming in fear, "Get away from me, you freak!"

I sit up dazed and confused. I am all alone in the dark. Hurriedly, I jump to my feet and begin to run back toward my house only two streets over from the park. When I get there, I realize that I dropped my purse and there is no way I'm going back to get it, not tonight most definitely, and maybe not ever. So now I am locked out of my house, and I can't imagine sleeping outside all night long. I don't know what to do. As I walk across my front lawn, I am still crying, and the tears streak my dirty face. I collapse down to my knees on the grass and bury my head in my hands. I can't believe my luck. I never do anything like this, and the one time I agree I'm set up with a guy who doesn't understand the meaning of the word no. All of a sudden I hear a noise on my front porch, so I look up from my hands through the haze of my tears. And there sitting on my front porch swing is someone. My heart skips a beat, and I'm afraid at first that it's Terry again but then I recognize him immediately as he looks up in my direction. It's the guy from the bookstore. The guy that I'm convinced is in my dreams. It is William, and he has my purse in his hands. I stand up and stare right at him with disbelief written across my face.

"Did you lose something," he asks holding out the purse for me as he gets up and begins to walk over to the edge of the steps. Our eyes meet, and I feel powerfully drawn to him. What strange effect does he have on me? Feeling as though it's an involuntary motion, I walk slowly towards him, my body reacting to his in a way that doesn't feel familiar to me and it feels like the first time that I have ever seen him. Through different eyes, I see him now. He is tall with a muscular build, statuesque. His skin is pale white, and it glows as the moon bathes him with a soft light. His hair is a deep auburn brown, and his face sculpted like a model. He possesses an alluring handsomeness that makes me shyly look away for a moment. His expression is serious and his eyes, oh, his eyes are his best feature, icy pale blue eyes that pierce straight through me as he stares in my direction, yet there is warmth within them as he gazes upon me. Of all the physical beauty that he retains, the one thing that overshadows it all is the goodness within his soul. It shines brightly like the stars in the heavens above me this night. I can see it as I stare deeply into his pale blue eyes.

"Yes, thank you, how did you…" I break off as I continue to stare into his eyes feeling mesmerized and conjuring up a feeling deep within me that makes me finally realize at that moment that I need him more in my life now than I was ever before willing to admit. And it suddenly didn't matter to me how he had found my purse because I know that he must have been the one that saved me from Terry.

"Are you alright?" He asks as he cautiously walks closer to me and touches my face softly with the back of his hand wiping the dirt-laced tears from my cheeks.

"Y...Yes, well, mostly I'm shaken up."

As William touches my hands, I notice that they are so cool to the touch, and it surprises me, but it feels good against my hot skin.

"I want to apologize for the way I acted the other night at the bookstore. It was rude of me," I step back from him just far enough away so he can't touch me as easily.

"The last time we saw each other things didn't go as I had planned. It got off to a rocky start," William says looking at me as though he sees straight through me.

"A rocky start, a start to what exactly?" I ask coyly.

But he doesn't answer my question, and he stands there very silent not saying a word or even making one single sound. He looks out into space as if he is studying the stars in the night sky and then looking back at me only this time with that same intense expression on his face that I had seen at the bookstore the other night. I sit down on the steps to the porch. He walks over slowly and sits next to me. I can feel my heart flutter.

"How did you know…" I stop, feeling like the words I want to speak somehow are lost off the tip of my tongue when I looked into his eyes again.

"How did I find your purse or how did I know where you live?' He asks.

"B…Both, I guess?" I stutter again over my words, and it makes me even more self-conscience to be so close to him as my heart starts to pound in my chest. I think he is beautiful, almost to the point of being unreal as I stare at his gorgeous features. His skin is ivory, and I immediately think about the dreams of my guardian angel. He smiles and shakes his head slightly as he turns his face and lowers his eyes to the ground as though he knows what I am thinking.

"What? Did I say or do something funny?' I whisper.

"No, it's nothing," he says as he continues to look down at the ground.

"Were you in the park tonight? Were you the one that helped me?" I ask as my body becomes tense and there is impatient anticipation to my tone.

"You ask a lot of questions," he turns and gazes deeply into my eyes. I sit very still almost as if paralyzed as my pulse quickens. Then slowly I speak softly.

"I've forgotten what I was asking you." I pause feeling somewhat befuddled.

"I'm scared," I admit this while thinking about what happened to me in the park earlier.

"I can see that you are still upset and I will stay with you until you feel better."

"Yes, if you don't mind?"

"I don't mind." He smiles.

"Here, give me your hand." He reaches over and holds his hand out palm facing up. I look at him not sure what he will do, but I trust him. I place my right hand in his, and it feels cold, but after a few moments, it starts to warm.

"Now, close your eyes." He tells me.

I look down at his hand holding mine and then back up into his eyes, and I close mine slowly. He starts to whisper in my ear, and I feel even further calmed by his soothing voice.

"Abigail, it's going to be o.k. You're safe now. You no longer need to worry."

I feel warm and safe as he speaks to me quietly and when he stops, I open my eyes to see him staring out across the front lawn still holding my hand.

"Where did you come from?" I ask with a bewildered tone to my voice.

"From the park, you already asked me that." He seems to be confused by my question.

"No, I mean…well, I don't know what I mean, I guess. I wonder if you are watching me, following me?" I can't believe I just asked him that question, but I feel compelled to know why he always seems to be around when I least expect it.

"Are you afraid of me?" He asks as he lets go of my hand.

"No. I might have been a little at first, but now, after tonight, I feel even more drawn to you."

I am a little embarrassed by my honesty and the moment suddenly becomes awkward as he stands in silence and doesn't say a word.

"Well, anyway, it's getting late. Thank you for bringing my purse to me. I guess I owe you one, maybe a free coffee one night at the bookstore." I start to stand up on the last step of the porch with my purse securely tucked under my arm. As he stands up next to me, I feel a magnetic pull towards him, and I don't want to walk away. I want to be closer to him. There is some sort of connection between the two of us that I don't understand. He reaches out and gently takes my hand into both of his. I am taken aback yet again by the surprising coolness of his skin as shivers travel up my arm, but it isn't because I am cold. His touch thrills me. He holds my hand for a few moments longer and then letting go, "I'm glad you're safe. Sweet dreams."

He turns and steps off the porch walking out into the yard a short distance. I stand motionless watching him as he moves gracefully across the front lawn.

"Don't forget about the free coffee," I say, but he is gone, disappearing into the dark. I look around the yard, but he is nowhere. Had he ever really been there at all? Then I hear the owl that I had seen in the trees a couple of nights ago. Watching as it starts to fly through the night air high above the house, I begin to feel scared again and wish that he was back by my side. Not wanting to waste any more time getting inside my house for fear that Terry and the others would pull up in the driveway at any moment looking for me, I quickly open my purse, pull out the keys and unlock the front door hurrying inside locking it securely behind me.

Walking, in a daze, into the bathroom, I start to undress. My shirt is torn and covered in dirt. My knees are skinned and bloody. The stockings that I am wearing have run in them, and the blood on my knees makes them stick to me as I pull them off slowly. The palms of my hands sting as I step into the shower and wash the dirt, the blood, the sweat, and the smell of that monster, Terry, off my body. I continue to shake as I put on a nightgown and slowly pull the covers back from over the bed and climb into it to get some much-needed sleep. The softness of the mattress against my tired, aching muscles feels good, but despite this, I still don't think I will sleep well. I toss and turn and dream. I dream about William.

He is there in the park watching me as I run through the tall, dark trees, the branches swooping down towards me trying to tangle my body in the limbs. He stands like a statue staring at me, and I feel like a hamster stuck on a wheel going nowhere trying to escape the voice that calls out from behind me in the dark. Just as a hand comes out of the blackness that surrounds me and grabs my arm, I am suddenly awakened by the sound of my alarm. I lay there for a moment, breathless, before reaching over and turning it off. The buzzing sound is deafening as my head pounds with pain. I must work the day shift at the coffee shop, and I feel like I haven't even slept.

Dragging my body out of bed and slowly trudging my way into the kitchen, I make some breakfast and a very strong cup of coffee. I take two aspirins in the process and think back at last night. I shiver inside for a moment at the horrible recollection, then wonder how William had found my purse and how he knew where I live. He must have been in the park watching everything as it happened just like in my dream. He had to have been the one who saved me from Terry. Now I wonder if all the nights I felt like someone was watching me if he was the one doing it. The thought of being watched by him should scare me, but instead, it is surprisingly comforting. I hope I will see him soon to find out more. I have a lot of questions for him. I am suddenly excited and hopeful at the idea of seeing him again. It makes my day almost bearable, and I notice something that I haven't felt in a long time, a smile forming across my face.

I finish eating and gulp down the rest of my coffee. I am running late for work, and I know that it will mean I will have a lecture waiting for me from Mr. Ackerman, my manager, which is the last thing I need. Just like I expect he is standing behind the counter of the coffee shop with his arms folded looking directly at me as I walk into the store. I make a beeline to the opposite side of the coffee shop from where he stands and go directly behind the counter to clock in.

"You're late," he says looking down at his watch.

"Tell me something I don't know," I mumble under my breath.

"What did you say?" He turns and looks in my direction with a scowl on his face.

"Oh, I said, good morning Mr. Ackerman. I'm sorry that I'm late. I had car trouble."

He stares at me as though he doesn't believe a word of what I just told him. Quickly, I put on my apron and step in beside him to work on the coffee orders that are piling up in front of me. Another girl is working with me. She is taking orders from the customers and running the register. I haven't met her yet because she is new and has only worked the day shift thus far. The time at work goes by very quickly for me because it is extremely busy, and I am thankful that I don't work the day shift all the time. I am a little disappointed that William hasn't come in for the free coffee that I promised him, but he knows I work nights, so it makes sense that I haven't seen him.

After work, I decide to walk to the park near my house. I feel safe being here during the day and it is busy with lots of people walking along the trails that wind around the outer part of the park in a large circle. I walk over to the swings and sit down on one beginning to push myself with my feet and legs back and forth faster and higher. For a minute I am lost in the motion of soaring through the air effortlessly. Then I stop pushing and pulling my weight with the swing and slow to a sudden stop. I stare out at all the people in the park with their families, and it reminds me of my parents. I begin to feel very sad. It is a feeling that never really leaves me for very long. It is always there tapping me on the shoulder and reminding me of the one most important fact, that I am all alone.

I hoped to see William here at the park, but I knew it was a long shot. I look down the path where I had been attacked the night before and begin to feel uneasy about being here. I quickly stand up and walk back home just as the sun is starting the go down in the sky. All is quiet this night. I lay in my bed staring out the window, and I can hear the faint call of the owl who has made a home in the trees next to my house. It is a soothing sound to me, and it makes me feel better. My thoughts drift to him again as I try to fall asleep. He's perfect. The way he walks, his looks, his calm, soothing voice, everything about him. He's intriguing and mysterious. I can't wait to see him again.

I have never had a serious boyfriend, and this is the first guy that I have been interested in since high school. I am a young woman after all, and I have wants and needs. I long to be near him, to feel his touch, and to see him gaze at me with his gorgeous blue eyes. There is something about him that is different from any other guy I have ever known, and it stirs up new feelings inside of me.

Chapter 6: Left

On this night, I wait impatiently and stare almost constantly at the front doors of the bookstore hoping that he will come in to see me again. I wait half the night, and he hasn't shown up yet. I start to think that I won't see him again tonight. It is almost closing time as I walk up and down the aisles returning several books to the shelves that customers have left in the coffee shop during the day. I stop and stare at a book that I have become very familiar with during my long quest for answers. It is titled *Past Lives*, and I must resist the urge to pick it up, flip through the pages one more time for good measure and place it neatly back where it belongs on the top shelf. Suddenly I am overcome by a strong memory. It is the same memory that I have had many times since the wreck. I can see a young woman crouching down on the floor in a dark room all alone, and she is crying. She has lost something very dear to her. I know the feeling, and I am sympathetic with a woman in the memory.

"That's a good book," a voice from behind surprises me, but I recognize it immediately. I turn around to see William standing slightly behind me.

"Oh, you startled me. Yes, I suppose it is a good book."

"You came back. I was starting to wonder when I would see you again." I beam.

"You wanted to take the book off of the shelf and flip through it again like you've done so many times in the past," he looks deep into my eyes, and I feel exposed.

"How did you know that?" I am very intrigued by his observation, and I suddenly realize that he must have been watching me before like I thought, but I am not frightened by him. I am drawn to him now more than ever.

"We need to talk, right now, if it's alright?" He looks intense as always and slightly nervous as he continues, "Can we go outside where we can be alone?"

"Uh, sure, don't you want that coffee I offered you the other night?" I ask, perplexed by his tone and not knowing what to expect once we walk outside. I do know that it will be the perfect opportunity to ask him questions about what happened in the park.

"Not right now, thank you anyway." He is always very polite, very gentlemanly and that is something not seen very often anymore. I follow him to the front door as he holds it open for me and I look back at Jenny behind the counter of the coffee shop staring with wide eyes at us and smiling a little-crooked smile. We make our way over to the side of the building out in front under a dim security light and stand awkwardly staring at one another for a couple of seconds until we both begin to speak at the same time.

"Sorry, you first," he says with a shaky grin. He looks especially attractive in the dark of night underneath the parking lot lights like he had the night before and I begin to get a little nervous.

With a quivering voice, I say, "Oh, well, okay, I was going to ask you about the other night in the park. Were you in the park the night Terry attacked me?" I know deep down the answer because he found my purse and brought it back to me, but I want to hear it come from him.

"Yes." He answers as he leans against the building with his arms folded in front of his chest.

"I did find it strange that Terry, that horrible guy who was attacking me, suddenly became air born and disappeared into the dark. Someone must have pulled him off me. It was done so quickly though, that I couldn't see what happened. Do you know anything about that? Did you see anything?" I question, but he stands silent and stares into my eyes looking a bit lost in them like he is searching for something inside of me. He doesn't say a word, so I continue my inquiry.

"You said that you were in the park that night, right, William?"

"Yes." He quietly answers now with his face turned towards the parking lot.

"Did you save me from that monster?" I direct the question to him as I stare up at him. He hesitates and then slowly shakes his head up and down as if to say yes without speaking the word. He moves away from the wall and stands close to me now. It makes my heart race to finally have it confirmed. I reach out to touch his hand, but he pulls it away and looks nervous again.

"I'm sorry. I want to let you know how grateful I am. I don't want to think about what would have happened to me if you hadn't been there that night. You saved my life."

He turns to the side just slightly out of my immediate view, but I can still see that he appears to be tormented for a moment by what I had just said. I am confused by his reaction, so I slowly and gently place my hand on his shoulder, and then after a moment, he turns back to face me. His expression is softer now as he holds my gaze and I feel weak at the knees. His eyes speak to mine, and I can feel that there is something he wants to tell me but is struggling to do so. He is different from any other guy I have ever met. He is so much more intense, but there is a sensitivity about him too. I don't quite seem to understand him half of the time. His behavior around me is odd at best. His skin is pale and cool to the touch. His eyes, strangely concentrated, stare at me, and I know that I should feel frightened when he looks at me that way, but I don't.

"How do you know where I live? Did you follow me home from the park? I ask trying to break the tension between us.

"It was something like that." He stands even closer to me now, and I notice that he seems to be breathing in deeply like he is savoring a wonderful aroma in the air, but I can't smell anything except for his cologne. I look longingly into his eyes, his icy blue eyes which are paler than they have ever been before as he continues to stare at me. I move away from him slightly and then pause as his face tenses up again like he is in pain as he hastily looks away. I stand in silence not knowing what to think or say.

Then I mutter slowly, "How did you know what I was thinking just now in the bookstore?"

"I just guessed." His tone is flat as he continues to look down at the ground and I know he isn't telling the truth. I look in the same direction as he does now. We are quiet for a few minutes, and then I break the silence again.

"How do you move so quickly?" My expression is curious as I wait for an answer.

"What do you mean?" He tries to play dumb.

"That night in the park, how did you get him off me as fast as you did? I didn't see anything, and then he was gone. And how did you get to my house before I did?"

He stares blankly at me. I feel as though I am asking too many questions and I can tell it is making him feel threatened. He gazes quickly into my eyes again. I stand there motionless and don't press him any further about the issue.

"William, I think about you all of the time." I inch closer to him feeling the magnetic pull again as my heart pounds in my chest. I look up into his pale blue eyes as they smolder now like fire and ice.

"I know. I can feel," he whispers and then abruptly stops short and falls silent again with an expression of pain on his face.

"What were you going to say? You can feel what?" I whisper moving even closer to him now as though I am under some other control besides my own.

"I want to be near you all of the time, Abigail. I feel you and think about you constantly."

I am overwhelmed by the intensity radiating off his body, and his demeanor throws me off guard. His body is rigid and tense as I move even closer to him now. I am drawn to him by an invisible force as I move in just close enough that our bodies touch ever so slightly. I can feel the electricity like little impulses connecting between us. I lean in and up as my head tilts back and with my eyes slightly parted and my lips puckered subtly hoping for his to meet mine in a first kiss. He stands there looking down at me as the corners of his mouth turn up by a very small margin into the beginning of a smile. He leans over and touches his lips softly to my forehead lingering for a moment as if he is taking in my fragrance. I feel very embarrassed and very disappointed. I back away from him as I feel my face turn a shade of bright red.

"Will you please stay and wait for me after work. I've been out here for a while, and I'm going to have to go back inside," my voice is pleading which further embarrasses me.

"Abigail, we can't... I can't ...it wouldn't be right for...," he stops again and doesn't finish. He stands and looks at me longingly seeming as though he wants to say more.

"What are you saying? You don't want to wait for me." My face flushed as the blood flows down to my hands and feet making them tingle.

"We're just too different, you and me. It would never work this way. We come from different worlds. I came here to meet with you this one last time. I didn't want to be inconsiderate and leave you thinking that I didn't care about you. I do care about you, I just...just trust me, please, it's for your good." He doesn't say anymore.

"What do you mean one last time? You just told me that you wanted to be with me all of the time." I can feel my stomach tying up in tiny knots as the rejection begins to set in.

"This is all wrong. It is not how I planned it. You weren't supposed to ever see me. I... I can't get anything started with you, it's just better this way," he says as he picks up my hands that hang down limp and lifeless by my side. He holds them for a moment, and his skin is like ice, colder than I have ever felt. I feel numb inside and very foolish too. I can't believe I am being dumped by a guy that I haven't even started going out with yet. He squeezes my hands and slowly lets them drop back to my side as he turns and leaves me standing by myself.

"Wait, William, don't go." I run towards him and grab his hand. He turns around and stops. His expression is one of distress.

"Why wasn't I supposed to ever see you? What do you mean?" I hold tightly to his cold hand. He is silent, not saying a word. He looks at my hand wrapped around his.

"Please, you can't leave me. I have only just met you, but I feel like I've known you all my life. I need to understand why I feel this way about you. It's something that is deep inside of me that I can't explain. Please." My whole body is begging him to stay, and my tone is desperate.

"I can't, Abigail, I'm sorry." He takes his hand back and turns around walking towards his car.

"I dream about you at night! I've been dreaming about you before I even saw you that first night here in the bookstore!" I yell.

He stops and with his back still to me I walk over to him cautiously. Standing as close as I can without touching him, I whisper, "Please, William."

He turns quickly and takes me into his arms, kissing me on the lips ever so softly, and then letting me go he jumps into his car and drives off leaving me standing alone in the parking lot. I watch in shock while he drives very fast down the street. Tears begin to well up in my eyes. I had warned myself not to get involved with the imaginations and dreams of my mind, and this is the result of not heeding the warning within myself. I watch him drive away and then walk slowly through the front doors of the bookstore. I make my way back over to the coffee shop counter. Jenny is waiting for an update on what has happened between us, but when she sees the tears, she doesn't ask any questions. She just continues wiping down the little tables in the dining area and feeling sorry for me from afar.

After work, I go home and fall into my bed pulling the covers over my head, crying myself to sleep and the dreams come. In my dream, I see myself standing in front of William. He stares at me with his gorgeous pale blue eyes, and he has a grave look on his face. I can feel an inner struggle deep within him as he looks at me. He turns to walk away like he had done so many times before in my dreams, but I don't call out to him this time instead I follow him. As we walk side by side, we come to a cliff, and I peer over the edge. It doesn't seem to have any end in sight. He turns and smiles, holding out his hand for mine. I take it. He gazes deeply into my eyes and says, "Don't be afraid."

And then we jump off the cliff together into the dark abyss.

Chapter 7: Sorry

The next morning, I get out of bed and make myself a cup of coffee. I walk out onto the front porch and sit on the porch swing sipping my coffee slowly. The temperature outside is already beginning to be hot, and the sun blazes brightly in the clear sky. My eyes are red, puffy, and sensitive to the light from all the crying I had done the last night. I go back inside where it is cool and dark. I keep the blinds drawn the whole day and stay in my pajamas until it is time to go to work. I want to call in sick, but I still have a little hope left in me that maybe he will come back, maybe he will change his mind. I walk into the bathroom and take a quick shower. The warm water relaxes my tense muscles only temporarily. After I shower, I dress and go into the kitchen. I see that I have missed a phone call. Listening to the voicemail message, I stand next to the back door looking out into the yard.

"Abigail, it's Samantha, I am so sorry about the other night. Terry had too much to drink, and I don't know what got into him. He doesn't normally act that way. You must think I'm horrible for setting you up with him. Please, call me back and let me know that you are alright."

The message ends and I stare at my phone with a blank look on my face. I don't call Samantha back.

As I pull into the parking lot of the bookstore, I scan it for his car. All I can remember is that it's a shiny black BMW with dark tinted windows, but there aren't any cars in the lot remotely matching the description. I go inside, and Jenny smiles dolefully at me but doesn't ask me any questions about William. Before too long she is talking non-stop about many things and I try to tune her out. I am heartbroken behind the counter filling orders for the customers. My mind is somewhere far away, and I am not paying attention to what I am doing. I mess up a couple of the orders and must redo them as the customers wait impatiently, glaring at me. Then I burn my hand when I spill hot water from one of the coffee pots. Jenny covers for me as I go to the restroom and wrap it with a paper towel soaked in cold water. The coolness of the water reminds me of his hands. I stare at my reflection in the mirror as I think back to the night in front of my house when he touched my cheek brushing away the tears from my face. Lost in the memory, I close my eyes, and I can almost feel him standing next to me. I can feel his breath on the side of my face as he whispers in my ear. A woman comes barreling into the restroom, and I am snapped back into reality. As I walk out of the restroom, I see Terry sitting at one of the tables in the coffee shop. I stop frozen in my tracks, and I feel my heart skip a beat. He looks over at me with a strange expression on his face. Trying to ignore him, I turn around and make my way down one of the aisles to the magazines hoping he doesn't see me. Samantha must have told him where I work. My temper begins to flare. I look back behind me, and he has left the table and is now following me. I walk faster, but he is right on my heels.

"Abigail." He says loud enough for everyone around to hear him. I ignore him.

"There has been a huge misunderstanding," he says.

I stop dead and turn towards him with fury in my eyes.

"What do you mean there was a misunderstanding the other night? I didn't misunderstand anything!" I say at the top of my voice, and people start to stare as I dart my eyes back and forth at them. I hurry down one of the aisles, and he follows.

"Hey, listen to me for a second." He grabs me by the arm.

"Get your hands off me. I'll call the police if you don't leave now."

My voice is shaky, and my tone is serious.

"Wait. I'll leave just let me say something."

My arms are folded tightly around my mid-section as I glare at him.

"I'm sorry for the way I behaved the other night. I was drunk, but it's not a good excuse for what I did. Please, tell your boyfriend to leave me alone and to stop harassing me. Tell him that I came here to apologize as he asked me to do," he pleads.

I am in shock and speechless. I can see the definite fear in Terry's eyes when he speaks about William. Terry is a decent-sized guy, but he appeared small and deflated at that moment. He also seems genuinely sorry for what he has done.

"Okay," I mutter. He turns and walks out through the front doors. I am trembling. My whole body was extremely stiff while I was face to face with him, but now that he is gone, I feel like I am having trouble standing. My knees are shaking under my weight. I head back over to the tables in the coffee shop to pick up the books that had been left during the day by the customers. The night is going by so slowly, and there hasn't been any sign of William. On the same table where William and I first spoke the night he came to see me, was a book. A book about vampires. I have never seen this book in the store before, but I have never spent any time searching for answers in books about vampires. I glance around and then slowly sit down at the small table. I pick up the book and begin to flip through the pages. I read about the appearance of the vampire and their cold, pale skin. I also read about their superior mind-control techniques and their piercingly hypnotic eyes. Then it hits me. William is pale and has cold skin. He has mesmerizing eyes that make me forget what I am saying or thinking most of the time. His behavior around me is always strange, the way he seems to be able to read my thoughts. I am stunned with disbelief as I slowly straighten myself into a rigid position in the chair. My heart sinks low in my chest, and my palms start to sweat. There's no way, I think. I shudder inside and then close the book quickly. I pick it up again and flip through the pages one more time. My heart begins to sound like a drum inside of me as the room begins to spin. Could William be a vampire? I entertain the question and then shake the idea out of my head. It's a crazy idea. Vampires don't exist. They are a thing of folklore not reality. Then I remember the last time I saw him when he told me that it wouldn't work between us because we come from two different worlds. I sit at the table staring out into the open space around me. I get up and walk over behind the store counter. Pulling my wallet out of my purse and holding the book I wander over to the front check out and pay for it. I stare at the cover of the book as I hold it tightly in my hands.

Swiftly I start cleaning up the coffee shop. When I finish, I clock out and run to my car more hopeful now than before that I might find him at the park. I drive fast down the streets thinking about what I had read in the book and the idea that William might be a vampire. It seems too crazy. It isn't real. It is too unimaginable, but the more I think about it, the more it begins to make sense to me, everything that I know about him leads me to believe it. I am very nervous but more than this I am very excited now thinking about seeing him again. I want to be with him again no matter what.

It is dark when I enter the park, but I am not scared. I run over to the swings and stand beside them looking all around.

"William!" I yell loudly, and then I wait for a response.

"William!" I yell again and wait, hoping that he is here.

A man and a woman walk past on the trail. They stop.

"Is everything alright, miss?" The man asks abruptly.

"Um, yes," I reply shyly casting my gaze to the ground.

"Is someone lost?" The woman questions with concern in her tone.

"Um, yes, well, no...not really."

They look at me strangely, and I feel the need to come up with an explanation.

"It's nothing, really, just my cat. He will come back. I'm sure of it," I start to walk back to my car feeling dejected. I begin to drive home.

I feel as though I am part of some bizarre alternate reality. I start to think that he must be playing a mean joke on me as I flip through the pages of the book, but I know better. I know that he would never do that to me. Now I am even more disjointed knowing that he isn't going to come back and the reason he gave for not coming back has me feeling dizzy as I lay in my bed peering out the window into the moonless night. I close the book and toss it to the side of the bed.

I slip into a slumber and begin to have dreams about him that aren't entirely unusual, but these dreams are more like nightmares. I can hear his voice in the dark calling for me somewhere in the distance, but I can't see him. Only the blackness that engulfs me, wrapping around me like a thousand stinging bees. I wake to scream in the middle of my bed not wanting to fall back to sleep, so I just lay motionless while my thoughts begin to torture me.

One month passes by achingly, heartbreakingly slow.

While I am at work, I wait behind the counter of the coffee shop wishing he will return to me and desperately hoping that he will change his mind about us being together. I keep my eyes fixed intently on the front doors of the bookstore expecting to see him walk in at any minute. I imagine him taking me into his arms, telling me that everything will be alright and that he has made a terrible mistake. I want to see him again, even if he doesn't want to be with me anymore if I could see him just one more time. I must see him, and it is tearing me up inside. It's as if there is a spell cast over me and all I can do is eat, drink, sleep and think about William. My heart aches for him. And I want to rip it out of my chest and toss it away because the hurt is too much for me. An empty void would be better than the pain my heart now causes me.

When I'm not at work, I find myself walking aimlessly around the park watching people pass me by as though I am invisible. I sit on the old wooden bench and wait. I wait for him to show up, but he never does. At night, I spend my time sitting at the little tables in the bookstore thumbing through magazines and drinking coffee. I have begun to drink large quantities of coffee hoping to ward off sleep because I don't want to dream. I don't want the nightmares of him anymore but inevitably I finally collapse on my sofa from pure exhaustion with the television blaring in the background.

Over time the nightmares turn back into pleasant dreams, and it is the only time when I can see his beautiful face and hear his sweet, soothing voice again. Dreams are all I have left of him. I long for him to be real to me again like he had been at one time. I am now hopeless and feel helpless to do anything about it. I don't know anything about William. I don't know where he lives or works. I don't know anything that will help me find him. It is like he never really existed and is becoming once again a figment of my imagination.

My life is a circle of ordinary events. Work, search, eat, drink, sleep, work, search…and on and on. I walk down the long aisles in the bookstore to the back wall. I am off from work this night and decide to occupy my now regular spot on one of the cushioned armchairs, but all the chairs have occupants. I glare at the person in my usual spot, but they don't notice. I grab a book from the new author's rack and sit down across from the same small table where William and I sat the first time. I stare at the two empty chairs. It has been over a month now, and yet it feels like it has been a whole lifetime.

"How are you doing?" A small voice came from the side of where I sat.

I look up to see Jenny smiling faintly.

"Um," I shrug my shoulders.

"Here this is for you. It's on the house." She hands me a cup of coffee.

"Can I sit down for a minute?" She asks

"Sure," I answer not looking up from my book.

"I know something happened between you and that guy. You haven't been the same since that night you went outside the store with him," she says in a soft tone.

I don't say anything to her. I look up slowly from my book at the front doors.

"Are you alright? I'm worried about you."

I manage a small smile and try to convince Jenny that I will be fine, but it doesn't work.

"Men are dogs. Just remember that Abigail. You'll find someone else." She speaks as if she knows from experience. She gets up and goes back to work. I know I won't find anyone else and I don't want to either. I sit in silence, flipping mindlessly through the pages of the book, sipping my coffee and thinking, thinking of all the things in my life that have gone wrong up until this very moment and wonder what my life might have been like if it had been different from the one, I feel trapped by now.

After I leave the bookstore, I drive back to the park one last time hoping to find him there.

Chapter 8: Offer

As I walk slowly along the edge of the lake looking out across the water at the lights on the other side, I feel trapped somewhere in between the dreams that have become my reality and a life that has become my nightmare. The night sky is dark and starless, and the humidity hangs thick in the air. The moon hides slightly behind the clouds shedding little light on the scene below. The old oak trees hang heavy with moss as their branches sway gently in the warm breeze. As I make my way through the park towards my house, many thoughts are racing through my mind, but the one that weighs the heaviest is the question of how I can live one more day of this life without him in it.

On this night, I am drawn to this place as if I am acting out a part in a play that I never wanted. I feel hollow inside, but still, I wait not knowing anymore what keeps me here. Mourning the loss of him, I would give up everything to have him back in my life. I contemplate my loneliness as I face the darkness around me. It is an inevitable moment, and I know he isn't here even though I can still feel him. I have been waiting long enough and know that I will not find him here, not on this night and not ever again. Even though he has left me, his presence still lingers here, and I can't seem to erase the image of his face from my mind nor do I want to. The sweet sound of his voice still rings in my ears and now that I know what I must live without I can't just be left behind to live alone again. My dreams are no longer enough. I sit down on the old wooden and iron bench as my thoughts consume me. I am numb by the thought of never feeling his touch again. I am pulled down, and my exhausting life is drowning me. My fears have kept me suppressed all these years, but he was a glimmer of hope, a light that shined in the dark for me. I want to cry, but the pain is paralyzing. I visualize jumping off that cliff in my dream, falling forever. I can't go on like this any longer. Slowly I stand up and begin to walk back towards my house.

As I walk towards the edge of the park along the little-pebbled path I notice shadows forming around me in the dark trees that surround on either side. I have been so wrapped up in my thoughts that I forgot about the danger of being in the park alone late at night. I don't know if my mind is playing tricks on me, but I think there is a shadow of a man in the trees to my right. I walk faster as my heart pounds in my chest, and my mouth goes dry. I hear the cracking of sticks and leaves off in the distance, and it sounds like someone is approaching from behind. I am fearful, wanting to jump and run as fast as I possibly can but I stand perfectly still looking all around. I don't know the direction from which the sound is coming. Then slowly and deliberately a shadow appears out from the thick cluster of pine trees to the right of where I stand, and it's at this very moment I see it. It is a man, and my stomach does a flip. I panic and can't think straight. I have flashbacks to the night that Terry attacked me. I should have never been out in the park alone after dark. I begin to run, fast, towards the exit that leads out of the park and to the safety of my home, but he catches me in his arms, and he holds tightly onto me. His grip is so tight that I feel I might suffocate and then he loosens his grip ever so slightly. This is it, this is the end, and I will die tonight by the hands of a crazed lunatic and not by my own. I begin to scream and kick, pounding with clenched fists at the arms that are wrapped tightly around my waist, and then I turn my head quickly to see the assailant hoping to be able to identify him if I do survive. But as soon as my eyes meet his, I freeze.

"William," I breathlessly whisper as I stop resisting. If I ever had any doubts before that he is the one from my earliest dreams after the wreck, those doubts are gone in an instant for I immediately know as he holds me close to his body that he is the one. He is my guardian angel.

"You came back," I exclaim as I remember all the countless nights that I laid awake in my bed thinking about him and wanting him there with me.

"I thought I would never see you again." I smile, catching up with my breath now. "Abigail, is it true? Are you thinking about ending your life tonight?"

"Yes, I am, or I was. I can't live without you, William! I don't want to live without you!"

I stop speaking as he places his finger over my lips. My heart begins to beat faster, and he feels it as he places the palm of his hand on the center of my chest. The beat is strong as it races almost out of control. His eyes are overcome with emotion for me. The beat of my heart begins to slow to a calm rhythm.

"I'm sorry, Abigail, I didn't mean to frighten you," he quietly says as torment fills his expression.

Unable to move or speak, I am caught in a trance by his eyes as he slowly begins to speak.

"We don't have to be apart, Abigail, but there is only one way we can be together. I can offer you a new life and a love everlasting. I can offer you a life beyond your wildest imagination. I know you have spent a long time feeling empty and searching as I have searched. You don't know how long I have searched for you. You will never be lonely again, and your emptiness will disappear. Don't be afraid. All you have to do is say yes."

I have waited for what has felt like forever for him to come back to me and at this very moment, I know what he is saying to me is true. I have been searching for him from the moment I woke up all alone in the hospital after the wreck until here tonight in this park. He is the answer to all the questions that I have been searching for. He has always been in my heart and my soul, a part of me. He will be my salvation from this lonely life, and I want to be by his side forever. I finally understand my destiny, and it is here in front of me. With tears in my eyes, I say, "yes."

He looks at me the way a man looks at a woman when he is in love and holds me now gently in his arms; he slowly leans his face in closer to mine. I am safe here, not fearful, feeling as though I am finally complete. He kisses me softly on the neck, sending chills up and down my spine, my heart pounds faster in my chest, and then I feel the pain, the sharp, shooting, white-hot searing pain. There is a burning through my veins and surprisingly, an unusual sense of pleasure at the same time. I struggle briefly and then I succumb to the moment. Staring up at him, pleading with my eyes for him to stop, and then my body suddenly goes limp. I feel him cradle me in his arms and with fangs buried deep in my jugular; he drinks in my blood draining it from my body, giving to me the mortal death that I had come to this place seeking and taking from me the life that I no longer desired to live.

Chapter 9: Dawn

I open my eyes slowly and everything around me appears distorted. I blink furiously until my vision is clear. I can't be sure at first about what happened because my memory is foggy.

"Abigail." I hear a soft voice coming from above me. I take one look at him and I'm confused. Then fear courses through my body.

"Stay away from me!" I cry out, my voice is hoarse as I twist myself off the bed trying to stand on shaky feet. My body seems to take on a life of its own, every cell screaming out with searing pain. It runs deep like the pain someone feels after losing the one they love and the burn in my veins is practically paralyzing. There is a hunger inside of me, an intense hunger like I have never felt before and it only adds to my confusion. I make my way stumbling down the hall into the kitchen as if I am being drawn there against my own will. I follow the pull towards the refrigerator feeling the pain twisting and gripping at my insides as I open the door. I quickly grab the raw meat in the drawer and sink my face into it draining it dry of all blood. Dropping it to the floor

I stagger to the bathroom and look at myself in the mirror, blood drips from my face, but the pain still lingers.

I feel empty like a shell without a center, a body without a soul. Something is missing. It is my heartbeat. I can't feel it anymore. My body wretches as I hunch over, tears should be streaming out of my eyes but there is nothing. They remain dry.

"What has happened to me?" I scream out, feeling betrayed as he stands next to the door of the bathroom.

"It isn't supposed to be this way! This isn't what I wanted!" I yell.

I make my way to the front door opening it, I step outside. The sun seems unusually bright to my eyes making it hard for me to see and my skin raw. He stands silently in the corner of the living room watching my every move. He seems concerned about me but keeps his distance.

The sun is low in the sky and there isn't a cloud in sight, so I turn around and stomp back inside, still confused. I pace the floor back and forth feeling like a caged animal. The walls close in on me as I glare at him from across the room.

I saunter over to the wall and look at my reflection in the mirror. I don't completely recognize myself. I turn and glance at the clock. It is 5:00 p.m. and I realize then that I have slept most of the day away. The burn continues in my veins as I slump down onto the floor. As I am lying here, I suddenly remember. It all comes back to me and I know what happened. I feel an urgent need for him now. The sun finally sets, and it is dusk outside.

"William," I call out as I sit up on the floor and lean against the wall.

"I'm here, Abigail."

He rushes to my side and helps me up off the floor and to my feet. His voice is soft and sounds like music to me.

I move closer to him until I am leaning on him and he supports me in his arms. I slowly raise my arm and touch the side of his face with my hand. A flood of memories rushes back. My mortal life is flashing before my eyes, all the memories that I could not remember layout in front of me. I see myself as a young girl with my family, smiling and happy, and then the loss of my parents, the grief, and the loneliness. I see the face of a young woman who I don't recognize followed by strange memories that don't seem to fit. Then I see myself in the park contemplating the unthinkable. He is there watching over me as he had done so many nights before and he waits to save me from myself. He wants me to be with him forever, immortal. I see it in my mind, every detail as vivid as though I am reliving every moment. Suddenly the memories end and I peer up at him. He is gazing at me affectionately and I lean in closer to him placing my weary head against his strong chest feeling very weak as he holds me steady in place.

"Let's go outside and get some air." He helps me out onto the front porch, and we lean against the railing.

"I am burning inside, please make it stop. I can't take the pain any longer," I bellow looking up at him with desperation.

"Here, you must drink my blood. It will complete the process," he says and with those words, I place my lips on his neck, I bite and the twisting burning pain that I feel in the pit of my core is gone. I take the blood into my body and the emptiness is gone. I can feel my heart beating now and it beats inside of me stronger than ever. The feeling of loss and all the pain that I have ever felt during my mortal life has vanished. I feel a deeply satisfying love from him that I have never known as he cradles me in his arms. I am whole for the first time during my existence. As though it were instinctive, I know when to stop and I move my lips over to his and we kiss with a passion that I didn't anticipate. We both have waited so long for one another and we are finally together. Our search is over, and my immortal life begins.

Chapter 10: Memories

"My mind keeps racing with memories of you from a time that seems so distant, so far away. I can't completely place them," I say as I reach for his hand and hold it in mine, not knowing why I have always been so drawn to him. I am stronger now and I can stand better on my own two feet.

"Some of your memories from when you were mortal will take time to come back. Others may never come back." He tells me.

"Come on, let's talk more inside. There is a lot that we need to discuss," he says as he leads me back inside the house.

He shuts the door behind us, and we walk over to sit on the sofa. A chill goes straight through me and I tremble. He reaches behind me grabbing the blanket off the back of the sofa and he places it around me hugging me close to his chest.

"Is that better?" He asks squeezing me tight against him. He is strong and his arms around me feel right.

"Yes, very much." I smile up at him.

"You've been through a lot. You need your rest," he suggests.

I place my tired head on his shoulder as I enjoy the security and the warmth of being in his strong arms. Even though he is as cool to the touch as I am now it still feels warm to me. A sense of contentment washes over me and a feeling of belonging that I haven't known in a long time. His body is hard but comfortable and his cologne smells like musk and sandalwood. My body aches but in a good way this time.

"I remember dreaming about you and I remember seeing you in a bookstore." I gasp as I suddenly remember the bookstore and that I am scheduled to work in the coffee shop. There is absolutely no way it is going to happen. I spring to my feet quickly and prance into the kitchen searching through the cabinet drawers for the phone number to the coffee shop. When I can't find it, I look at my phone and see that it is in my contacts.

"I just remembered that I have to work tonight," I announce as I pick up the phone and press the button to place the call. It rings three times and then there is a voice on the other end of the line that I don't recognize.

"Thank you for calling Ultimate Coffee, this is Jenny, can I help you?"

"Um, yeah, this is Abigail Dubois. I won't be coming in to work tonight...I... um...have come down with a stomach virus, I think." My voice is raspy and hoarse.

"Alright, Abigail, I'll let the manager know. I hope you feel better soon. It's not going to be any fun working tonight without you here." The voice on the other end exclaimed.

"Uh okay. I'm sorry." I reply a little confused because I clearly don't remember Jenny but I should.

"Don't apologize silly. Thanks for calling," she says and then hangs up.

I drop my phone onto the sofa and sit back down next to William.

"The last thing you need to worry about is work," he says with a smile on his face. I smile back at him and remember how much I love his smile.

"I feel so connected to you, William, do you know why? Please tell me."

There is a sense of urgency to my voice that I don't quite understand but I so desperately want to know why I have always felt a supernatural force between us.

"Yes, I do know why," he says leaning in to kiss me again as we embrace with the most passion that we have felt between one another yet. Our cool skin pressed together feels warm.

"I am your maker," he whispers in my ear.

"I feel like it goes deeper than that. I feel like I have always known you my whole life."

"That is a typical feeling for a newborn to have towards their maker."

Turning my head and looking up at him slightly, I ask, "How did you know what I was thinking last night in the park?"

"I could feel it, not hear it," he says. His brow creased and his mouth turns downward in a grimace.

"I finally found you. I couldn't lose you," he confesses.

"Why did you leave me?" I ask. My tone is sad from the faint memory.

"Just one more kiss before I explain." He leans in to kiss me. He then stares across the living room as he starts to answer my question.

"I was a vampire and you were a mortal. I wanted to be with you more than you can know but I knew it just wouldn't work. I was too tempted by your blood and by your scent. When I was close to you the hunger inside of me was almost too much to handle. When you would stand too close to me, I would begin to envision taking you in my arms and draining the life out of you so that you would be mine forever. It was all I could do to resist the blood pulsing through your veins and throbbing in your neck. I can resist mortals when I need to, but you were different. I wanted you for reasons other than just your blood. The temptation was just too great. I never wanted to hurt you or use you in any way. Leaving you that night in the bookstore parking lot was the hardest thing that I ever had to do, and I thought it would be the best thing for you, but I know now that it wasn't. I never actually left you, though. I was always there, Abigail. I told myself that I would continue to watch over you and protect you from afar. But my love for you was too strong and I knew that I wouldn't be able to stay away for good. I found myself wanting and needing to be near you more and more every day. When I wasn't watching you at work, I would stay outside your house at night waiting in my car hoping to see you, to catch a glimpse of you, just to be near you. I was there every night that you waited for me at the bookstore. I watched you and you never saw me. I could feel your pain and it tore me up inside. I had hoped that over time you would have forgotten about me or even learned to hate me, but you didn't. Your love for me somehow grew stronger and so did your pain. Last night I followed you to the park and kept watch over you ...waiting to make you mine." He pauses and his eyes are intense as he stares at me.

"I could feel the despair in your heart, and I feared what you might do if I let you go back to your house alone. I knew that I had to protect you from yourself. I waited in the shadows feeling what you were feeling. When I realized that you were willing to end your life because of me, I knew I had to offer you this life. It was the only way we could be together. I knew that I could no longer stay away from you. I wasn't strong enough and I didn't want to lose you for good. I needed you and I wanted you with me, immortal, but I feared that you might not accept it. I had to give you the choice, though."

"All I want is you, William, all I ever wanted was you. I had given up on my mortal life. There was nothing for me in that life anymore. I would have never turned you down. What happened after you turned me, I don't remember any of it?" I ask.

"Afterwards I carried you to my car and drove you to your house. I laid you on your bed and I stayed with you for the rest of the night, watching and waiting, making sure you would be alright and that the process wasn't too painful for you. I watched as you thrashed around violently in your bed, but you remained unconscious during the worst of it, thankfully. I held you in my arms to keep you still and I tried to offer more of my blood to you, but you were too far into the change to know what was going on around you."

"More of your blood?" I question.

"Yes, I had given you some from my wrist after I turned you. That is what starts the process. Usually, during the changing process, the memory of how it happened is lost and it can take a little while for it to come back. I knew you would be confused and I would never want you to fear me so when you started to wake up I almost left your side thinking that it might be best for you if I weren't here but I couldn't bring myself to do it. I couldn't leave you again not when you might need me the most. I promise to never leave you again, Abigail. You have my word. "

His melodic voice is soothing to me as I lounge by his side and when I think about how strong his feelings are for me, I can't help but understand how he feels because I feel the same way about him.

"William, you are my destiny." I touch his face gently with my hand caressing his smooth cool cheek. "I would never be frightened of you," I say as I move my head and place it on his chest. We sit in silence for a long time, enjoying the moment. He runs his fingers through my hair and twists them gently around the dark blonde locks bringing my hair closer to his face to savor the scent.

"Are you still drawn to me by my scent?" I ask.

"Yes, but it's different now. It isn't your blood but your perfume." He says and we both laugh.

"When was the first time you saw me? Was it the night that I saw you in the bookstore?" I ask sighing with elation as little shivers travel through my body from his touch.

"When I first saw you, I knew my search was over. It was nearly three years ago when you first started working at the coffee shop. I felt my heart drop in my chest at the sight of you. It was as though I had known you forever. You're so beautiful to me, Abigail, inside and out. From the first moment I laid eyes on you I knew. I saw deep into your soul and I just knew." He confesses.

Slowly he continues, "You reminded me that I could love again. I felt the icy façade that I had built around me over many years melt away. There was something about your eyes that drew me in from that first moment. I hadn't seen that look in anyone else's eyes in many, many years. I could see the soft warmth in them and a special understanding of things that most mortals never get. You were different, unique. I stood in the aisle that night and just watched you as you worked. The way your body moved gracefully and the way your long blonde hair gently flowed with each movement you made. You were the first mortal to mesmerize me the way you did." His attention seems to wander to a place far away.

We look at one another for a long time and then finally the silence is broken.

"Why did it take you so long to reveal yourself to me?" I ask.

"I never meant to reveal myself to you. I knew that it would complicate things further for you and I didn't want to be a complication in your life. I envisioned holding you in my arms and telling you how I felt. We would live happily ever after, a mortal's fairy tale, but I knew that it wasn't possible for me, so I had decided that it was enough for me to just know that you were in the world and that I was near you. I decided that I would love you from afar and watch over you. But then you saw me at the bookstore that night watching you. I had hoped that maybe I was mistaken and that you hadn't seen me after all. But after the day in the grocery store, I knew that wasn't the case. You weren't supposed to see me. It wasn't part of my plan for you to ever see me but as time went by, I became careless." He admits without any regret in his tone.

"Why did you come to see me at the coffee shop later that night then?" I question him.

"I could feel how upset you were after the grocery store incident when you saw me there and I didn't want you to feel that way. So, I went to see you at the coffee shop that night to apologize and make you aware that I wasn't just some figment of your imagination and that you weren't going crazy. I only wished that I could have explained things to you to clear up your confusion, but I knew that was impossible for me to do. I could feel how desperate you were to know why I seemed familiar to you. I knew you were having dreams about me too."

"It seems like such a long time to have only watched me and to have never approached me not until I saw you," I respond but not quite understanding the inner strength that it must have taken for him to stay away from my sight for so long.

"Well, immortality can be an extremely adequate teacher when it comes to learning a good lesson in patience. And as you will become aware of since being made immortal yourself, time does seem to pass by a little faster for us than it does for the mortal human. It is only illusionary of course," he says, and I nod in agreement.

"So, three years wouldn't feel like the same length of time to an immortal as it does to a mortal?" I ask, trying to understand my new life.

"No, it's more like half of that," he replies. We sit on the sofa in each other's arms and it is relaxing. I am noticing that it is always such a relaxing feeling to be around William. He calms me most of the time except when he looks at me in that certain way with his gorgeous pale blue eyes or when he kisses me softly along the nape of my neck.

Chapter 11: Reflection

The next morning the sun breaks past the horizon and the soft light of day comes filtering in the room through the opaque curtains on the windows. I sit silently staring at the beautiful man who lounges next to me. His eyes are closed as he rests peacefully. In the soft light of day, his skin isn't quite as pale as it had seemed when I saw him by the light of the moon on my front porch. It has a muted glow in the morning light with a slight blush to his cheeks. His lips are slightly parted, and they seem to tremble almost unnoticeable. His chest rises leisurely up and down with the breaths he takes in and exhales out. His dark auburn hair shines with the light and is cropped just below his ears. He slowly begins to open his pale blue eyes to catch me studying his exquisite features. Smiling with rested contentment and reaching out, he pulls me over and across his lap until I am lounging semi-upright with my head resting gently on his chest.

"Good morning," he whispers.

The faint activity of a heartbeat is all that I hear as my head lays gently at the base of his chest.

"William, why is it that our hearts beat so faintly to the point that it can hardly be heard or felt?" I quietly ask.

"Well, let's see," his voice is low in tone as he closes his eyes again, thinking.

"The immortal's body is one of the most efficient and physically fit of all the creatures on this earth. As one's body becomes more physically fit, this includes mortals too, the less often your heart contracts, therefore, saving heartbeats. Since the immortal has probably the most physically strong and fit body of all, it is only natural that the heartbeat is almost undetectable. Our hearts only average about 35 or fewer beats per minute.

Is it hard for you to hear my heartbeat? Is that why you are asking me this question?"

I nod sheepishly at him in agreement with a small smile on my face. He smiles back seeming to be taken with my inquisitive nature.

"As your abilities begin to take effect you will be able to hear and feel even your heartbeat better," he tells me.

"I almost forget how it feels to be a newborn because it has been so long ago since I was turned." He gets up from the sofa and stretches. I watch his strong body and I think it is the most magnificent one that I have ever seen. He is tone and muscular. And the way his shirt clings to his chest showing off his chiseled physique makes me feel warm inside my cool body.

"Is that enough questions for now?" He asks as he leans over and kisses me on the forehead.

"Yes, enough questions for now," I state and watch him wander over into the kitchen.

I stand up and move towards the mirror that hangs on the wall in my living room. I stare at the strange woman looking back at me. Although my eyes had once been brown as a mortal, they are now a piercing pale amber color, unlike the pale icy blue that I see gazing at me from William's face. The woman in the mirror isn't the shy, weak, and unsure woman that I once knew. This new image is confident and strong. My muscle tone is tight, almost hard, like I had been working out at a gym for months, maybe years. During my mortal life, I had been plain but now I am beautiful, seductive. My hair is the same long wavy dark blonde that it had always been, but it seems to shimmer now with a subtle glitter as the light streams in from the windows and dances around it. And unlike the dull flat skin color of my old body, this new body is the color of porcelain. It is radiant, nearly translucent, it almost seems to glow. I barely recognize myself as I stand here mesmerized by the gorgeous reflection in the mirror, desirable to the point of almost being hypnotic. I admire my new image for a long time, my new appearance, thinking of all that has happened to me in the last twenty-four hours. It is incomprehensible and bewildering but mostly it is unbelievable. I am now immortal and a vampire.

Although my confidence level and outward appearance have changed for the better it's my insatiable thirst for blood that makes me feel uneasy. And it hasn't been tested yet around mortals because I haven't left my house since I was turned or saved as I like to think of it. I don't know how I am going to react when I am finally around them. I can still smell the meat on the floor in the kitchen but by now its scent is no longer inviting, it's putrid.

There is still so much that I don't know about my new existence in this life. I know that I will be learning something new every day from now on and there are so many questions that I need to answer. Some of those questions have already been answered by just living this new life of mine. For instance, I know that it is uncomfortable but not impossible to go outside during the day. The sun seems too bright to my eyes and it makes my skin feel raw, but I figure with the right amount of sunscreen, long sleeve shirt, pants, and sunglasses, an immortal can tolerate it. Although, I would imagine that most of the time the choice is not to. I can already tell that I will enjoy the cloudy days better and during my mortal life, I always preferred them anyway, so it seems to suit me just fine. I know that I no longer need sleep only rest. I know that my body doesn't require mortal food for nourishment any longer and I wonder if I will begin to miss it. Although immortals still can eat and drink if they wish or if the situation depends on it. I wonder if food will taste as good as it did when I was mortal. Although, somehow, I highly doubt it. I feel like I will probably try until I find the things that I can still enjoy. I know it will take some time to get used to my new life and all the changes that come with it. Time is one thing that I have plenty of now. I know that I will never really miss anything from my mortal life because being with William forever is more than enough for me.

I turn and look around the room. Focusing my eyes on every little detail as they become much clearer and more apparent to me, my senses are slowly becoming heightened as I stand here. My sense of awareness for everything around me is more intense and I can feel myself becoming much stronger physically. As I run my fingers along with the console below the mirror, I am more conscious of my sense of touch. The grain on the wood feels alive as I caress it. The feeling creates little impulses that shoot through my fingertips like electricity. My vision, smell and hearing are developing into a magnification of their former state as I stand here in my living room. It is like someone is turning up the volume on the control panel of my senses. The minuscule cracks in the plaster on the walls stand out more than before and the tiny particles of dust that would normally be almost undetectable to the mortal eye float

freely across to the other side of the living room. The musky smell

coming from outdoors is stronger than usual and it

invades my nostrils. I am strangely aware of everything and all at

the same time. I can even feel the faint beat of my own heart

in my chest once again.

Although my hearing is more sensitive than it had been as a

mortal, I don't hear William walk back into the room after cleaning

the mess that had been left on the floor in the kitchen from the

other morning.

I am noticing that William is very graceful, very quiet, and cat-

like and I, too, have also become more graceful since becoming

immortal.

"There you are, I was just helping out in the kitchen. You

left a pretty good mess on the floor," he says with a wink.

I don't think that I will ever get used to seeing him. It

feels like the first time every time. He is the most handsome man

that I have ever seen. Breathtakingly gorgeous and the love that I

feel for him makes my chest want to burst open with happiness. He

walks over to me and takes me in his arms, kissing me on the

cheek ever so gently. His eyes are warm and full of love for me.

"Am I dreaming?" I ask.

"What? You never heard of a man cleaning the kitchen before?" He teases and then leans in and whispers in my ear, "If you are, I don't ever want you to wake up."

His cool breath sends shivers down my spine, filling me with a longing for more. He kisses me on the lips softly and slowly before walking over to the built-in shelving along the wall standing and looking at the framed family pictures.

"This is you and your parents," he questions as he picks up the frame to get a closer look. I walk over next to where he is and put my arm around his lower back.

"Yes, that was the night of my high school graduation at the restaurant where we ate," I answer. William turns and glances in my direction while placing the picture frame back on the shelf. I stand to stare at the photo for several minutes. Then I sit down in the chair next to the sofa. I look up at William as he leans against the wall in silence.

"Have you ever wondered about where my family is?" I ask him suddenly. He shakes his head in agreement and looks down at the ground. His expression is hard to read.

"They died," I say flatly while still eyeing the picture. William doesn't say a word. He just continues to stare at the floor.

"Anyway, I don't remember all of the details about it nor do I want to talk about it right now. It's all very hazy in my memory. Tell me your story, Will. I want to know everything about you. All of the details."

"What do you want to know?" He asks as he sits down on the sofa.

"Everything and then some, like, when were you born, where, what did you do during your mortal life?"

"Well, as you know, mortal memories can be hard to remember and since mine was so very long ago I will try my best. I do know that I was born sometime in the summer of 1788 in Bordeaux, France. I've always used August 5 as my birthday, but I don't know. I am certain of the year, though. My parents named me William Francois Delaflote. My childhood is pretty much a blur to me but in my mind's eye, I can still see the faces of my parents as I left them behind for the new land. Of course, I'm talking about America and I wasn't much older than you. I was 22 years old, so young. When I arrived, along with my brother, in New Orleans it must have been around January in 1810 because I remember it was very cold. My memories are a little more vivid during my mortal life in New Orleans. I got a job working down at the docks and eventually, I was introduced to Captain Lafitte. He offered me a spot onboard one of his ships and I gladly accepted. It worked out well for some time. Back then it was an appealing way of life for someone such as me. Anyway, we would sail the Gulf of Mexica all around the Caribbean and from New Orleans to

Galveston and made stops in between, one of those stops being here in Lake Charles. The voyages took a lot of hard labor, but the evenings made it all worthwhile. Being out on the open saltwater as the sun was setting in the sky, painting it with colors of pink, yellow, and orange. I can still taste that salt in my mouth as the sea spray gently misted my face. It was the life. We would stop here along the Calcasieu River quite often because it was almost midway between the two destinations. This region became known as the Neutral Strip around the year 1806 when the boundary between Spanish Texas and the United States was being disputed. A treaty was signed, and the area was left unoccupied by law enforcement and troops from either side. The area soon became a haven of sorts for the lawless and social outcasts from the two countries. Over time the strip became home to some of its earliest settlers who would eventually sail on the ships with us. Lafitte loved the bayous along this area, Contraband Bayou was his favorite. He had hideouts all along the bayou. He also had several friends that lived here along the lake and they would provide us with food and much-needed rest during those long voyages."

I am silent and in shock, staring at him for what feels like the longest time, repeating in my brain what he has just told me. He has been alive for so long and yet only appears to be in his mid-twenties, all the things that he must have seen and done during his existence are sending my mind spinning.

"Y…You are over two hundred years old and you were a pirate?" I finally murmured in astonishment.

"Yes, well, it was a job and it did pay well. It provided me with a good living. I helped operate the ships most of the time. I wasn't the type of pirate that you are probably thinking about although I did find myself in many a precarious position from time to time that required a pistol or sword as a quick solution. But I liked to think of myself as more of a Privateer than anything else."

"I feel completely speechless. I don't know what to say except that I almost can't believe it," I admit, being amazed by it, and then suddenly a memory washes over me like a strong ocean wave. "I know what happened to you. It was awful. When you worked on the ships a long time ago, you were accused of stealing something of value. Some of the crew members wanted you to give back the missing treasure that they believed you had stolen from Lafitte. They thought you had buried it along the bayou to hide it for yourself and when you couldn't tell them where it was, they didn't believe you and therefore they attacked you. They left you for dead along the edge of Contraband Bayou." The memory drains me.

"That's right. I can't believe you know that! I didn't steal the treasure. I was set up. They had suspected another pirate of stealing it at first, but he pointed the finger at me. The other men on the ship didn't like me too much. I was different from them because I didn't like to drink and stay out all night carousing and causing problems for the locals. So, it was easy for them to blame me." William's lips hardened into a thin crease and a look that I have never seen before possesses his face and his eyes are ice cold with intensity. The memory has him visibly upset so I move from the chair and sit next to him. I wrap my arms around his shoulders with a hug and gently stroke his back.

"I am sorry, Will. I see how it still upsets you after all this time," my tone is soft and sympathetic.

"This is great! You must be able to see into the past. This must be one of your capabilities, Abigail."

"I have a capability. Is that a vampire thing?" I am confused.

"Yes, it is." He smiles and laughs loudly.

"No more talking about the past, let's go out into the night, there is something I want to show you. It has probably taken effect by now. You need to see!" He says with a mischievous look on his face as he grabs my hand in his.

Chapter 12: Ghost

The day disappeared into the night so quickly. Time seems different to me in this new life, it goes by faster than it used to when I was mortal, just like William had told me. He places his arm around me, and we step out the back door of my house and into the black of night. The crickets chirp softly, and the air is warm and moist as it clings lightly to my skin. As I look out at my surroundings I am in complete surprise, it isn't dark to me at all. I can see everything very clearly now as an immortal. It's as though I had always been wearing a veil over my eyes during my mortal life that kept me from seeing in the dark and now it has been lifted. The particles of light from the stars and the moon bounced off every solid object around me and create a type of night vision for my eyes.

I look out across the back lot and can see deep into the woods that stretch out in front of me. It wasn't this way the other night, only now is my eyesight different. This is what he meant when he said it should have taken effect by now. I look around slowly using my newly acquired sight as my guide as I step down slowly onto the damp ground beneath my feet. Walking around the trees on the wooded lot, I turn to William to share the excitement I feel about my discovery of nocturnal sight. He is standing on the back porch a few feet away from where I now stand, and he is staring up into the tall pine trees.

"I can see in the dark. I can't believe it. This is so amazing!" I exclaim looking all around me and spinning in a tight circle until I feel slightly dizzy.

"I know isn't it marvelous. It is one of the best qualities of the condition," he says as he continues to look up at the trees. I stop to see what he is distracted by and suddenly without warning, I feel a rush of air pass quickly by the side of my head blowing my hair every which way, and then again it came from the opposite direction. I scream, duck and start to run back to the porch where William stands. I cower behind him with fright. I then look up at the night sky as I scan the pine trees above me. They are tall and thin, seeming as if they go on forever. I quickly look for whatever it is that has just flown past me and then on one of the branches above I see the owl. I look over at William as he says, "He's flirting with you, Abigail."

"What are you talking about?" I question. My voice is a little edgy and I don't know what to think only that he is joking with me and it makes me a little upset after the owl has practically dive-bombed me. I peer back up in the pine tree above me to the right of the large lot and there it sits, the owl, the one I had seen before in the trees. It is large and magnificent, majestic. It calls out to the night as I stare at it and then it seems to fall from the branch in a downward spiral speeding towards me amazingly fast. I close my eyes bracing myself and hiding behind William expecting to feel the full impact of it as it hits both of us with its massive body, but nothing happens. I don't feel a thing. I open my eyes to see William standing there facing me with the owl on his right hand, smiling from ear to ear. In sheer amazement at the sight of the beautiful creature with him, I too begin to smile.

"He thinks you're the most beautiful woman he has ever seen," he states as the smile stays fixed at each corner of his lips.

"Who does? The owl," I ask not understanding his joke. "You're teasing me, stop it."

"Am I?" He is amused as he meets my gaze directly. "Abigail, would you believe me if I told you that I can hear his thoughts?"

A hush came over the crickets and the night suddenly seemed too quiet. I have no idea what he is talking about.

"Oh, no, don't you for one minute expect me to believe that you can talk to animals."

"After everything that has already happened you don't want to believe that these things are real?" He questions, surprised by my reaction.

"These things only happen in stories, it is supposed to be made-up stuff written in books or seen in movies, and it isn't supposed to be real!" I shout, feeling like I have come unraveled by all that had taken place in the last twenty-four hours.

As I turn to run back into the house, William grabs me by the arm gently and turns me back around towards him. He looks concerned as he places his hand on my cheek slowly caressing my face before moving his fingers to my mouth and tracing my lips softly.

"I'm sorry. I didn't mean to upset you. I wasn't thinking. You have had so much to process in such a short time. It wasn't fair of me to pick on you that way, please forgive me," he sincerely pleads with me. Reluctantly, I smile and tell him it is alright. Not being able to resist his eyes.

"Does he have a name?" I ask looking at the owl.

"I named him Ghost because he flies silently through the night usually unseen and sometimes his call sounds like he is saying boo," he says looking at me again with those irresistible blue eyes.

"I found him one night in the trees around my house. He was calling out as though he was talking directly to me. I went outside and that is when he flew down and landed directly in front of me on the banister of my front porch. He has stayed near me ever since. My favorite bird since then has always been the owl. It is the most logical and appropriate nocturnal creature for me to communicate so easily with since I like to spend most of my time outdoors during the night. That is how I kept an eye on you a lot of the time. Ghost can go farther and without being noticed as easily." William smooths the bird's feathers with his free hand.

He whispers something to the owl.

"Watch this, Abigail," he says.

"Ghost, fly to the top of that pine tree and bring me back one single pine needle." And with a gust of wind from his wings, the owl propels himself into the flight, soaring high into the tree above while landing on a branch and plucking one insignificant needle from the limb. Then he is back to gliding through the night air and landing back into William's waiting hand. The owl drops the single pine needle into William's other empty palm. I assume that William must have spent a lot of his spare time training this beautiful bird to do this trick for him. I'm not quite convinced.

"That's an easy trick," I reply with a look of skepticism written across my face.

"Oh, Ghost, we have a tough audience. Let's show her something that will impress," he says then commands the owl to do something just by looking into the creature's eyes. The bird was off and up in flight quickly out of sight from both of us.

"What did you tell him?" I ask curiously.

"I told him to fetch something for me from my house and to bring it back to me so that I can give it to you."

"What is it?" I smile.

"A rose from my garden." He moves closer to me and takes my hand in his. "I'm going to tell you something else, but you probably already know this one." He gazes into my eyes and leans in closer as I stand very still slowly closing my eyes as my head slightly tilts back. I can feel his breath softly against my cheek as he whispers in my ear, "You are so beautiful in the moonlight, Abigail." I open my eyes briefly and am met by his icy blues. I pull him towards me and kiss him for the remainder of the time until Ghost appears with the same gust of wind from its wings as before and lands on the banister that surrounds the back porch with a red rose nestled in his beak for me. I smile at the owl and then up at William as he takes the rose from Ghost and hands it to me.

"Thank you, Ghost," I say looking over at the owl. The bird nods his head to me which causes me to giggle.

"I'm impressed," I admit to him. William leans in and kisses me once more.

"How long have you been able to do this?" I ask breathlessly, staring at him and realizing what a truly wonderful gift it is to be able to communicate with nature the way he can. The owl blinks his brilliant yellow eyes slowly at me and then turns his head around to look out into the night.

"I have been able to read the feelings and sometimes the thoughts of most living things since the very beginning of my immortal life. I possess an inner strength that most immortals do not find until much later in their existence. I found this magic by accident one evening in the woods where I had been camping behind my home as it was being built. I watched the birds in the trees above me and as I looked up at them wondering what it would feel like to fly as freely as they do, I began to feel it. I felt what the birds were feeling as they flew around in the trees above me that night."

"I remember now that I had seen him outside of my house a couple of nights before all of this," I respond with my eyes wide. "Has he been watching over me?"

"Yes, as I would also. He would come back and tell me what you were up to."

"You were spying on me," I say, laughing.

"No, I was worried," he says as he lets Ghost fly back to the trees and leans in against the banister. William holds my gaze for a long time until I feel like I will melt from the love that simmers inside of me for him. I step over in front of him and he wraps his strong arms around my waist. His arms are strong like stone and being this close to him always makes me feel safe.

"How do you do it?" I ask.

"Do what?" He replies.

"Hear the thoughts of others." I lean my head backward from him ever so slightly to look up at his pale blue eyes.

William continues to hold me in his arms tightly and says, "Well, it comes pretty easy for me to tell you the truth. It does take a good amount of mental strength and energy. It is more like I can command a certain loyalty from him at the same time I can hear and feel what he is thinking. There is a certain magic that is found deep inside of me and only a few of us possess it. If the immortal does possess the magic it can usually take years to acquire the talent for it to become successful. I focus intently on the mortal creature that I want to listen to and then I begin to visualize what it is feeling. Over time and with practice it can be done without so much intense focus. I begin to feel what the mortal is feeling as it starts to happen slowly at first, there is a churning of little bubbles inside the pit of my stomach, and then I begin to feel what the mortal or creature is feeling and sometimes thinking. Sometimes it can be hard to feel what others are feeling." He furrows his brow but then starts to laugh. The sound comes flowing out of his throat like music amid the air. I love hearing it.

"Can you still read my feelings?" I ask looking down at the ground a little embarrassed at the idea.

"No, not anymore, I can't read immortals' feelings, unfortunately." He winks at me and I sigh with relief.

He continues, "We all have different capabilities. There are, of course, the basics that all immortals possess such as added physical strength, enhanced hearing, graceful agility, ageless beauty, and mind control. Some immortals do eventually develop special capabilities. Some are body shapeshifters, while some read thoughts and feelings, like me; others might run fast or have super physical strengths. The possibilities are endless, really, but like most things that are possible in life, even if the life is an immortal one, it can and usually does take time to develop them."

"You mean that there are immortals out there that change shape?" I ask in astonishment.

"It's true, but I have only seen one during my two hundred years in this condition."

My special capability, the only one that I have come to realize thus far, is the ability to see into the past and I wonder if I will be able to see the future. I am excited about the possibility of one day being able to find this magic that William speaks of within myself and be able to do some of the things that he has just told me. I try to imagine myself as a shapeshifter and what shape I would take. I would be an owl and I would fly alongside William one day. The thought makes me giggle to myself.

"This is truly a dream, William, to be here with you now. My life has only just begun," I whisper.

"What do we do now?" I ask, hoping it will involve more time alone exploring our new-found feelings for one another. I feel a strong longing to be his in every sense of the word and it is tearing at me almost to the point of being uncontrollable.

"I don't know. What would you like to do now?" He asks as he bites gently at my earlobe.

"William, I can hardly control myself around you, when we are this close all I want to do…" I stop speaking as I find it hard to find the words while he kisses the spot on my neck where he had given me this new life just a couple of nights ago.

"I know. I feel the same way, but we have to be patient," he whispers.

I can't help but feel a little disappointment but also excitement at the same time. I am thrilled by the thought of being with him completely. Always and forever.

"Do you want to go back to my place," he asks as he stands back from me slightly which breaks some of the physical tension between us.

"That sounds like a line," I laugh. "Where is your place? Please tell me it's not a cave or a perch high up in a tree somewhere," I say playfully.

"No, I live in a house. Can you believe it?" He laughs out loud.

"I don't know what to believe anymore, to be honest."

I take his hand and follow him out of the backyard to

his waiting car. A new shiny jet-black BMW coupe with dark

tinted windows sitting in the shadows of my driveway parked next

to my old blue 1997 hatchback. The interior is black leather and it

has that new car smell. I ease into the smooth comfortable

passenger seat as he sits on the driver's side and begins to back

down the driveway. He pulls out fast and speeds down the street

turning the corner sharply. I feel a rush of excitement inside

of me as I watch him control the car with effortless precision.

Speeding towards Shell Beach Drive and turning left onto it

following the curves in the paved drive down until he turns onto a

narrow driveway is hidden in a thick layer of trees.

Chapter 13: Questions

It is a very short distance to William's house from mine, probably only a mile away from where I live. As he drives the car along the driveway, I can see the house is hidden from sight behind a dense layer of tall pine trees. His home is an older, historic two-story probably about a hundred feet back from the road that runs in front of the lake. The outside of the home is painted antique cream with a large wraparound porch that extends out on both sides. It looks like arms open in a welcoming gesture
for me, inviting me inside. The home can use a fresh coat of paint and if it were restored it would be beautiful. I instantly fall in love with the home. It has a romantic quality about it, a true southern gem just yearning to be polished.

"I built this house shortly after I first came to settle here many years ago. It needs some cosmetic work on the outside but I keep it that way so it will appear abandoned." William states.

I can't help but wonder why he would want it to appear this way. As we step up onto the front porch the pine needles and leaves blow past our feet with the breeze.

"You really should give it a new coat of paint, it would be lovely," I observe, looking around at the exterior walls as I cross the porch to the front door.

"I will think about it, maybe I will do it for you." He winks at me as we make our way to the front door which he unlocks. I think about how long William has lived here along the lakefront and how I had grown up only a mile away from him here in the same town. I think about how mysterious and cruel fate can be sometimes but that it can also be wonderful. I know that fate has dealt its hand in both of our lives and has eventually brought us together.

William holds the door open as I step into the house. As I enter the home, I am astounded by the large two-story foyer that sprawls out in front of me. It holds the most beautiful furnishings and tapestries.

"I had all of the furnishings brought back with me when I left New Orleans," he says.

The ornate crown molding details the high edges of the walls near the ceiling. The floors are made from polished pine and the staircase is the grandest thing in the house sweeping down seamlessly in a gentle curve from the second floor. The inside of his home is very well kept compared to the outside and it is very modern in many ways, but it still maintains the nostalgic feel of the centuries past. William walks over to the fireplace and lights it.

Even though it is the month of May and the weather is warm outside the fire still feels good to me as I have not yet become used to my body's recent temperature drop. I walk over and stand next to him.

"You have the most beautiful home that I have ever seen," I say breathlessly as I continue to look around at every detail.

"Thank you, I'm glad you like it," he says. "I would like it if you stayed with me here tonight...every night from now on."

The fire crackles in front of us, it is the only light that fills the room, and its heat suddenly becomes too hot for me all at once. I back up quickly and move over to the couch. William follows and sits next to me. I can see by his expression that it is obvious to him that something is not right with me as I sit and stare at the fire glowing warmly in the fireplace.

"What's the matter? Did I say something wrong?" He reaches up and with his hand gently moves my face towards his. He can see the worry in my eyes and that bothers me.

"This is all happening so fast, it is all so new to me. It feels so unreal, too perfect," I say hesitantly. We sit silently for a few seconds and then he says, "I know, it's alright, you don't have to make a decision tonight. Just think about it, but please"

I place my finger on his lips and stop him in mid-sentence.

"Oh, William, that isn't what I meant but I do love that you are so generous, and you always think of my needs first. I don't ever want to be away from you not even for one second, so, yes, I will stay with you tonight here at your home."

"Can we make it permanent?" He grins with the most handsome smile that I have seen on him yet.

"Let's go get my things tomorrow." I smile with a slight gleam in my eyes.

He kisses me on the forehead and then walks over to the stereo system on the shelves next to the fireplace. There is also a large flat-screen television mounted on the wall over the mantle of the fireplace.

"Some music?" He asks and I nod. He puts on a slow song, one that I have never heard before. It sounds like something from the nineteen-fifties.

"Can I have this dance?" He asks as he reaches for me.

I stand up from the couch and walk over to where he is and take his hand, he twirls me around in a circle and then slowly pulls me close to his body as we sway in time with the music.

"You're a romantic, William Delaflote," I whisper in his ear. "What song is this?"

"Darling, Je Vous Aime Beaucoup by the great Nat King Cole," he whispers and then asks, "Do you speak French?"

"No, not fluently. I only know little bits. I have a pretty good idea what the song title means, though," I say quietly as we spin around slowly in a small circle. "Darling, I love you very much."

He nods in agreement with my translation and gazes deeply into my eyes. He begins to sing along softly and when he sings the words in French his voice makes me want to melt in his arms. There is electricity between us as we dance closely. He dips me once quickly as I giggle and then with determining slowness, he brings me back up as my back arches the whole way until I am straight, facing him eye to eye. We continue to dance until the song comes to an end and then we dance some more to the rhythm of our bodies.

"Would you like a glass of wine," he whispered to me.

"Can we do that?" I question as he leads me by the hand across the living room to the spacious kitchen. The next song begins to play in the background, and it is something more current. I feel as though I recognize it.

William makes his way around the kitchen counter and bends down to grab a vintage bottle of red wine out of the built-in wine refrigerator under the custom cabinetry.

"Do what? Oh, you mean, drink wine," he replies trying not to laugh but I can tell that he can't help but be amused and the look takes over his face.

"Of course, we can, you are twenty-one, right? Do I need to see some I.D.?" He asks as he chuckles.

"William don't make fun of me, I don't know all of the vampire dos and don'ts yet," I respond with a pout but it is funny to me so I just laugh it off.

I watch him as he effortlessly pulls the cork out of the bottle with the corkscrew. Taking two clear crystal wine glasses out of the cabinet he pours the red wine into both.

I take the glass of wine that he hands to me and he raises his glass to make a toast.

"To your new life, Abigail Catherine, may it be all that you hope for and more!" He winks at me.

"Thank you for coming back to me," I say affectionately as we touch glasses making a tiny clinking noise with them. The wine tastes good to me and I haven't thought that anything other than blood would ever taste good again, although blood does taste better.

"Well, since you mentioned vampire etiquette, there is a lot that you need to know about your new life?" He tells me as he walks around the bar to stand next to me. We sit down on the stools.

"Do you have any specific questions?" He asks me and takes another sip of the wine.

"Tell me what I need to stay away from. Like garlic, crosses, etc," she says.

"Those things are only myths, Abigail. You won't have to worry about any of those. The only thing that I know about that can be dangerous is silver. It will render you worthless and if it wasn't removed from your body in time you would eventually waste away." He says matter-of-factly.

The idea of that scares me. I finally have something real in my life to exist for and the alternative is not something I ever want to think about ever again.

"So, I guess all of my silver jewelry is going in the trash," I laugh nervously.

"That would be best," he agrees.

"What about sunlight? I tried to leave my house after I woke up the other morning and my eyes were so sensitive to the light and my skin felt raw."

"You will outgrow that. You probably already have. The sunlight is usually only that bothersome to a newborn after they first awaken. Over time your skin won't feel that way when you're in the sun, but your eyes will always be sensitive just not as bad as they were the other morning. You will learn that sunglasses are a necessity. Naturally, our kind, are drawn to the dark and we love the cloudy overcast days. It is a part of our genetic makeup, our DNA."

"That's good to know. I was worried that I would always feel that way in the sun." My tone is one of relief. "I've heard you refer to us as immortals, why is that?" I question and take a sip of wine. I had never been much of a drinker while I was mortal and now, I wonder why because this wine tastes wonderful to me.

"Well, we are vampires and that is what most mortals refer to us as. But among our circle the preferred term is immortals." He pauses and I sit quietly listening.

"Most of us with this condition prefer that term instead of the word vampire. The word vampire conjures up the idea of a monster and most of us don't want to be considered monsters. The term immortal is used loosely because as immortals we do reserve a very long lifespan, hundreds and sometimes even thousands of years, but immortality does not mean living forever and never dying. Our condition allows us to heal faster from injury than the normal mortal rate but severe injuries or being drained dry of our blood can kill us. The immortal condition enables us to age much slower both physically and mentally than mortals. It is because our minds naturally work differently than the mortal's mind and we are constantly in a state of perpetual physical regeneration, it is mind over matter most all the time. The immortal mind is a very powerful thing. So, indeed, our condition allows for us to live much longer, and because of the reasons I just stated we are called immortals. Unfortunately, we are not indestructible. We are not immortal in the true sense of the word."

"William don't refer to it as a condition. You make it sound like a disease or something." I wrinkle my brow and frown at him.

"I'm sorry. I don't mean to upset you by it. That's just how I refer to it." He leans back on the bar stool and looks across the kitchen.

"You're not upsetting me. It just sounds a little peculiar but since you explained everything now then I guess it does make more sense to me."

When I don't ask anything else, he continues, "Our appetite is sanguinary meaning that we must consume the blood of mortals or animals. It is the living cells inside of the blood that nourishes us. We can go about a week between feedings if we have to, but we never usually wait that long. When you start to feel weak you will know it is time to replenish your blood supply."

"There are three different types of vampires." He says as he looks at the surprise on my face.

"Three different types?" I respond.

"Yes, the most common is the Sanguine such as ourselves. Then there is the Psychic or Psi vampire who feeds only on the life force energy of the mortal and not the actual blood within the mortal. They can even feed off an immortal's energy. There aren't too many of them, but they can be dangerous. All they must do is touch their donor with their hand to receive the energy. I've only run across one Psi in my whole existence. And lastly, there are the

Hybrids. They feed off both the blood and the energy from mortals. They are truly unique. Their existence is purely an accident. Legend has it that the first Hybrid had two makers, a Sang, and a Psi, which ultimately created the Hybrid Vampire. There are more Hybrids in existence than are the Psi but far less than there are the Sang. Their covens are more often found in Europe."

My head feels like it is spinning by all the information that is being thrown in my direction.

"Honestly, it all sounds like it comes from one of those science fiction novels somewhere on a shelf in the bookstore where I worked." I laugh out loud and I can tell William is amused at me. The sound of my laughter is something that hasn't been heard by anyone in a very long time.

"I drank the blood straight from a piece of raw meat out of my refrigerator yesterday afternoon before I remembered what happened to me. It didn't completely satisfy my thirst. It only eased the hunger slightly."

"That is right, animal blood will only prolong the inevitable feeding on a mortal, and in the case of that raw meat, it didn't come from a live animal so it was pretty much worthless to you," He looks warily at me as if he is waiting for a response to everything he has just explained and probably not knowing what to expect because since he had turned me that night in the park he can't read my feelings as easily. My eyes suddenly freeze on him as he stares at me with concern. And then I begin to panic… the realization has hit me at what this truly means. I have been so wrapped up in the forever part of my immortality that I have completely overlooked one important factor. I will have to kill innocent people just to keep myself fed. I don't want this, and I didn't ask for this. I stiffen in my chair and become fixed with fear at the thought. The idea of the blood that I now hunger for is appealing to me but if it means killing to get it then I don't think I can do that. I know that I can't do it. It is making me sick to my stomach thinking about killing someone.

"What's wrong, Abigail?" William watches me as my face is stricken with panic. He places his fingers on the side of my hair tucking it behind my left ear.

"I don't want to kill anyone. This isn't right!" My voice sounds shrill and filled with terror as I face straight ahead and away from his gaping stare.

"It's alright, you won't have to. You didn't let me finish. The way most immortals choose to feed is the most humane and desirable way possible. When a mortal or donor as they are usually called, is chosen it is done through mind control and hypnosis. Only enough blood is taken to satisfy the thirst, which you will learn doesn't take much, a pint or less, and the donor never remembers what happened. The bite mark is instantly healed with our saliva."

William waits quietly to see how this news will register with me. I turn back to the side to face him and throw my arms around him and hug him tightly.

"A good vampire, I'm impressed. I had envisioned all the horror stories that I had heard about as a child," I smile at him gratefully and I am very relieved. I lean in closer to him and place my head on his shoulder hugging him tightly as it sends little pulses of electricity through my body to be so close to him.

"Now don't get me wrong. It does take a certain amount of self-control especially when you are new to this life but there are some immortals out there that don't live this way. They were already evil, sinful people during their mortal lives, and it carried over into their immortality. I have met some immortals who like to drain a mortal dry just for the fun of it and quite possibly because they are just gluttons. But they don't usually get away with it for long. Eventually, the ones who break the rules, which is the immortal code of honor, are dealt with harshly. So please remember, Abigail, there are bad immortals out there but most of us do our best to coexist with the mortal inhabitants of this world in which we live," William warns and I can't help but think it sounds funny that there is an immortal code of honor.

I nod understandingly and quickly ask, "Explain this immortal code of honor to me, and who enforces it?"

"It's the code that must be abided by all vampires and it has been passed down from maker to newborn throughout the centuries. It ensures that we are never discovered to be coexisting among the mortals. It helps maintain our anonymity. It is the same moral law that all humans live by, like the Ten Commandments for example. Not much has changed just because we now have a different diet. We still try to live moral lives and abide by the code of honor. The ones to enforce the code are the immortals in the area at that time. If a rogue immortal is found in an area causing problems among our kind or the mortals, they will be forcibly detained and a council of his or her peers is assembled. The one in charge of the council will always be chosen based on seniority. Anyway, the council hears the violations that the rogue is accused of, and then if their guilt is determined they are dealt with immediately."

"How are they dealt with?" I ask lowering my eyelids slightly as I bite my bottom lip.

"Usually they are beheaded, and their bodies are burned but if the crime is deemed particularly heinous then the immortal could be drained of their blood little by little causing a slow and excruciatingly painful death." William shifts a little on the bar stool and seems unnerved at the idea of it.

"Wow. That's harsh," I comment, and my eyes are wide with astonishment.

"Well we can't have immortals going around drawing attention to our kind like that and anyway it is a moral disgrace to us," his tone is serious. I wait a few minutes, trying to let it all soak in and then I ask, "Why doesn't the donor turn into a vampire after they have been bitten as you read about in books?"

"That's just a myth, we choose who we want to turn. It is not something that is done very often. Our numbers are relatively small around the world. To turn someone, the maker must drain the candidate of all their blood down to an inch of the mortal life without losing that life completely and then return to them a small amount of the blood that has been intermingled with the maker's immortal blood. The candidate then loses consciousness and must feed again within several hours of their newborn life for the process to be completed."

I think for a moment about what he has just said, and it occurs to me that I am a part of him now. The two of us are as one. The bond between us will never be broken but I also know that it goes much deeper than this for us. I know that it is a love story that had been started centuries earlier with William as he passed through time unnoticed until he finally found me.

"Now it is your turn to share some things about yourself," William says. "Tell me what you remember about your mortal life."

I stare at him for a moment and then say, "Well, I was born here in this town. I have lived here my whole life. I was always the shy one. My childhood was typical and nothing out of the ordinary ever happened. I was an only child and at times it could get lonely. I lost both of my parents three years ago around the time you say that you first saw me. I had started working in the bookstore about a week before the wreck happened. I had been on my own since that time or so I thought." I smirk at him playfully and he smiles back at me. "I continued to live in the house which is the same house that I grew up in. It was left to me in the will. I had just turned eighteen when it all happened. It was the night of my high school graduation. I spent that last night with my parents before they were killed on our way home in a car wreck. It had been raining that night and the roads were very slick, but it wouldn't have mattered because there was nothing my father could have done differently. The car came straight for us so quickly..." I say as I sit staring out into space. "It feels like so long ago now, so distant to me, another life. I guess when I think about it, it was another life. But you know the one thing that I never figured out was how I got out of the car that night. The paramedics assumed I had been ejected but I don't remember. I know that I must have been wearing my seatbelt at the time of the wreck so that just didn't seem like a possibility to me. They told me that I must have hit my head but yet there was no bump or mark. That must be why I lost my memory of everything, I guess. I must have hit my head on the way out."

William sat there looking down at the floor not saying anything, lost in thought.

"Are you alright? You've become quiet all of the sudden," I inquire.

He looks up at me and says, "I haven't told you this yet. I was waiting for it to come up and I guess now is the best time as any. I was there that night. I saw the other car lose control and wreck into your parent's car. I had been following in my car not too far behind and when I saw the wreck happen. I quickly pulled out my cell phone and dialed 911. I jumped out of my car and ran to where your parent's car had overturned in the ditch. I pulled you out of the car and then went around to the other side to check on your parents…" he looks over at me as I stare blankly at him. He swallows hard. "I had to make sure you were alright. I thought I had lost you that night. Your mom and dad were already gone. There was nothing I could do for them. I'm sorry."

"William, why didn't you turn them?" I ask in a slightly elevated and panicked tone.

"You know I couldn't have done that. Your mother was already gone, and your father was too close at the time." He says in a very low voice, almost a whisper, and then picks my hand up and holds it in his. I look at him with tears in my eyes at the thought of my parents lying dead in the ditch.

"You saw me when I pulled you out of the wreckage... but I had to leave quickly because I didn't want to be around when the paramedics arrived. You asked me who I was and without thinking I told you my name. I couldn't let you remember seeing me so I erased your memory of that moment and then suddenly I felt a strong urge to protect you from the grief that you would inevitably feel when you realized that you had lost both of your parents. So, I erased some of the memories of your life that you carried with you in your mind. I thought in that split second that it was the right thing to do. That if you couldn't remember exactly what you had lost it would somehow ease the pain that you would feel."

I stand up and walk over to sit on the couch in front of the fireplace. I don't know how to feel about what he has just told me. I am in shock and feel a little numb.

"I...I can't believe you did that." I stumble to find the words.

William stares across the room at me and the intensity of the moment begins to build. From his expression, I can tell that he is starting to wish that he hadn't told me about his intentions the night of the wreck, but I know that he doesn't want to keep anything from me either. He sits down next to me, brushing my hair away from my eyes and gently turning my face towards his.

"Abigail, I only did it out of concern for you. I know the pain of losing someone that you love very deeply, and I didn't want you to suffer that same pain. I only wanted to protect you. It was a dumb thing to do, I know that now." He says in a soft tone but with a tensed brow.

I turn my face away from his and silently stare into the flames of the fire as I feel my body temperature slowly rise. I don't speak for several minutes. I just sit and stare.

"Please, say something. Are you mad at me?" William pleads with me.

I answer him, saying, "No, I'm not angry. I don't know what to feel. I know that it didn't completely work or help. I'm sorry but I think it only made things harder for me. I was so confused about my life after the wreck. I couldn't remember my past, only bits, and pieces of it."

"I'm the one who is sorry, Abigail. I didn't know how it would turn out. I shouldn't have done it." His tone was remorseful as his eyes begged her for forgiveness.

"I know you are, and I also know that you meant well. You know, I still remembered that night you saved me, William, because it came through in my dreams. I dreamed about you almost every night after that, seeing you there at the wreck with me. I dreamed of you that night in the hospital. I saw you as my guardian angel."

"Well, that is an interesting way of looking at it. I guess in a way I was your guardian at the time. Since the wreck, I had been keeping an eye on you an awful lot. I was always watching over you and protecting you, but I didn't save you that night. You survived the wreck on your own. I was only making sure you were going to be alright," he replies with noticeable relief that I'm not angry with him.

"And if I hadn't been alright, would you have turned me?" I look into his eyes to gauge his reaction. He sits quietly for a moment, staring at the fire.

"There would have been nothing that I could have done if you had died but if you were mortally injured and near death anyway, then yes I would have."

"I started having strange memories after the wreck too," I admit to him.

"What kind of memories?" He asks as he leans back onto the couch.

"Memories of a young woman, she was always so sad in these memories."

William stares at the fireplace and watches as the fire crackles. He gets up and pokes the logs once, causing them to burn brighter. Then he stands by the mantle silently.

"What are you thinking about?" I glance over at him. He is in deep thought, seemingly somewhere far away. The music still plays softly in the background.

"Oh, nothing, what did you ever make of the memories?" He questions.

"I don't know. I didn't know what to make of them at the time. I started to think of all kinds of explanations. I thought that I had lived another life at one time, a past life, possibly. I started to think that I had been reincarnated but it sounded so silly to me. I didn't know what to think. It was very strange."

"Well, the only explanation that I can come up with is that you were able to see into the past as a mortal." He suggests.

"I hadn't thought of that you must be right. It's the only reasonable explanation." I am relieved to finally have some sort of explanation for the memories that don't belong to me. William sits down next to me on the couch.

"It only started after the wreck, though and why do you think I couldn't remember my past?"

"Well, it's probably because I erased most of it." He says with a remorseful tone.

We sit silently for several minutes just staring at the fireplace.

"Do you ever miss anything from your mortal life, William?" I ask.

"No, not anymore, but when I was first turned my maker didn't stick around to help me figure things out, so I did end up missing some things, especially companionship. Some things from the mortal life you never miss, and others can take some time to get over but I would give up everything all over again to be here with you right now," he confesses and I smile gently at him.

"Are you missing anything, Abigail?" He questions quietly, appearing not sure if he is ready for whatever answer I might give him.

I admit happily, "Absolutely nothing, everything is perfect when I am in your arms."

I can see that he is happy to hear me say this and from what he has told me I know it is the first time since he has become immortal that he feels the same way.

I have been alone for so long before you came to be with me, and I know you can barely remember what it even feels like to be without me near you since you don't remember much of your mortal life. I realize that this life is new for you, Abigail, but at the same time, it is also new now for me too. William says softly.

"What do we do now?" I ask with bated breath, hoping to stay close to him like we are for the rest of the night.

"We feed!" He announces with excitement. I stare at him with wide eyes and feel unsure about whether I am ready. It will be my first time to feed on a donor and I am very apprehensive about it. He sees that I am nervous.

"It's time, Abigail, you have to learn. Don't worry it will be alright." He says as he hugs me close to his chest.

Chapter 14: First Time

There is a first time for everything and over the past couple of days, I have been doing a lot of firsts. I am extremely nervous about my first feed though and I'm not even sure I want to do it. I know that my survival hinges on this one major detail and it can't be avoided.

"Can't you do all of the hunting and I can share from you when you return home?" I suggest. He watches as I squirm out of his arms and sit up straight.

"Are you serious?" He chuckles.

"Sort of," I frown.

"I have to give you credit. It is a novel idea, but we wouldn't get enough nourishment and I would have to feed more often, which would mean I would have to be away from you more." He pulls me back to his side and kisses me softly.

"I know you wouldn't want that, right?" He whispers in my ear. I can feel the coolness of his breath.

"I would only agree to something like that if you were incapacitated for some reason or maybe…I would let you share if the mood struck me just right." He laughs.

"You're such a tease, William." I give him a nudge with my elbow.

"Sorry babe, you have to learn to hunt for yourself. It is detrimental that you learn." He stresses the point.

"I know." I pout for a minute, my eyes locked on the fireplace, thinking who had ever heard of a vampire that didn't drink the blood from a mortal donor? I know that it has to be done for my good.

"It's alright we can wait for a little while before we go." He rubs my arm trying to comfort me.

"Where will we go to do this?" I probe.

"There is a nice heavily wooded and secluded area south of town where mortals like to jog and walk. I think it will be the best place for you to start."

"Will you stay with me?" I ask with a look of worry on my face.

"Yes, of course. I will be right by your side the whole time. I will even go first to show you what to do but I'm telling you that it will come naturally."

"Are you ready?" He asks, standing up and walking over to the fireplace to extinguish the fire.

"About as ready as I'll ever be, I guess." I slowly rise from the couch.

The drive takes less than ten minutes and when we get there William pulls the car into the first parking spot nearest to the entrance of the wooded walking trails.

I turn to him and say, "I'm a little nervous. No, that's not true. I'm a lot nervous. I don't know if I will be able to handle my first feed and I am worried that I might not be able to control myself and stop in time. I don't want to be the cause of someone's untimely death."

William reassuringly says, "It will come naturally to you, I promise. Just like a baby nursing for the first time, it is an instinct."

I am pretty sure he can tell that I am not completely convinced.

"You are not a killer at heart, Abigail. You will be able to resist the temptation to drain the donor dry." He says.

I don't know if it makes me feel any better, but I decide to believe him. I trust him and what he tells me. We get out of the car and step into the woods walking along the narrow pebble path for a little way and then we disappear further into the forest. There are only a few mortals on the dimly lit trails that night but to anyone that would see us, we will look like any other regular mortal human. There is nothing about our appearance that will suggest that they are anything different. For hundreds of years, probably thousands, vampires have possessed the distinct ability to remain anonymous and to blend in well with the society around them. Mortal humans still think that they are only a myth, that vampires are just mere legends.

As we reach a tiny clearing in the woods off to the right of the small narrow path, we stop and wait. William looks me in the eyes and says, "Wait here behind this tree and watch what I do."

I shake my head with nervous anticipation and watch as he walks several feet away from me. He takes his place a couple of trees away from me and stands perfectly still, like a statue, waiting ever so silently. He looks like a leopard waiting for his prey.

"Here comes one," he whispers so quietly that only I could hear him due to my newly acquired sensitive hearing. The donor is alone and on his way up the path. I smell him before I even see him and he smells delicious. I don't know if I will be able to just stand by and watch as William feeds on the donor's blood after I get a whiff of his aroma. I can feel the burning and twisting hunger start deep inside of me in anticipation. It is unreal to me the power that has taken control of my senses. I dig my fingernails into the bark of the tree that I am leaning against.

After a few seconds a tall thin man comes jogging down the pebbled path alone and William poises himself for the attack. Quick, like lightning, he steps out from the trees and stops the donor cold in his tracks just by the look in William's eyes. The donor just stands there stunned in what looks like a trance to me from where I am hiding. William extends his hand and slowly walks back into the wooded area behind him with his eyes never leaving the donors. The man follows as if he is obeying some unspoken command from William. As they wander farther into the woods away from the path, William without pause or hesitation sinks his fangs into the man's neck. I watch with a high level of pleasure at what I see as William looks up at me with blood-red pupils and then within seconds, he has the donor back to the trail never to remember what has just happened to him.

William steps over to where I am. His eyes are the same beautiful pale blue that I love and not the deep red that I saw while he was feeding. He takes my hand into his and says, "I will remain close by just in case you need me. Just do the same as me and everything will be alright. It will come naturally, I promise." He kisses me on the forehead, smiles, and quickly steps back behind me into the trees, watching.

I am silent, barely breathing, watching, and waiting. I am nervous but also excited. I don't know what to expect except for what I have just seen William do. Several mortals pass by but they were in pairs, I have to wait for one to be completely alone before I can make my move. It only takes a few minutes before a mortal, who is all alone, comes walking towards me. She is short and plump. She appears to be in her early forties and has brown shoulder-length hair that is pulled up into a ponytail. How convenient that her neck is already exposed, and I can see the blood pulsing rapidly as she walks. She is dressed in black exercise pants and a pink tee shirt. Her scent is so powerful, and it overtakes me instantly. I feel more crazed this time by the smell of the blood. Watching William feed on his donor was a tease to my taste buds. The hunger starts again immediately and my insides writhe with pain, my body begins to burn. It takes all of my strength not to jump out and attack the poor woman, draining her dry of all life.

"Control, I must have control," I whisper to myself. I can hear the donor's heart beating fast and hard as she walks closer towards me. It is a sound that briefly strikes a simple sadness deep within me for the sound of a mortal heartbeat that was once my own. As the donor approaches the sound gets louder and I continue to wait quietly behind the trees. When the woman is even with me on the path, I move slightly crunching the dead leaves under my feet. The donor turns and looks in my direction. Our eyes lock immediately, and the woman's eyes are wide and frozen, void of any acknowledgment of what is happening, she only stares deeper into mine. I never look away, and she can't. I have her in a trance and she is under my control. I reach out for the donor's hand and I walk slowly towards her, I take the woman and lead her deep into the woods away from the path and away from anyone's sight. William watches as I breathe in the woman's intoxicating aroma and then, as if I, myself, am under control, the blood's control, I bite down on the donor's neck. I bite hard and sink my fangs into the woman as her blood, warm and thick, flows out of her veins and down my throat, filling my body's cells with new revitalized life. It tastes sweet and salty to me as I moan with delight. The hunger inside of me goes away instantly and my body doesn't burn anymore. Instinctively, I know when to stop. I heal the bite mark with my saliva and lead the donor back to the path where she rests for a few minutes and then continues her way never to remember what happened to her.

William walks over to me and we continue our stroll down the crooked little pebble path.

"I'm proud of you. Your first feed. It was a success," he says with pride in his voice.

"Yes, it was hard to control myself at first, but I managed. Her blood tasted so good," I admit. We walk back to his car. William drives effortlessly along the winding roads, as we sit in satisfied silence. I am enjoying the feeling from my first feed. It was exhilarating and euphoric. On the drive back we stop by my house so that I can pick up a few of my belongings because I am now going to live with William at his home. We go inside and rest for a few moments at the table in my little kitchen.

"Are you alright?" Williams asks as he watches me from across the table.

"I am better than alright. I feel powerful. It's a bizarre feeling but it feels so good." I say full of adrenaline. I feel stronger than ever. I also feel a surge of dopamine that has taken over my whole body. I never had experimented with drugs during my mortal life, but this must be what it feels like to be high. I begin to rummage around my house packing up the things that I will need to bring with me, and I notice that there are several messages left on my answering machine. I suddenly remember that I haven't been back to work in a couple of days. Pressing the button on the machine I listen carefully. The first message is from Jenny at work.

"Hey, Abigail, um, you haven't been back to work since you called in sick. I was wondering if you are alright. Just call back when you can." Beep.

The other messages are just hang-ups but the caller id confirms that they have come from the coffee shop. I think for a minute about what I should do as I stare at the phone. Picking up the receiver I dial the number to the coffee shop and Jenny answers on the other end.

"Thank you for calling…" Jenny begins but I interrupt.

"Jenny, is…is that you?" I stutter while twisting my hair around my finger trying to think of what to say next.

"Yeah, Abigail, oh, my goodness, are you alright?" Her tone is riddled with worry.

"No… well, sort of. I'm still sick." I turn around and see William standing behind me listening.

"When do you think you will be back to work? Mr. Ackerman thinks you skipped out on us and he has been talking about firing you."

"I don't know…it's hard to say."

"Are you sure you're alright? Does it have anything to do with that guy you said was stalking you? I know you were still upset about him the last time I saw you." Jenny is serious for once and I have never heard her talk this way.

"No… everything is okay I have to go now. If I'm not back in one more day just tell Mr. Ackerman that you talked to me and I said that I wasn't coming back but wait a day before you say anything. I need time to think…I mean get better. Okay, bye," I say quickly and hang up the phone.

"You think you will go back to work?" He moves closer to me and leans against the kitchen cabinet by my side.

"I don't know. I don't need to but I did love working in the bookstore." I stare down at my feet. It is hard for me to concentrate when I feel so good from the blood that courses through my veins.

"You might find it hard to be around mortal humans again so soon, but I know you can probably handle it." He encourages me. "And I would be there with you for added support if you needed it."

"Well, I'll think about it." I smile at him.

"I guess the place has sentimental value for me. It is where I saw you for the first time and you do look pretty cute in that apron." He flashes his brilliant smile at me and I laugh loudly.

"Come on. Let's go back to your place now," I say.

William speeds down the road and within seconds we are pulling up into his driveway. I am still high on the energy I feel from the feed and it is like nothing I have ever felt before as we make our way up to the house. The night air is cool, and I can't wait to stand next to the fireplace. As we step up onto the front porch of the house William puts the key in the lock and turns it. He opens the door and immediately goes over to the fireplace to light it for me. He kneels poking at the wood to gets it started and I walk into the kitchen to pour two glasses of wine. I meet him in front of the fireplace handing him one of the glasses. We both take a sip and then simultaneously place our glasses on the mantel. He takes my hand and kisses it as our eyes meet and sparks ignite between us. He moves in closer and kisses me gently on the lips. I, in turn, with my newfound strength, kiss him back deeper and longer. I don't want it to end. I hold on to him tightly and kiss him with an intensity that shoots straight through me like fireworks. I press my body close to his as he cups my face with his hands. I pull him down with me onto the couch as I slide my hands up his back pulling his shirt off. His skin is smooth. I kiss him along his broad shoulders and up his neck finding his lips waiting for yet another. As he starts to undo my buttons on my blouse kissing down my neck passionately, he stops and sits back on the couch.

"What's wrong?" I ask him breathlessly.

"Abigail, we have to wait." He says looking at me with a serious expression.

"Why?"

"I want it to be perfect not the result of being high after a feed."

"Oh, William, I don't think I can. I want to be yours in every way possible."

"I know…believe me I know, and I feel the same way, but I want our first time to be special." He moves closer to me and I can see in his eyes that I am not going to get my way.

"You're a hopeless romantic." I smile sweetly and he places his head on my chest to listen to my heart beating faintly.

Chapter 15: Legend

William sits on the edge of the bed and I lay next to him tangled up in the sheets. He smiles looking at me and says, "Well someone was feeling frisky last night, pretty typical after a feeding, though. Your donor must have had a lot of life in her blood." I laugh, agree, and say,

"Will I always feel that way afterward?"

"Most likely, I know every time I feed that's usually the way I feel. It is like a high, a drug. It can become addictive. You have to be careful. You will learn to control it in time." He tells me.

"I think it was from being so close to you last night. You are so irresistible, I couldn't control myself," I say reaching for him. He leans over and kisses me slowly. Then suddenly he lifts me out of the bed without any effort and brings me back down gently to my feet. I stand on my tip toes wearing his black silk pajama top and he wears only the matching bottoms.

He whispers in my ear, "Do you want to go outside today? It's a wonderfully cloudy day and I want to bring you somewhere to show you something very special to me. I know you will love it and tonight we can go to the Contraband Days festival along the lakefront."

"Yeah, that sounds like a lot of fun. It feels like forever since I went to the festival." I admit and start to think back at the last time I had gone to it when I was mortal. I vaguely remember that the festival is always held every year around the end of April or the first of May. I know that it is based on the history of Jean Lafitte and the legend of hidden treasure along Contraband Bayou. I barely remember a time when I had gone with my parents. It seems to me that we had gone to it more when I was young, but I can't be sure. I have a fuzzy memory of being at the festival and watching as the Mayor of the city was captured and forced to walk the plank of a ship into the murky waters of the lake. That would always be the official start and all the locals would go out to enjoy the carnival-like atmosphere. I am lost in the hazy mortal memory of being there with my parents and having fun when it dawns on me that William and what he went through over a hundred years ago must be the reason it is rumored there is a hidden treasure somewhere along the bayou. I had grown up hearing about the legend but now that I know his story it sheds new light on it. I feel like an insider to something top secret that no one alive today knows about. I sit on the edge of the bed while he walks into the closet and picks out some clothes to wear. William walks out holding a pair of jeans and a brown graphic tee shirt with a pirate skull on the front of it.

"What are you wearing?" He smiles slyly.

"My clothes are in the trunk of your car." I wrap my arms around my body.

"Oh, well, I guess it's not fair then if I get dressed and you can't. I'll race you." He throws his clothes on the bed and heads for the door to the bedroom.

I jump off the bed and run for the doorway wearing only the pajama top. He chases after me and we race down the staircase.

"I won!" I cheer.

As we walk outside, I glance over at William catching his eyes with mine and looking like I know some very important secret. I will surely burst if he doesn't ask me what I am thinking and soon. I slowly start to speak not being able to contain it any longer. "William…" he can see it in my eyes, and he must know what I am thinking. He answers the question before I can finish asking it.

"Yes, it's partly because of the treasure I was accused of stealing that the legend was born but also because Lafitte did have a few members of his crew bury some of Napoleon Bonaparte's riches along the bayou too. I never actually saw it happen with my own two eyes but it was the buzz on the ships for the longest time afterward," he says and then he stops at the bottom of the staircase and turns to me. "Many years after I had been living here, I would navigate my boat over the waters of the bayou at night. I would dock along the edge of the sandy Chenier and sit under the old oak trees on the land and think about how my life had taken such a drastic course from what I thought it would be. While I was lying there one night looking up at the stars, I felt the presence of someone nearby and when I sat up to see who it was, it was Lafitte, well, his ghost. He was walking along the edge of the land near the bayou still searching for his lost treasures, I suppose."

I swallow hard with my eyes fixed intently on his face.

"What's the matter?" he asks.

"Ghost stories have always scared me," I reply feeling a little silly.

"You're not supposed to be scared of ghosts anymore, Abigail, you're a vampire now."

He laughs and I do too as we continue our way outside. He opens the driver's side door and pulls the trunk release latch in his car. I start to pick up one of the suitcases.

"Here, let me," he reaches over and grabs the luggage placing it on the ground next to me. There are three large suitcases of clothing and toiletries. William unloads them out of the back of his car and carries them inside the house. He insists on carrying them up the stairs for me even though I am strong enough to handle it. I quickly change into my favorite jeans and a white tee shirt. I wear a thin long-sleeve button-down shirt that I leave open over the tee-shirt. I put my tennis shoes on my feet and tie the laces securely. Then I call him from the bedroom to see if he is ready as well. I am very excited to see what he wants to show me. He steps out of the bathroom to see me waiting for him in the doorway to the bedroom.

"Are you excited, because you look excited?" He grins. I smile and follow beside him back down the stairs and out into the front lawn.

"Are we taking your car?" I ask him.

"No, it is close enough that we can walk. I'm just going to grab our sunglasses," he answers. He reaches into the car and retrieves the sunglasses out of the glove box. He hands me a pair and I put them on. He holds my hand as we stroll down the long driveway to the street out front. The leaves and sticks snap beneath our feet as we walk. The tall trees around us provide shade and as we near the end of the driveway cars passing by on the street in front of us can be heard. We stop at the edge of the road and look both ways before crossing hurriedly to the other side. I look out across the road and see a pier located several yards away in the water with a large boat beside it. As we get closer to the pier, I can see the boat more clearly and it's the most gorgeous boat that I have ever seen.

"Is it yours?" I question as hope fills my voice.

"Yes, and it is now yours also. I have named it, *Abigail*," he says with a smile. I hug him tightly and then walk closer to get a better look at the detail.

"I've never seen a boat like this before," I say.

It is white with a thick black stripe along the sides and it has tinted glass which proves to be useful for a vampire.

"It's a brand-new sports yacht to be exact." He replies with pride.

"Thank you for naming it after me. I'm flattered." I say. "How long have you had it?"

"Not long, maybe a month now." He answers.

We walk out onto the pier. The water gently laps up against the sides of its pillars making a soft splashing noise. It feels strange to me at first to be outside again during the day in the wide-open space of the lake without feeling the sun sting my skin or cause my eyes to burn the way they had the first day I was turned. I look up at the clouds in the sky and it is nice. I take off the long sleeve shirt that I am wearing over my tee shirt and tie it around my waist. William helps me into the yacht and unties it from where it is docked. He steps into the boat.

"Let me show you around." He says as he motions for me to follow him below deck.

The interior is decorated with dark mahogany wood and tan leather upholstery. There is a master stateroom forward with a queen-size bed and an ensuite bathroom.

"This is gorgeous." I walk around taking in all the yacht has to offer visually.

"I'm glad you like it. Let's go back up." He says.

Back on deck, I see there is a six-seat leather lounge bench with a cocktail cabinet, a table, and flat-screen television. There is also a sound system that he turns on allowing soft music to play as he passes through to the front. I follow closely behind and sit on the leather lounge.

Williams sits down in front of the controls.

"Have you ever been out on a boat before?" he asks as he looks out the windshield and begins to press buttons on the control panel.

"Only once. I have lived near the water my whole life and have only once been on a boat when my father's company had a family day on the lake on a rented commercial party barge."

"Well, today will be your second time," he says as he places the key in the ignition and then starts the engine. He pulls the boat away from the dock and starts slowly. Every which way I look there are several boats, sailboats, speed boats, and pontoons. There are mortals all around and they are enjoying the day on the water.

"The festival usually starts every year with a pirate ship bombardment. There is a band of actors playing the roles of the Buccaneers and one of them always dresses up as Jean Lafitte. They overtake the city and then they proceed to raise a Jolly Roger, you know, a skull and crossbones flag. That marks their conquest. Do you remember this, Abigail?" He speaks a little louder than his normal tone because of the engine noise.

"Vaguely," I shake my head from side to side as if to say no. I know how strange it must be for William to watch the things that used to be a real way of life for him acted out now for entertainment. Off in the distance near the seawall, I see that the mock pirate ship is docked, and the actors are in the process of making the Mayor walk the plank. It is a funny sight to see.

William picks up speed as he guides the yacht across the lake and then circles back around towards the ship channel, being out on the water feels good as a surge of excitement rushes through my body. He accelerates the boat across the water, and it feels almost like it is hovering over it, not touching it. It glides smoothly across the water. William has a huge grin across his face. He begins to slow the boat down just a bit and says, "It has been amazing to watch all of this area change so much throughout the years. It seems like yesterday that its inhabitants were a small tribe of Attakapas Indians, led by Chief Crying Eagle. Long ago this area was also inhabited by bears, black panthers, and many more alligators than you will see today. We had a run-in one night with a black panther coming off our ship into the marsh. One member of the crew was attacked by it and we were forced to shot and kill the creature," he says loudly over the hum of the boat motor.

"It sounds very exciting to think about this area being like that so long ago. That makes me wonder about something, William, how have you been able to go this long without people noticing that you aren't aging?"

"Mind control, as soon as I leave a room, they forget that I was even there. Of course, I can let them remember if I chose."

He flashes that gorgeous smile in my direction, and I know that he is talking about me.

"Oh, that's right. I forgot," I mutter slightly embarrassed.

"You're still learning, it's alright," he pulls me closer with one arm while he steers the boat with the other. I lean in and kiss him on the cheek. We round the bend in the river and make our way towards the bayou. He slows the boat down to a crawl as it drifts past the Cypress trees that hang out over the murky brown water. It is quiet and peaceful as the sound of nature surrounds us. A lone alligator pops his head up quickly to watch as we glide past.

"It happened over there."

He points towards the land to the left of the boat.

"That is where they left me for dead." He steers the boat closer to the edge of the bank and then anchors it in place. He jumps to the ground and then turns to hold his arms out to help me out of the boat and safely onto the ground beside him. We make our way hand in hand through the tall grass with a small blanket that he had stored in the boat.

"Where are we going?" I ask.

"You'll see," he answers.

After a few minutes of hiking, they entered a large clearing. The ground beneath us is covered with dry brown soil and patches of soft green grass. Besides the Cypress trees, there are a few old oak trees whose long-curved branches hang low flirting with the earth. They must be over a hundred years old. The trees provide us with a small canopy of shelter from the sun whenever it peeks out from behind the thick white clouds that cover the sky above. The air smells sweet as the breeze gently dances with the tall marsh grasses in the distance. Small sparrows fly from the trees and a blue heron sits perched on one of the highest branches keeping watch over us. At the edge of the clearing, under the most beautiful majestic oak tree of all, is a small simple white cross.

William spreads the blanket out over a grassy spot, and we lie down next to one another under the oak trees as we stare up at the cloudy sky.

"Why is a cross over there in the distance under that oak tree?" I ask rolling to my side and leaning on one elbow as I point in the direction to where the cross is located.

"One night I took my old boat and came out here to be alone and I saw the cross. I didn't know who had placed it there but I later found out from one of my old crew mates that it had been placed there for me when they thought that I had been killed by the others. They knew me better than to believe that I would have stolen anything much less my own boss's treasure. I used to despise this place. I viewed it as something ugly and profane because it reminded me of what I had become. As time went by, I started to come here to find a resolution to the loneliness and misery that had become so much a part of me. I wanted to come to grips with the reality of my unending situation. This place ultimately became a sanctuary for me where I could escape for a while and think. That cross was meant as a memorial to the end of my mortal life but instead, it became a reminder of my immortality." He turns towards me and rolls onto his side looking me directly in my eyes. "You don't know how long I've waited to share this place with you, Abigail," he whispers to me. "I have learned through the many years of my existence that I have to embrace the wonderful things that I have in this world and see them through grateful eyes. That is when I discovered that this place where everything ended for me so long ago was, in fact, a very beautiful place."

"William, how did you become immortal?" I ask him, wondering at the same time if the memories may upset him too much.

"After they left me here to die, I laid bloodied and bruised for what felt like hours, not being able to move, I waited, waited for death but it didn't come quickly. I must have been slipping in and out of consciousness because at one point I woke up to see my brother hunched over me. I thought that he was there to help me. I stared up at him, but my vision was blurred. I had a hard time making sense of the things around me. As he leaned over me and got closer, I felt a sharp pain in one of my wrists. Then an excruciating burn started to course through my veins. There was a hunger growing inside of me, ripping its way out of me. I didn't know what was happening to me. I then saw him kneel over me and cut his wrist letting the blood drain into my open mouth. I couldn't control the hunger any longer. I took his wrist and wrapped my mouth around it drinking the blood into my body. I remember hearing the sound of the ship's horn starting to blow and then the next thing I knew he was gone." William recounted the memory as though he had stepped back in time and seemed to be reliving the experience somewhere locked away within his mind.

"How old were you when it happened?" I ask out of curiosity.

"Twenty-six," he says in a low reflective tone with a sullen expression on his face.

I just lay silently beside him and then I finally ask, "Your brother was a vampire? Did you know about it?"

"No, he kept it hidden until then," he says staring across the clearing at the small cross.

"But why did he leave you here by yourself?" I question not completely understanding.

"He had no other choice. The ship was leaving and if the ones that attacked me had known I was still alive they would have come back to finish me off. He kept quiet and his only choice was to turn me or else I would have surely died right here on this very spot along the bayou. He gave me this life but at the time I can't say I was thankful to him for it. I descended into a personal hell after that night."

"Do you still see him?" I place my arm over his waist as he rolls over onto his back. I rest my head on his chest and listen to the faint beat of his heart.

"No, I try to stay far away from him as much as possible. He has changed. He's not the same anymore," he answers as a cold cast occupies his eyes.

"I am sorry, William," I whisper. He places his hand on the side of my face slowly caressing my cool cheek and gazing into my eyes.

"Don't be, I never want to see him again."

It saddens me to know that he has born this burden all of these years, but I feel somehow as with my past that the load is somewhat lighter since we have found one another. We continue to lie here in each other's arms in silence enjoying the rest of the beautiful day.

The sun starts to set, and it is time for us to leave our sanctuary of peace and solitude. William stands up and stretches. He turns to me and I'm still lounging comfortably on the blanket.

"Are you ready?" He asks looking down at me.

"No, I don't want to leave this place. I love it here." I said staring up at the darkening sky. He kneels beside me and slowly crawls over the top of my relaxed body until he is face to face with me. He kisses me passionately on the lips and my body reacts unyieldingly to his touch. "I would love to stay here with you longer, but don't you want to go to the festival?" He whispers.

I kiss him and then feeling defeated, shake my head in agreement. We slowly get up and William grabs the blanket, both of us working to fold it back into a neat little square. We stroll across the clearing towards the water and he helps me up into the yacht. He jumps in and raises the anchor, then starts the engine. Turning it around, he steers down the bayou slowly. Other boats are passing by as we make our way back towards the lake. The sunset is lovely and I begin to think about the one that he described to me when he was on the ship out over the open water many years ago wondering if it was as spectacular as the one, I watch from the yacht this evening.

William maneuvers the yacht up to the side of the lakefront seawall and docks it. When we step off the boat, I am suddenly hit with the scent of the blood in the air around me. I am very tense as we walk up the grassy incline I wonder if it will ever get any easier for me to be around mortal humans again. I sense that William knows what I am feeling from the strained look on my face. He leans in and says, "It will be alright, just stay close to me."

I do as he says and holds tightly to his arm as we walk out across the busy fairgrounds passing many mortals along the way. I grasp his arm with more pressure as they get too close to me and he has to place his hand on mine to loosen my vice grip.

"I'm sorry. Do you ever get used to it?" I ask with a wild look in my eyes as I watch around me closely, feeling very guarded.

"Yes, but it does take some time." He responds with a small amount of sympathy for me in his tone.

"How long?" I ask to hope for some reassurance.

"Well, after the first hundred years it does get easier," he smiles at me and I don't appreciate his humor. "If it makes you feel any better, I have trouble with it too. It just takes some time to build up a little tolerance to it. Remember mind over matter."

"I'll try but that is easier said than done." I look up at him with wide eyes.

"Yes, I know and you're a newborn so it will be harder."

I remain close to his side. The carnival rides light up the night sky with multi-colored rays of artificial light and the midway games are lined in long tight rows with mortals yelling from inside their canopies, inviting everyone young and old, big and small to try their luck. We walk hand in hand past them not paying attention to the chants until we step near the baseball midway game.

"Oh, I love baseball. Do you mind if I throw a couple of pitches?" he asks.

"Not at all," I answer smiling to myself at the boyish charm that exudes from him that very moment. He pays the man behind the counter five dollars for five pitches and then the man hands him five baseballs.

"Wish me luck," he says as he turns to me with a lively look in his eyes.

"Good luck, although I doubt you need it," I reply with a look in my eyes that mirrors his expression.

The man behind the counter can't believe what he witnesses when William throws the first pitch. The ball fires past the man with lightning speed and all that can be seen is a blur of white. William aims perfectly each time and makes it into the fast-moving cylinder far in front of where he stands. I know that the games are purposely set to be nearly impossible to win but they are like child's play to him. With each turn, he wins a large stuffed animal for me, five in all. He reaches into his wallet to pay for another five pitches, but I stop him.

"I have enough stuffed animals already," I say as I raise my eyebrows at him. He laughs and says, "Are you sure, because I can win all of them for you if you want me to."

"I'm sure." I am amused by him.

"Here, let me hold a few of these for you." He reaches out and takes three of the stuffed animals from me. As we wander away from the booth the man stares bewildered at what he has just seen. He studies the baseballs and then checks the functionality of the game itself. William eyes the hammer strength test and he moves towards it like he wants to try his luck at it.

"No way, you will break it," I laugh, and he pulls me gently by the arm towards the game.

"Watch this." He puts the stuffed animals down beside me and picks up the large padded hammer. Holding it high above his head, he slams it down on the button without any real effort. He hits the game with the hammer and the multi-colored lighted display shoots up to the top, but a score doesn't register. He has hit it too hard and it starts going berserk. I look on in disbelief as the buzzer sounds and the old man that operates the game stands there wide-eyed and in shock. The buzzer is stuck and won't stop ringing. It is making the loudest noise and everyone around starts to turn towards the commotion.

"Whoa! How did he do that?" shouts a boy in the line behind them. There are several young kids in the line, and they all start cheering as the old man goes running to unplug it. Then it is those same kids who immediately start booing once they realize the machine must be reset and it will take a while before they can test their strength. I start handing out the stuffed animals that William has just won to make them happy. I keep one for myself. They all begin to cheer. Laughing loudly, they quickly make their exit from the area as everyone stands and stares at us.

As the hours pass, I start to feel more comfortable around the mortals. Their scent is always on the back of my mind, teasing my senses but I'm not clinging to William for support anymore. The sound of music comes from the outdoor concert being held across the grounds at the amphitheater as we walk along the lakefront looking out at the boats in the water. The smell of food fills the air as we walk past the concession stands and I am briefly reminded of what I used to enjoy during my mortal life.

"William, I want to try some barbeque," I announce with excitement in my voice.

"Are you sure? I don't think..." but before he can finish, I pull him over to the concession stand and order one small plate of barbeque chicken for the two of us to share. He pays for the mortal treat and we walk over to sit at a picnic table nearby.

"Well, here goes nothing," I say as I open my mouth and take a big bite of the chicken. The sauce clings to my lips as I sit there holding the bite in my closed mouth. I don't chew it. I just sit with it in my mouth and stare across the table at William.

"How is it?" He asks already knowing the answer to his question from the look on my face. I suddenly spit it out into my napkin and make a horrible noise.

"Ugh...I don't understand. I used to love barbeque!" I slump my shoulders staring at the piece of chicken balled up in the napkin in front of me.

"That was when you were a mortal," he replies waiting for me to work through my confusion. I know these things are true because it goes against every instinct, I have to think that I will enjoy food again as I did in my other life, but I feel determined to try anyway.

"I know. I just thought maybe it wouldn't taste so bad," I get up and throw the rest of the food in the garbage can. "Now I have this sickly-sweet tangy taste in my mouth." I protest.

He walks over to me and leans in kissing me deeply and then says, "Is that better? Now I have a sickly-sweet tangy taste in my mouth too." He winks at me. "Maybe as time goes by you will not be so repulsed by mortal food."

I figure that he is just trying to make me feel better because even he made a sour face when he tasted the sauce from our kiss.

The music from the outdoor concert continues to fill the air around us and it leads us automatically over to the amphitheater. We listen to the southern rock bands that are playing on stage as William lays a blanket, he brought from the boat over the soft grass near the top of the hill away from most of the mortals so that I can feel more relaxed. He holds me close to his chest with his arms casually placed around my waist as we sit side by side enjoying the concert. The band starts to play "Brown Eyed Girl" by the Rolling Stones and William coaxes me to my feet gently guiding me closer to him as we begin to dance. He twirls me around as my laughter fills in the space around us, then dips me once and slowly raises me to his eye level, and kisses me softly on the lips. We continue to laugh and kiss as our bodies gracefully sway to the music. As I gaze up at the night sky and see all of the stars shining back down to the earth, I think, while dancing in William's arms, that I would have never believed anyone if they had told me a year ago that I would be here this very moment having the time of my life.

When the concert ends, we fold the blanket and walk over to the Ferris wheel, riding it a couple of times. I look out over the city at all the bright lights. My newly acquired night vision doesn't seem to interfere with the beauty of the small skyline around me, it only enhances it. During my mortal life, I had been afraid of heights but not now. It feels good to me to be high above the ground and I feel free, free as a bird. As the wheel turns around and around sending us up towards the heavens and then back down to earth my stomach does little flips but I don't mind it. I snuggle up to William and never want the night to end.

Stepping off the Ferris wheel and onto the carnival grounds once again we walk over to the seawall where the boat parade has just started and find a place to sit on the steps. The boats are all decorated with tiny colored lights strung along their sides and tops as they pass by slowly on the water. The mortals in them are dressed as pirates and throwing candy and beads to the small children sitting on the grassy incline. Suddenly and without warning, a sinking feeling comes over me. I had never given much thought about children before but at this moment I quickly realize that I will never be able to have children of my own. I try to shake the thought from my mind not wanting it to ruin our perfect night as I scoot closer to William. He is looking out at the boats and the children running around as they excitedly catch the candy and the beads that are being tossed in the air. Try as I may though I can't rid myself of this nagging feeling. I watch William as he smiles and looks out at the parade. I study his face for a few minutes until he turns towards me to see that I am watching him.

"William, do you ever wish you had been able to have children?" My eyes wander back to where the children play. I can tell that he doesn't seem surprised by my question and I think for a moment that maybe he can still feel what I am thinking.

"Yes," he says shaking his head up and down slowly as a pensive look washes over his face. "Do you?" He asks in return.

"I had never given it much thought until this very moment, but I think I would have loved to with you," I say looking deep into his eyes now trying to force a small smile. He kisses me on the forehead and then we continue to watch as the boats maneuver past.

Of all the things in the whole world that we look forward to during our long future together, it seems as though children will never be a part of it.

"It's almost time for the fireworks. Let's go back to the boat. They're beautiful when viewed from the water," he stands and holds his hand out for me, and I take it. Within minutes we are back on the yacht and slowly drifting out to the middle of the lake. The water is a murky black as he navigates the boat to a quiet secluded area away from the noisy mortals in the boats around us.

"You seem distant. Is everything alright?" He asks as he gets up from the controls and sits down next to me outside on the deck.

"I'm fine," I answer.

"Would you like a glass of champagne?" He asks.

"Yes, that would be nice."

William walks over to the saloon room and pulls a bottle of chilled champagne out of the small compact refrigerator. Stepping back out onto the deck he twists the cork and sends it sailing into the air out over the water. He pours some into two crystal flutes and hands one to me as he sits back down by my side. The fireworks begin to explode above us. The colors sparkle and fall like glittering rain down from the dark sky. It is a glorious sight. We spend the rest of the night on the yacht afloat over the open water of the lake, together, under the stars.

Chapter 16: Work and Pleasure

We make it back to the pier across from William's house just as the sun is starting to rise over the horizon. The sunrise is splendid, and I can't remember the last time I had been up early enough to enjoy the sight of one. I stand on the bow of the yacht watching as William ties it to the dock and then, chivalrous as always, he helps me out onto the pier. We make our way up the long and winding drive to the house.

Once we are inside William turns to me and says, "Let's go out tonight and have some more fun. I'm a little hungry too. If you remember I used up a lot of energy last night." He winks as if to remind me of all the stuffed animals that he had won throwing baseballs at the carnival.

"Would you like dinner and dancing? There is a nightclub nearby where I like to feed sometimes." He walks into the kitchen and places the keys to the yacht in a drawer near the back door.

"Yes, that sounds great. You can pick me up after work." I admit and watch him closely to see his expression.

"You decided to go back." He inquires and is pleasantly surprised.

"Yeah, you convinced me to go back the other night at my house. I figured after being around all of those mortals at the festival last night that I will be able to handle it for a few hours at work and anyway how can I resist the idea of you watching me work from the aisles in the bookstore. Jenny thinks you're a stalker." I laugh as he staggers towards me with a crazed look on his face and arms stretched out in front of him like a zombie. Then he grabs me by the waist and as I continue to laugh, he whispers, "I love you, Abigail."

The words stop me silent and my expression is serious as I stare into his pale blue eyes. I know that he does but it is the first time that he has said those three words to me.

"I love you too," I whisper back as he holds my chin with his cool hand and kisses me softly. I don't want the moment to end but we hear a noise on the front porch and William goes over to the window to see what it is. He opens the door and I see the mailman walking back down the driveway.

"It's just the mail." He leans around the corner of the door and reaches into the box on the outside wall near the front door and pulls the envelopes out of it. Shutting the door behind him he shuffles through the stack.

"You get mail?" My eyes are wide with surprise. He looks up at me from the letters in his hand.

"Yes, and I have a phone and a computer and email…" he smiles, and I feel silly.

"It's mostly junk mail." He passes by me and throws it away in the trash can keeping one envelope for himself. I am curious as to what it can be, but I don't want to be nosey.

"I'm going to go take a shower. See you in a few," I blow him an air kiss and run up the stairs to the master bathroom.

It is beautifully decorated and like everything else in the house, very modern. There are Italian marble countertops throughout with Travertine tile flooring. Glass enclosed stand-alone shower that is so large it can easily fit several large people all at once without being crowded. I try not to imagine the idea. The tub is oversized, perfect for a man such as William. I do, however, begin to imagine William in the tub soaking after a hard day's work. For a moment I fantasize about him coming home from a long voyage on one of his ships and then relaxing in a nice hot bath while I massage the sore muscles in his back. And then I realize that there is so much that I don't know about him. I know about his past, his very distant past, but what about the present. It sounds funny to think of a vampire having a job but of course, I am about to go back to work tonight so I figure it is plausible. He did say that he had made a lot of money while he worked as a privateer but how could it have lasted for over a hundred years.

I turn the water on in the shower and let it run for a few minutes while I take off my dirty clothes. The water is very warm as I step in and it feels good against my cool skin. It stings for a few quick seconds but then my body becomes acclimated to it. I'm not used to being warm anymore and it is one of the things that seems to be taking me some time to get used to in my new life. Standing under the steady stream of water that sprays from the shower head I let it run along the length of my body. It is relaxing. I shampoo my hair and then lather up with a bar of soap as I wash yesterday down the drain. The steam from the shower has fogged up the entire bathroom and when I turn off the water and open the shower door there is a towel waiting in front of me with William on the other side holding it up in the air. He wraps it around me as I step out of the shower.

"I'll leave you to get dressed. I'll be in the bedroom." He turns and walks out of the bathroom.

I rummage through my suitcases in the huge walk-in closet and find a tee-shirt, some leisure shorts, and a comfortable robe. I run a comb through my wet hair and hang the towel up over the hook on the wall. When I open the door into the master bedroom, he is laying on the bed watching some television. I walk around to the other side of the bed and lay down propping myself up with some pillows to see what he is watching. He has it on the weather channel getting an update of what the weather will be like for the rest of the week. This is one thing that I have learned is important to an immortal, keeping track of the weather. Most mortals like sunny days but immortals love cloudy ones. This day is going to be partly cloudy which is good too.

Looking over at William I begin to think of the questions that I had come up with in the shower. With slight hesitation, at first, I quietly ask, "What do you do for a living?"

"What do you mean?" He mutters and continues to watch television, flipping through the channels.

"You know, what do you do for a job?" I sit up a little straighter in the bed and stare right at him waiting for an answer.

"Oh, I don't have a job," he states plainly while still channel surfing.

"How do you afford all of this?" I ask looking around me, "the yacht, the car, and the house, they're all very expensive things."

"Most of the money I have is old money and a lot of it I invested well in various stocks and bonds over the years. I dabble in real estate from time to time also," he answers as he looks at me with slight amusement in his inquisition.

"Did you think I was still a pirate?" he chuckles to himself.

"Well…" I say looking at him with a smirk on my face. He grabs me and starts to tickle me.

"Don't! Stop! I surrender," I laugh uncontrollably losing what little breath I have left in me.

"You surrender? Does that mean I win?" He speaks softly in my ear sending those always familiar shivers up and down my spine yet again.

"Yes, I guess I do. What do you want as your prize?" I tease while showing him my bedroom eyes.

"I already have my prize, it's you." He gently kisses the same place on my neck where he had made me immortal.

We rest for a little while and watch some television. After about thirty minutes William says, "I'm going to take a shower now."

"Alright," I answer as I roll onto my side and watch him walk into the bathroom. While he is taking a shower, I lay peacefully for a moment in the center of the king-size four-poster bed but then start to feel restless. I begin to wonder about this beautiful house that I am now going to live in and realize that I don't know much about it yet. I have only seen the living room, kitchen, and upstairs bedroom and bathroom. I haven't seen the other rooms and decide that I will take a self-guided tour of the rest of the house.

I sit up quickly and swing my legs off the side of the bed reaching with my toes until my feet touch the floor. I turn off the television and walk out of the room. There is a long hallway that opens on one side to the first floor and I can see all the way downstairs into the foyer. There are two other doors down the hallway. I open the door to the room next to the master bedroom and peer inside. It is a normal-looking bedroom with normal-looking bedroom furniture. There is a full-size bed with a nightstand on either side with matching lamps, a dresser, and a closet. I close the door to the room and walk a little way down the hall to the next door. I open it and see a room filled with boxes. It is being used for storage. I shut the door feeling somewhat disappointed by the normalcy of the rooms. As I make my way down the stairs, I study the detail of the walls and the stair railing tracing it with my fingers as I pace myself gracefully along.

The walls are painted in soft beige with white trim and the staircase railing is a black wrought iron scroll design. I step lightly down off the last step and make my way across the foyer. There is a room off of the living area that I haven't been in yet. I quietly open the door and it squeaks as I push on it. It is a study. The walls are all brown paneled wood and there is an old mahogany desk in the middle of the room with a high back black leather chair behind it. The desk appears to be an eighteenth-century antique stained in a cherry finish. There are various papers neatly organized on top of it. I walk over and pick one up. It is a financial report of some sort and there is information about stock quotes on it. On the corner of the desk are a computer monitor, mouse and keyboard. The contemporary intermingled with the antique, I think to myself.

On the wall behind the desk is an oil painting of William surrounded by an ornate gold frame. He stands straight and looks very regal. He wears a light blue cravat that is tied into a small bow inside a high white shirt collar and a dark royal blue double-breasted waistcoat with brass buttons. He wears dark ochre trousers that are neatly tucked into black leather calf-high boots. In his left hand resting straight down by his side, he holds a brimmed black hat that is tall and conical in shape. His left leg is crossed in front of the right one and his right hand, he holds a walking cane. His hair is the same dark auburn brown and fashionably tousled. It appears to be close to the same cut that he still wears but with longer sideburns.

On the shelves to the right of the room are many books. Some are very old and appear to be in a fragile state and others are new. I recognize them from the bookstore where I work and know that he had spent a lot of his time there before I had met him. Above the books on the highest shelf are two Flintlock pistols preserved in glass cases and on the walls around the room hung various swords and daggers. They are very old and appear to have been well used. As I turn slowly around the room gazing at all of the intricate details of the past I notice William standing in the doorway watching me. My eyes meet his and I can't quite interpret his expression.

"I see you found the best room in the house." He says as he walks in and stands next to me by the desk.

"Yes, it's amazing. I feel as though I have stepped back in time." I marvel.

"I especially love the painting," I reply and glance over in the direction where the painting hangs on the wall behind the desk.

"Yes, I was a dandy back then." He grins and looks at me because he knows the terminology is very old-fashioned. I peer over at him and smile, understanding his humor.

"You were quite dashing, absolutely handsome." I agree.

"Were," He jokes and glances at me with a humorous expression on his face.

"Of course, you still are." I muse and he smiles looking up at the painting.

"So, this is your home office," I state.

"Yes." He answers.

"Do you like it?" He asks.

"Of course, what's not to like. It's like being in a museum." I scan the room eyeing all the antiques.

"Hey, now, watch it. You're making me feel old." He stands behind me placing his hands around my waist.

"I'm sorry. I didn't mean…well, it just came out wrong." I struggle to make up for what I said.

"I'm just giving you a hard time. I like to watch you squirm…" He chuckles and then tickles me once on my right side above my hip.

"Tell me about the painting," I ask after wiggling out of his grasp and walking behind the desk.

"The memory is hazy at best, but I do remember paying a lot to have it commissioned. It was painted in 1813 just one year before I was turned." He stops and stares at the painting lost in thought.

"You were mortal," I comment as I study the painting closely and notice that his skin tone was tan and his eyes didn't have the same pale blue cast to them. They were a darker blue and they matched the coat that he wore.

"That was a different time, so long ago." He silently looks out the window located at the end of the room.

"Come to see, I want to show you something outside," he says as he motions for me to follow him out of the room and over to the back door.

"What is it?" I ask.

"You'll see," he says as he places his hands over my eyes and starts to guide me down the steps of the large wraparound porch. We pace our way slowly about half the distance of the back lot while William helps me to maintain my footing. As we come to a stop, he uncovers my eyes, and sprawling out in front of me is the most perfect rose garden that I have ever seen.

"It's wonderful." I reach for his hand and step to his side. I wander over to the edge of the garden and peer over the green hedges to get a closer look.

"Go on in," William tells me standing a few feet behind me now. I walk underneath a white arched garden arbor that is weighted down with fragrant yellow jasmine and into the beautiful garden. There are climbing roses on lattice work trellises in the far corners and to the right and left of me are the most gorgeous full-grown rose bushes that I have ever laid my eyes on.

William steps in close and begins to call out the name of each one.

"This rose here is named *Braveheart*," he says as he touches one of the blooms with his palm. "I planted it because it reminded me of my long voyages at sea. This rose here beside it is named *Imagine*." He takes a small step and points in its direction. "It reminds me of a time when I imagined what my life would be like here in America as I boarded the large ship for the long journey from France." He moves across the garden and reaches out touching the rose bush directly in front of where he stands. "This rose here is named *New Orleans*. It's obvious why I chose this one and over there are two

named *Generosity* and *Memories*. I planted *Generosity* because it is what was shown to me by the good people of New Orleans when I first landed there many years ago and *Memories* is the one that shares all that I have just spoken about. All of my roses are heirloom varieties."

"What about this one here? It looks newly planted." I hold one of the full blooms beneath my hand. The petals are soft like velvet.

"*April Love.* That one holds the most special meaning of all for me, for it is the month in which we came together as one, eternal." He touches my hand that holds the rose.

As I near the middle of the garden admiring all the beauty that surrounds me, I see a pond with white water lilies and pink lotus flowers. Tall cattail plants border the pond and large orange, white and black spotted koi fish swim effortlessly around in the clear green tinted water. There is a fountain statue of a small boy sitting on a jug that spills water out into the pond directly to the farthest end of it.

"This is the most beautiful garden I have ever seen. It's so well established. When did you plant it?" I question turning to face him as he points over to a small stone bench where we can sit by the side of the pond.

"Many years ago, when I first came to live here after I had finished construction on my house which took me about a year to finish. I did most of the work by myself although I did have some of my old crewmates help me when they were in the area. They would bring things that I needed off the ships in return for a hot meal that I would prepare for them. We would camp out here at night and things were as close to the old days as they could be before everything went awry. Some of them were very surprised to see that I was still alive. They had heard about what happened and thought I was dead. They believed in my innocence. They told me of the stories about the ones who attacked me all had their date with fate meeting their demise, mostly in violent ways. One was murdered for shooting his mouth off one night in a bar in New Orleans, shot dead on the spot. Another one died at sea after he fell overboard into shark-infested waters in the Caribbean and was eaten alive as the crew watched from the deck above. And the others I never heard what happened to them, but I know that they met their demise because my old crewmates, the ones who would come to help me with my house, kept me updated. I went back out on the ship one more time after I was turned but the long voyage didn't accommodate well for someone with my condition. When the rats, which I might add taste extremely foul, aren't plentiful on a ship and my appetite for blood can't be sustained then I ended up resorting to feeding on my crewmates and that was something I wasn't comfortable doing. When we made it back to New Orleans, I left and didn't board the ship again for another journey.

I made my way back to Lake Charles on horseback. After my house was finished and the guys that I knew from my old pirating days eventually stopped coming by, I found that I had a lot of free time on my hands. So, I decided that I needed a hobby and that is when I took up gardening. I toiled the ground and planted vegetables at first. I would sell them at the market nearby. When I stopped doing that and I started to plant all the rose bushes I could get my hands on as they would sell them at the market. I added the pond later when a ship from the Orient had entered the river selling exotic goods and koi were a part of the products that they were selling. This garden has been a source of pride and happiness for me during the lonely times of my long existence."

"It must take a lot of your time to keep it looking this nice," I respond.

"Not really, it's for my enjoyment now. It doesn't take as much time anymore and it is very easy to maintain now. Sometimes I have a gardener come when the days are long, and the sun is too hot for my liking." He looks over at the pink roses growing up the trellises against the back corner of the garden. The warm breeze gently rolls past.

"And the house, do you take care of it all on your own?" I turn back towards the home.

"No, of course not," he smiles. "There is a maid service that comes from time to time, but I have to repeatedly call them to come out because before they leave, I erase their memory of ever being here. It's kind of funny because when they come out here each time it's like the first time they've ever been here. I must admit that sometimes when I am feeling rather lazy and I don't want to hunt, I feed on them too. I guess you can consider its delivery as opposed to takeout," he laughs loudly.

"You're naughty! That is the most devilish laugh I think I have ever heard come out of you!" I giggle at the thought with a slight gleam in my eye.

It is now close to 5:30 in the evening and I know that I will have to get ready to go to work at six o'clock. It is going to be the first time back since I have been saved by William in the park. I trudge upstairs to the master bedroom and change into my black jeans and bright red collared uniform polo. The color of the shirt reminds me of the diet that I am now required to live by. I am a little apprehensive about being around mortals again, but I feel like I am strong enough to withstand the temptation. Though I hope it won't be too distracting for me as I try to work. I enter the master bathroom and check my appearance in the large wood-framed mirror. I don't need much makeup now since I have become immortal. My skin is radiant and flawless. I trace my eyes lightly with a black eyeliner and dab a small amount of blush-tinted lip gloss onto my full lips. I smile at my reflection in the mirror baring my teeth so that I can see them more clearly. My canines are slightly sharper than they had been when I was a mortal, but they don't appear to be extremely unusual at first glance. It is nothing a mortal would notice as being out of the ordinary. They are sharp enough to get the job done when it comes time to feed on a donor. I pick up a bottle of perfume and spray one small mist over my body and go downstairs to meet William. He is outside setting the sprinkler system to water the garden while we are away from the house. I stand at the window and watch him. His physique is like that of a Greek god and his muscles flex under his clothing as he steps up onto the porch. I feel a surge of warmth inside of me as I watch him.

"Are you ready to go?" He steps into the house through the back door.

"Yeah, I guess so." I am feeling unsure all of the sudden.

"You're nervous?" He walks over to the kitchen sink to wash his hands. I nod my head up and down with little movement.

"Do you want me to stay with you?" He suggests.

"No…it's alright. I'll be okay." I respond as I walk over to the bar.

"What will you do while I'm at work?" My expression feels thoughtful yet tense.

"Oh, I don't know. I have a few errands to run. I'll meet you at the bookstore when I'm done." William grabs the car keys off the table, and we leave the house. The drive to my job only took about ten minutes. William knows all the back ways around the city, and he drives very well and fast.

"Have you ever been pulled over by a cop for speeding?" I look out the window at the swiftly passing landscape.

"Yes, but I don't get tickets. I never do. Remember the mind control thing. When I do get pulled over it's just more annoying than anything else. I try to catch their eyes in my gaze either in their rearview mirror before they step out of the patrol car or as I pass them on the street because then I can get them to just drive away. Mind control comes in very useful don't forget about that while you're at work tonight. You could use it to your advantage. Get Jenny to do all of the hard stuff." He chuckles and pulls the car to a stop in front of the bookstore doors.

"I'll try to remember," I say, and we lean in together and kiss. I hop out of the car and look back at him as I walk inside the store. He waves reassuringly to me and I know that I will be alright.

As I enter the store the aroma hits me like an iron curtain, the smell hangs extremely thick in the air and I suddenly feel panicked. I look back through the doors, but William has already driven away. That's when I realize that I had been outdoors both times when I was around mortals and the smell was able to dissipate to some degree. Now I am indoors in an enclosed space with them and the smell is the strongest I had ever encountered. I stand at the front of the store feeling like I want to hyperventilate but the more I breathe in the more the smell causes me discomfort. I back against the wall while the mortals closest to me stand and stare.

"Are you going to be alright, honey?" A medium-sized woman leans over me with concern in her eyes for me. I gasp, standing frozen and wide-eyed. Then the woman's face falls blank as she turns and walks away suddenly.

"Control, Abigail, get control," I whisper. Just then Jenny spots me from behind the counter of the coffee shop and starts to wave for me to come over. I dizzily stand straight and slowly saunter in her direction.

"Hey, Abigail, you look different. Your eyes are a different color." Jenny tries to get close to me as if to offer a hug, but I back up quickly and Jenny backs off too.

"I'm glad your back. It's been hell working this shift by myself." She grimaces.

I don't say a word. I just clock in, go stand at my place behind the counter and start filling orders.

"You're quiet. Are you sure you are feeling o.k.?" Jenny asks in between ringing up customers.

"I'm alright," I reply while keeping my eyes down on the coffee machines and trying to concentrate on the job.

"You seem tense, are you sure?" Jenny harps.

"Yes, I'm sure…" I scold and look directly into Jenny's eyes. Jenny stands frozen for a moment and then goes back to her job, this time without saying another word to me for the rest of the night unless it is work-related.

I stay as close to the machines as I can while working because the smell of the coffee camouflages the aroma of the blood. Only when a mortal stands too close to me, I tense up again. I am working so intently that I don't notice much of anything going on around me but when William walks through the front doors I can feel him here. I look up immediately to see him walking down the aisle gracefully towards me and smiling. My eyes light up when I see his beautiful angelic face. He is my soul's mate.

"How's it going?' He walks over closer to me where I stand.

"It's going," I say with a flat tone to my voice.

"That well, huh?" He replies and I frown at him.

"I'll be over there looking at books and staring at you in a stalker kind of way, okay?"

He chuckles and I start to laugh as he walks over to look at books. From time to time I look over at Jenny who is wide-eyed and staring in his direction. I have a hard time keeping a straight face.

When it comes time to close, I walk into the back office and sit down at the manager's desk. I pick up a pen and piece of paper and start to write a note. I fold it in half and leave it on the desk for the manager to find in the morning. With my eyes, I command Jenny to finish closing the shop without me and walk out to meet William who waits for me outside in front of the building. We slowly make our way to his car arm in arm. I know after tonight that there is no going back to any part of the life that I had once lived. There are certain things from my mortal life that are over and done. I leave the coffee shop and the bookstore behind me for the last time this night, never to return.

The sun had gone down hours earlier and it is dark outside. I am upstairs getting ready for our date. I am ravenous after being around so many mortals the night before at the festival and then tonight at work. When I descend the staircase, I am wearing my best short black dress. It is low cut in the front exposing a small amount of cleavage and I am wearing my black patent leather stiletto heels. The scent of my perfume lingers in the air and William turns around immediately to see me.

"You look exquisite!" He walks across the room to where I stand on the last step of the staircase. He places his hands on my sides and picks me up swinging me around in the air and back down onto the floor in front of him. I laugh loudly as I feel the air escape my lungs and then I breathe back in again with a long sigh at the end of the exhale. The desirable nature between him and I is most intoxicating as he pulls me closer to his chest pressing our bodies together firmly and holding me there in place without letting me go. Our lips touch softly, and I feel sparks rush up and through my body as we kiss long and hard.

"Maybe we should stay in tonight instead," he whispers in my ear sending shivers up and down my body.

"I thought you said you were hungry and after being around those mortals last night and tonight because I am too," I reply with a tiny giggle.

"I'm hungry for something else now," he says.

"But you're right, we should go," he grumbles reluctantly and feeling the slight burn of hunger pains.

The clouds have cleared, and the brilliance of the night sky glitters with stars in the darkness above. The moon is full and bright. It lights the landscape with a soft iridescent glow. Sitting in William's car out in front of the nightclub, we watch as all the mortals file into the dimly lit building. It is very busy, but it is a Saturday night. I turn to William looking nervous again, thinking that I will never get used to it.

"I don't know if I can handle being around so many mortals indoors again. The smell of their blood may drive me crazy," I say.

He answers me with a crooked smile on his face, "You'll be fine. Just remember it's like it used to be when you were around your favorite foods as a mortal. You would smell the mouth-watering aroma, but you weren't allowed to eat because you were on a diet." He laughs. I glare at him in disbelief.

"Yeah, some diet. This should be interesting!" I rolled my eyes and ask, "Are you amused by my suffering?" I begin to pout.

"You know that's not true." He smirks and then becomes more serious.

"I know, I know. Well, here goes nothing and I can hear the headlines tomorrow, vampires do exist and one of them went crazy in a nightclub last night." I step out of the car and follow William closely behind holding onto his hand for support.

The music is loud as it pulsates against my chest reminding me of the strong mortal heartbeat that once occupied the now mildly beating chambers. It feels good to me but in a strange way. William pays the cover charge at the door and the doorman lifts the velvet rope and lets us through. The club is dark but not to us, of course. The lights on the dance floor blink and flash in different directions. Mortals are everywhere, standing along the sides of the walls, on the dance floor, and over at the long bar. I feel drunk from the intoxicating aroma of the blood coursing through their veins and it is almost making it hard for me to see straight. I pull William out onto the dance floor and our bodies naturally follow along with the beat. He is a very good dancer and I am not surprised because of the unique grace that he possesses at everything he does. He makes walking look like art in motion.

The music seems to be playing only for the two of us. The aroma in the air is maddening to me and it seems to act as fuel for me on the dance floor. William keeps up without any problem. Our movements, just like our eyes, are hypnotic. We never break a sweat even after dancing through an hour's worth of long electronic dance music.

"I'm hungry," William says leaning in closer to me. I agree and we leave the dance floor to find a spot to sit near the back of the club, out of plain sight.

As potential donors walk past us, William spots one across the room makes eye contact, and motions for her to come over to where we sit. He senses that this one is here alone. He takes the donor's hand and tells her to sit next to him which she does obediently. Her eyes stay fixed on his as he leans in closer enjoying the aroma that entices him to feed on her. I sit across the table from them watching intently as he sinks his fangs deep into the tiny woman's throat and drinks in her blood.

The club is so busy that night that no one even notices as he feeds slowly and with a pleasure that makes me twinge inside with a small pang of jealousy. To anyone at the club who might see them it just looks like another couple making out.

When he is finished, he lets the donor go back to her place against the wall on the other side of the nightclub.

"I'm impressed." I have a slightly annoying grin on my face.

"It's just the result of over a hundred years of practice," he says satisfied.

"It seemed to me that you enjoyed it a little too much, though," I comment with a frown and tilt my face downward looking up at him from underneath my eyelashes.

"Abigail Durand, are you jealous?" He questions with a degree of astonishment to his tone.

"Maybe just a little, I have never watched you feed like that before. You were so seductive, and she was so pretty," I confess sheepishly. He slides over next to me in the booth and puts his arm around my shoulder, kissing me softly on the forehead.

"You have my heart. She was just a meal, that's all."

And with those words, he presses his lips against mine and we are lost to one another in a long deep kiss.

"Will you share with me?" I whisper between kisses. He nods and offers me his neck. I bite and drink, sipping slowly being careful not to take too much. The pleasure is almost too much for either of us to contain.

"I'm still hungry," I whisper.

William motions for a young man that stands alone not too far from where we sit. The man walks over methodically and sits next to Abigail while William keeps the man's eyes connected to his gaze until I lean over and make a midnight snack out of him. When I am finished the donor is released. I lean back in the booth feeling completely satisfied. The surge of adrenaline is starting to build in my muscles.

"Now I'm jealous." William grins with a sly look in his eyes and moves closer to me as I rest my head against the back of the seat. In return, he takes a little bit back from me. Pleasure courses through my body as he bites my neck and drinks slowly.

"Now we're even. Let's go work some of this energy off on the dance floor!" He quickly motions for me to follow him towards the middle of the crowded room. We dance together the rest of the night without a care in the world.

Chapter 17: Sketches

As dawn breaks, the birds begin to sing the sweet songs of morning and William rests by my side on the couch in his house, now our home together. We sit silently staring at the fire that glows from within the fireplace while I rest my head on his shoulder feeling as though I ought to be tired from such a long night of dancing but to my pleasant surprise I am not. Some of the energy from feeding is still coursing through my veins but not to the degree that it had been when I was at the nightclub. As I lean against William, there is a stillness that seems to possess us, barely any breath or heartbeat, still, just like statues. Skin like marble, so exquisite, a work of sculpted art.

As I rest with his arms loosely placed around me, I reflect on the past few days of my new life and everything that has happened. One day I am just a plain Jane, all alone and working at the bookstore serving coffee to strangers and now I am in the arms of a vampire, I too, a vampire. It is still so surreal to me and sometimes I wonder if it is all just some strange dream that I will wake up from.

William sits half slouched beside me with his head back on the couch not making a single movement or sound. I turn to him and watch him as he quietly relaxes by my side. He is so peaceful and still, so perfect. I can see the sun coming up outside from the front windows. It will be another sunny day.

"Would you like to go to New Orleans for a few days?" William asks breaking the silence and I am surprised to hear his voice suddenly out of the quiet that surrounds us. It is soothing as always and I think for a moment about what he has just asked me, not knowing if I am ready for what might wait to be discovered there. It has been a question that lingers in my brain since I found out that his past had begun there so many years ago, a past that I should uncover, even if I am not the one who had lived it.

"I think I would like to do that, yes, let's go," I answer his question with confidence that I didn't have just moments before. Suddenly I am excited to learn more about his life long ago.

"We will leave tonight then. Let's pack," he says as he kisses me on the lips, and he takes me by the hand and leads me up the stairs to the master bedroom to start packing our things.

"I'm going downstairs to get my favorite jeans out of the dryer. Be back in a sec." He leaves the room in a hurry. I step into the large walk-in closet and start to pack my clothes into the suitcases that I had brought from my house. I fold each one of my shirts and pants neatly into little rectangles. Then bending down I place them one on top of another in the smallest of the three suitcases. I don't know how long we will be out of town, but I don't want to bring too much with me either. I figure that will go shopping if I need anything else. As I stand back straight and look up at the shelves in the closet, I notice a small shoebox. On the front of the box, the word Sketches is written in black ink. I pull the box down and carry it to the bed. Opening the top carefully I look inside and can see that there is a collection of four charcoal sketches. The first one I see is a sketch of a young woman sitting in an armchair by a fireplace. The next one is of the same young woman standing near a window looking out of it and the other two are portraits. I immediately recognize the woman as being the same one from my memories after the wreck.

"I found the jeans that I was looking for they were in the dryer like I thought."
William walks into the room and stops suddenly to see me holding one of the old sketches.

"What's her name?" I whisper as I look at the old piece of paper with the woman's face drawn on it.

"Her name was Elizabeth…. Elizabeth Rose." He looks down at the floor with a sullen expression across his face.

"She's the one from my memories," I say as I stand stunned and then turn to look at him.

"Who was she?" I question slightly confused by my present discovery.

"She was my fiancée a long time ago when I lived in New Orleans." He lumbers over to the bed and stands next to me peering at the sketch that I hold in my hand.

"Did you sketch these?" I can barely make out the initials in corner of the paper and it appears to be the letters WD.

"Yes." He says and then falls silent.

I place them back into the box and sit down on the edge of the bed. I am very still for a few minutes quietly contemplating everything he has just told me and then with a small amount of reluctance I whisper, "Tell me about her."

He looks at me intensely searching deep inside my eyes, as if he is wondering if I am ready to hear about his past love. Elizabeth had been the one he loved so many years ago. After searching my eyes for the answer to his unspoken question, he slowly begins to speak while sitting down next to me.

"She was petite. She had dark brown hair and light golden-brown eyes. She was always so full of life and very outgoing. She came from a very noble aristocratic family in New Orleans and we met one night at one of the many social events that her parents frequently hosted for the wealthy elite in the town. I just happened to be there because Sir Lafitte had been invited and he brought me along. I began to court Elizabeth and after some time went by, I wanted to propose marriage. Her father was aware of what I did for a living, but he approved of my profession because he respected Lafitte, the Gentleman Pirate, as he was known as around the city. So, he deemed me good enough for his daughter, and over time he gave me his blessing to marry her," William pauses for a moment as he seems to reflect on the memory, and then he continues the story. "It took some time for me to make the journey back to New Orleans after I regained my strength from being turned. I made it halfway on foot and the other half by hitching a ride from a generous boat captain on his passing boat. I was dropped off at the docks and walked the remainder of the distance to Royal Street in the French Quarter. That is where Elizabeth and her parents lived. I remember that night vividly. It was bitterly cold for early November and damp from an earlier rain shower. It was an unusual night in the city as I made my way back to their house. There wasn't any light coming from the house. It was completely dark inside and out which I remember at the time was strange. I knocked on the door to the Devereaux home and waited patiently but no one answered. I slowly entered as I had always done in the past when I came back from a long voyage at sea. Elizabeth would usually be waiting for me there in the living area with open arms," he gazes out into the empty space seeming to be lost somewhere far away in his mind and then glancing at me for a moment, and then he continues, "but instead of Elizabeth it was her parents standing near the kitchen to the right of the living room and they were not expecting to see me. That was evident by the look of shock on their faces when I walked into the house. They looked as though they were staring straight into the eyes of a ghost. I was confused by their reaction and asked if I could see Elizabeth. Her mother started to cry, and her father was the one to break the horrible news to me that she was gone." He looks directly into my eyes to find some solace within them. I know it is painful for him to remember this part of his life, but I need to hear about it. I place my hand on top of his for comfort.

"Take your time, it's alright," I reassure him, and he picks up my hand kissing the top of it firmly.

"I rushed past them, hoping it was all just a terrible nightmare and wanting desperately to awake from it. I bolted up the stairs calling out for her but there was no answer. I remember pushing the door open to her bedroom and running inside only to find it empty. The only thing left in her absence was a small memorial in her honor. Several small candles were burning in front of a painting of her that was propped carefully on top of her writing desk in the corner of the room and the smell of fresh-cut flowers permeated the air around me. I turned back towards the door sadly realizing that it was not a dream, that it was real. I stormed back down the stairs into the living quarters where her parents stood by the fireplace holding onto one another for comfort. I remember yelling out at them while feeling the anger and grief welling up inside of me. I asked them how and why it had happened. That's when Elizabeth's father told me through his shaking voice that Lawrence had come by a few weeks sooner and told her that I was dead. That there had been a tragic accident on the voyage home and that I was lost at sea, never to be found. Her father told me that Elizabeth had believed him and that she ultimately died in vain. Her father cried out loudly as he smashed a vase that had been on top of the fireplace mantle. The fragments scattered around his feet. He was suffering greatly from the memory of his daughter's untimely demise. He looked like he could have killed someone. I remember thinking that I couldn't believe my ears. Why would Lawrence say such a thing to Elizabeth, he knew that I wasn't dead? Well, then I asked her father how it had happened. How she had died because I still wasn't quite clear on that point. He told me that she had taken her own life, that she loved me so much that she couldn't bear to live another day without me. I can still see her mother sobbing inconsolably behind him. I asked him where she was buried and I could feel my eyes glazing over with rage, rage against Lawrence. Elizabeth's mother told me that she had been buried in the St. Louis cemetery as she cried. She held out a ring in her the palm of her hand. It was the engagement ring that I had given Elizabeth only two months earlier. She told me to take it, and so I did, placing it in my pocket. I ran out the front door into the night. I ran faster than I had ever run in my whole life, mortal or immortal, and when I got to the cemetery I stopped, hesitating for a moment before I entered through the open gate. I knew exactly where she rested. I could feel it deep down in the pit of my core. I walked straight ahead into the dark damp cemetery."

William sits silently for a long moment as I look sadly into his eyes at the pain that the memory causes him.

"Who is Lawrence?" I ask.

"Oh, yeah, that would be my brother." He answers as a blank expression occupies his stare.

"What? Why would he do such a thing! He knew you weren't dead because he had turned you." I sit up straight and my face is frozen with shock.

"He loved her too. He wanted her for his own. He had this wild idea that if he told her that I was dead he would have a chance to make her love him."

"But he was a vampire," I gasp.

"I know. That was the worst part of it all. He had planned to turn her and he was going to do it against her will if he had to, to make her his forever."

"Did she know what he was?" I ask.

"No, she didn't." He takes my hand and holds it in his, palm up, tracing with his fingers the little lines and creases.

"That's why you said that your brother has changed, and you no longer want to see him."

"Yes." He answers and then brings my hand to his lips and kisses it.

"I'm sorry, William. It must have been so hard for you all of those years after learning about what he had done." I place my hand on the side of his face and feel the smoothness of his cheek. He leans in closer to my hand pressing it firmly against his cool skin.

"Yes, it was. Of course, he had no idea she was going to kill herself, but I still blamed him for it." He sighs.

Then I remember what it all means for me.

"I had memories of her when I was mortal, you know that because I already told you. I never understood why I was having them at the time. I didn't recognize the woman in them, and it was very confusing for me. I now know that it was Elizabeth. It was her life and her memories that became my own. It was her loss and her despair that I ultimately shared with her. I always felt connected to her because of the sadness and the emptiness that we both felt. The memories didn't make any sense to me at the time. I even started to think that I had lived a past life. Remember that book you saw me staring at on the bookshelf in the bookstore that night?"

He shakes his head in agreement.

"And now to think of all the time I spent searching in so many books for the answers and never finding them, it almost seems like it was a waste when all of that time the answers were waiting for me to find in you. I knew you held the answers to all my questions, William. I could see it whenever I looked into your eyes."

"What do you think triggered the memories?" He asks curiously.

"I don't know. It must have been something that happened the night at the sight of the car wreck when I saw you for the first time. Even though I didn't remember any of it in a conscious state something must have triggered the memories to surface. What do you think it was?" I ask him.

"Hum…I'm not sure. Do you think it had something to do with me erasing your memory? Or it could have been the wreck itself. Didn't the doctors tell you that they thought you must have bumped your head based on the concussion they said you had?"

"Yes, they did but I was wearing my seatbelt. I don't know how I would've done it." I answer him and stare intently at the floor concentrating.

"It must have had something to do with me erasing your memory then." He concludes.

"Maybe you transferred the capability to me unwittingly." I theorize looking into his pale blue eyes now.

"Yes, I guess that is possible." He agrees and turns to meet my gaze.

"I don't think we'll ever really know what triggered it." He says looking at me.

"Well, either way, it feels amazingly good to have the answers. I feel like a weight has been lifted."

I feel a freedom that I have wanted for so long, freedom from feeling trapped by the past. I can now live with the past, William's past, as a part of my future.

"Yes, I am so glad that you finally have the answers that you so desperately sought after." He lays back on the bed and looks up at the ceiling. "So, you could see into the past long before you became immortal."

I twist myself around to face him and contemplate what he just said for a moment. Then I scoot myself off the bed and walk over to the window pushing the sheer curtains back and peer out.

"Did you have any other memories besides those about Elizabeth?" He asks rolling over onto his stomach as he watches me stand near the window.

"No, only the ones about her, I would like to go out into the garden for a little while," I say staring longingly out the window and down at the wooded back lot to the house.

"Alright, I'm going to start packing. I'll be out there in a little bit." He springs up off of the bed and walks into the closet pulling his suitcase down from the shelf in one quick flawless motion.

"Make sure you grab your sunglasses out of the kitchen. There is plenty of shade in the backyard, just not much in the garden though," he says.

"Wait...Abigail..." He darts quickly from the closet and places the suitcase on the bed turning to meet me near the bedroom door.

"I love you very much." He confesses.

"I know. I love you too." I kiss him and then proceed down the stairs. I pick up my sunglasses off the bar between the kitchen and the living room before going outside into the garden. The shade from the tall trees is nice as I step off the porch into the soft green grass. There is a nice warm breeze that makes me feel comfortable in my cool skin. I walk a little way across the back lot and enter the garden. The sun begins to shine down on me with its prickly heat teasing my skin. The sunglasses come in handy because the light is a little bright even with them on. I sit on the little stone bench and stare at the crystal clear green-tinted water of the pond. I start to feel a little lightheaded and there is a dull hum in my ears. I wonder if I am having a reaction to the sun but then I quickly realize it is something else. The memory lurches over me swiftly and without much warning. I fall deep into the vision and it is something and somewhere that I have never lived. I see a man and a woman dancing in a large room off in the distance of my mind's eye. The vision is blurry at first and I have a hard time making out the faces. The pair held each other closely and they are very happy. The young woman wears a long dress that brushes the floor as she sways back and forth in her partner's arms. It starts to become clearer as I watch the two continue to dance and smile at one another. They turn and twirl to the sound of a piano being played in the background and I can smell the scent of roses all around me from the garden where I stand. Then I see in my vision that the young man is William and he is very happy. They begin to slowly turn around to where I can almost see the young woman's face. I have just started to see the side of her face and it becomes clear to me that it is Elizabeth. She is beautiful and her smile is contagious. I smile along with the vision. Then Elizabeth's face suddenly disappears and is replaced with my face.

Then the vision ends, and I am left staring into the water of the pond in front of me. I touch it with my fingers and make tiny ripples on the water's surface. The koi swim around freely and effortlessly near the bottom. The memory is comforting to me. It makes me feel as though everything is as it should be and that Elizabeth would be happy too.

William quietly approaches from behind me and is dressed in a cream-colored button-down long sleeve shirt with faded blue jeans. He walks around and sits next to me with a can of koi food in his left hand. He starts throwing one piece of fish food into the pond at a time.

"Penny for your thoughts." He continues to feed the fish watching as they swim to the top and quickly snatch up the little pellets.

"Oh, I was just thinking about how I no longer mind the sunny days," I answer thoughtfully.

"The sun doesn't irritate your skin. It will only be a matter of time before it doesn't bother you anymore."

"No, not anymore but I used to dislike sunny days for a different reason. It reminded me of the day I buried my parents. It always made me feel very sad to see the sun shining brightly in the sky and now I don't seem to mind it. It's because of you." I turn my head slightly in his direction. My expression doesn't match my mood. Inside I am happy to be here next to William and feel wonderful after realizing the truth behind the memories, but my expression is forlorn.

"What's the matter, Abigail?" William notices my expression and I feel betrayed by my face.

"I was thinking about our trip to New Orleans. I'm excited about going but I will miss being here at your…I mean, our house," I say.

"We don't have to go if you don't feel comfortable about it." He turns his body towards mine as he moves closer to me on the stone bench.

"No, I want to go." I cast my gaze out across the lush garden.

"Good, I promise I will make it worth your while. You will enjoy it."

"I've never been," I state sheepishly.

"You've never been to New Orleans? Well, you're in for a real treat, then, Ms. Durand." He runs his fingers through my hair as he winks at me.

"I'm going to go back inside; do you want to come?" He asks and appears to be more excited now.

"Yes, let's go pack our things," I say.

Standing up and walking past the pond I turn my head quickly to the water's surface. I think about the vision that I just had and quietly smile to myself. We walk back inside the house and finish packing up all the things that we would bring with us to New Orleans.

Chapter 18: Real

The drive takes about three hours and we reach New Orleans around midnight.

William parks the car in front of a stunning two-story brick home located on Royal Street in the French Quarter.

"This is the house that once belonged to Elizabeth's parents. They left it to me after they died."

He stares out the window at the home then turns to me as I peer out the passenger side window he asks, "Are you ready?"

"Yes," I answer as I continue to stare at the old house next to us.

We get out of the car and head towards the trunk to retrieve our luggage. I brought a medium-sized suitcase and a small cosmetics bag. William brought one small suitcase. He picks up the two suitcases in one hand and I carry my cosmetics bag. He shuts the trunk door. Then we walk carefully along the slick sidewalk that leads from the street through an old iron gate into the courtyard and up to the front door of the house. Although it needs some tender loving care, the garden within the courtyard is a tropical paradise of various plants and vines that trail their way up

to the second-story balcony that overlooks the area below.
Standing in front of the door, William reaches in his pants pocket
for the key. He opens the door and then enters first, turning on a
lamp. He sets the luggage down on the floor and then takes the bag
that I am carrying, placing it on the floor next to the others. As I
step into the house I stand and search with my eyes around the
room at the familiarity of it. I feel as though I have been here many
times before, knowing every inch of the home in my mind.
William looks at me and can see in my eyes the look of amazement
and wonder. He also sees that ever-familiar crease of concentration
on my brow as I stare at the room around me taking it all in with
one intense glance.

"I have always known from the first time I saw you that I
was in love but in this very moment I realize how completely,
absolutely, and hopelessly lost I would now be without you in
my life." He admits to me.

"Are you alright?" He walks over and whispers, wrapping
his arms around me in a gentle embrace. I look up at him smiling
in a slightly delicate way and I can tell that he knows that I am.

The house hasn't seemed to have changed since the early
eighteen-hundreds except for a few modern updates and
renovations. The only modern appliance in the kitchen is a
refrigerator. William never needs to cook so there isn't a stove or
oven. There are a small television and a new sofa in the living

room. As I walk into the living area, I notice an oil painting hanging over the fireplace mantel. It is a painting of the family who once occupied the home. One member is immediately recognizable to me. It is Elizabeth. She is so young, in her late teens or early twenties, and very beautiful. Her eyes are big and brown, innocent. They call out to me from the painting and from another time long before I had lived.

"If it's alright with you we will stay here the rest of tonight until the afternoon and then we can see about getting a room at a hotel somewhere nearby," William says as he walks over to the fireplace to light it. I look at him for a moment and then respond, "If you don't mind, William, I would like to stay here. It feels like home to me."

"It's alright with me if you are sure?" He says with a hint of concern in his tone.

"Oh, yes, I am sure about it." I walk over to the mantle of the fireplace and touch the frame on the painting with my fingers ever so carefully.

"Elizabeth was so beautiful and so young," I observe.

William nods in agreement and looks down at the fire poking the logs to get them burning stronger.

"Do you think I look like her?" I ask as I look up at the young woman's face in the painting noticing a small resemblance.

"No, not really," he answers not looking up from what he is doing.

"These logs are old. I don't know if the fire will keep."

"Her bedroom is upstairs to the right when you first enter the hallway, isn't it?"

I turn towards the staircase.

"Yes, you're right but it's been closed off for so many years now. I don't ever go in there," he answers as he continues to work with the logs in the fireplace. I look over at the wall where a Grandfather clock stands next to the entryway of the home and its hands are resting permanently on the four and the twenty. Knowing that it isn't the right time I look at my watch and it is 12:35 a.m.

"I know you remember but let me show you around anyway." He stands up next to me in front of the mantle now, looking over and meeting my gaze. I nod in agreement.

He leads me across the living area and through a pair of double glass French doors into a small room that appears to have been a study at one time. Presently, though, the room is the occupant of a full-sized bed in the center of it.

"This used to be the study, but I converted it into a small guest room. I haven't been here in years, but this is where I sleep when I am."

I look around the room and see that the walls are lined with shelves that hold many different old books mostly dealing with financial topics and in the corner of the room is a worn leather armchair. William must have learned a lot about the financial market from Mr. Devereux's extensive library.

"This is where we will rest if that is alright?" He asks.

"That's fine. As long as I am in your arms I can rest anywhere." I smile warmly up at him and he leans over to kiss me. He takes me by the hand and turns to leave the room. He closes the doors behind him, and we walk back across the spacious living room and down a small hallway near the staircase.

"The first door to the left is the bathroom. It isn't anything fancy." He says pointing in the direction of the bathroom door. "That's it."

"What about upstairs?" I ask, slightly confused.

"Oh, there are only two bedrooms and a bathroom up there, nothing to see really," he walks back over to check on the progress of the fire. I know why he avoids the upstairs, so I don't push him to show me. I walk over and sit down on the sofa next to the fireplace.

"Do you feel like stretching your legs after the long car ride?" I ask.

"Yeah, sure, what do you have in mind?" He inquires as the fire begins to flicker and then slowly puts itself out with the dampness of the old wood.

"I would like to go visit her grave." I look directly at him to see his initial reaction, but he doesn't seem surprised by my request.

"Alright, let me put our suitcases in the guest room, first." He walks over and picks up the luggage carrying it into the room behind the sofa.

"Okay, then," he closes the French doors behind him. I stand up and follow him out the door.

We walk with a determined pace down the streets of the French Quarter. I admire the charm of the city at night as we hold hands the whole way in content silence. After several blocks, we turn onto St. Louis Street and then continue until we approach the corner of Basin. To the north is where St. Louis Cemetery No. 1 is located, the oldest cemetery in New Orleans. Stopping in front of the wrought-iron gates, William lingers for a moment. I stop alongside him momentarily to see if I can read his expression, but it is blank, he is deep in thought.

"We have nothing to worry about, but the cemetery can be a dangerous place at night, just stay close to me," he says.

We enter the city of the dead through the slightly rusted wrought iron gates and continue to move cautiously past the tall sun-bleached tombs adorned with dried flowers and melted candles. The marble figures atop the houses of death seem to stare at us, following our movements with stone-cold eyes as we pass by weaving in and out of the maze-like rows, the undead among the dead. Some of the tombs are brittle with age and the red clay bricks are caved in on themselves in heaps on the ground. Then solidly erected in front of where we stop, carved out of marble and elaborately decorated, is the crypt with a praying angel on the top of it gazing toward the heavens above us. The Devereux family is buried here, all three, Alexander Claude, his wife, Josephine Follet, and their daughter, Elizabeth Rose.

I stand quietly, afraid to blink, not sure if it will all disappear if I do. It is all real. Elizabeth was real. Before this moment it had only been a memory, a sketch, or a painting. I always knew that she had been real at one time, but this allows it to finally sink into my brain, and standing here in front of her grave confirms it. All the memories that I have been living with since the time of the wreck are real memories of this young woman and the life that she once lived. Sadness takes over me in this dark space of realization, deep sadness for the loss of this young woman's life, who feels more like a sister to me than anything else. I stare at the words written on the marker to the crypt and read them aloud sorrowfully.

Elizabeth Rose Devereux
Born March 23, 1793 – Died October 12, 1814.
Beloved Daughter

I turn and look at William knowing exactly what it means, that even in death she will always be a part of our life together. He is standing to the side of me looking regretfully at the tomb.

"I always wished I could have saved her." He whispers. "For many years I felt guilty about it."

"Everything happens for a reason, William." I place my hand on his back.

"You're right." He answers.

"I hope you still don't feel guilty about it. You're a wonderful man and she loved you very much. She wouldn't want you to feel that way."

"You're amazing, Abigail. How did I get so lucky?" He smiles warmly at me.

As we both turn around to leave the cemetery, we hear a deep guttural voice coming from proximity behind us. William spins around swiftly and is met face to face with a tall, heavy-set figure of a man with a knife pointed in his direction.

"Give me your wallet and that pretty heart necklace that she is wearing, and no one will get hurt." The thief demands as he inches closer to William.

I look at the man with a slight alarm across my face but then William glances in my direction with a smirk on his and a gleam in his eyes.

"Can you believe this guy? He wants my wallet and your necklace. Well, I'm afraid this is your unlucky night sir." As William turns his head to catch the thief's eyes in his hypnotic gaze the knife enters his side. The man has lunged forward and stabbed William. Suddenly, with extreme force, William sends the man sailing through the air. He hits the ground, hard, several feet away and then William is upon him pinning his arms to the ground and beating the knife out of his hand. Growling from deep within and bearing his canines he catches the man's eyes with his own and the man falls motionless. Jumping to his feet with the man held tightly in his grasp he demands his immediate departure from the cemetery without as much as a single word. The man immediately turns and walks away. William kicks the knife out of sight, and I run to his side.

"You've been stabbed!" I scream looking down at the blood on his shirt. I lift his shirt to see a small wound just above his right hip.

"It's alright. I'm fine." He says examining the puncture.

"How are you alright, you've been stabbed. You're bleeding" but before I can finish my sentence, I witness the cut heal rather quickly in front of my own two eyes. I look back up at him in pure astonishment. "But…what…"

"I told you that I was alright." He smiles.

I am in shock for a moment and then I touch the smooth skin on his side where the cut had just been.

"Are you sure everything is o.k.? You aren't in any pain?" I question in disbelief.

"Yes, I'm fine and no, I'm not in any pain." He watches my face fall from shock to relief.

"Now, let's get out of here." He suggests and I take his hand as we begin walking in the opposite direction back to the street. It is nearing daybreak as we make our way back to the old Devereux house. The sun is starting to rise in the sky and the glow from the sunlight is a gorgeous orange. We sit for a moment in the courtyard of the old home and watch it rise. I find myself staring at the blood on his shirt from time to time.

"It looks like it will be a sunny day." He observes seeing a clear sky above us.

"Let's go inside."

William pours himself a glass of water.

"Do you want anything?" He asks and then takes a sip of the water.

"No thank you," I answer.

"I'm going change out of this shirt." He walks into the guest room and I watch as he pulls the dirty shirt up over his head and then puts a new one on. I sit down at the table in the kitchen when he returns and throws the ruined shirt in the garbage can. He sits down next to me, breathing a heavy sigh. We sit at the kitchen table in silence and I watch him drink the rest of the water in one long gulp.

"Why did her parents leave the house to you?" I ask.

He looks out the window next to the kitchen table at the three-tiered fountain in the middle of the courtyard and says, "I had always been like a son to them. Elizabeth and I were engaged as you know and... well, they decided after her death to give me her dowry even though we hadn't had the chance to get married. It was more than generous of them and I tried to talk them out of it, but they were determined, saying that Elizabeth would have wanted it that way. They didn't have any other children so when they both passed away many years later, they willed everything to me. I was very surprised, to say the least."

"What did her father do for a living? I assume it had something to do with finances judging from the books in the guest room," I ask as I stare out the window at the sunny day and then I pull the curtains closed just slightly.

"He was a banker. He worked right here on Royal Street at The Old Bank of the United States. Royal Street was the center of the financial hub in New Orleans during that time. The family was quite wealthy." William looks across the room at the painting of Alexander Devereux above the mantel.

"Did they ever know about you…being immortal?" I inquire quietly.

"No, I was able to hide it from them since I didn't live here anymore. I came back less and less to visit as the years went on," he answers with a tinge of remorse in his tone.

"Did you stay here long after you found out about Elizabeth?"

"Just long enough to find Lawrence and confront him about what he had done."

"What happened?" My curiosity peeks now more than before.

"We had a nice gentlemanly duel in the city park." He replies plainly with a hint of annoyance at the memory. "I wanted to chop his head off."

"But you didn't…" I watch him closely, keeping my gaze intently placed on his.

"No," he chuckles. "I couldn't bring myself to do it, but I did pierce him straight through with my sword." He seems full of delight thinking back at that day but also annoyed that it wasn't enough to kill him.

He turns his face over toward the door for a minute and then says, "Hey, listen, I know you like bookstores and I was thinking that maybe later this evening we could take a stroll over to a really good one that isn't too far from here. I know you will love it."

I nod in agreement.

"Maybe we can check out some of the antique shops along Royal Street. I saw them as we were walking earlier." I suggest.

"Yes, anything your heart desires." He leads me to the guest room where we can rest for a while.

We lay down on the bed and snuggle close to one another. I press my lips against the side of his cheek and then bury my face into the curvature of where his shoulder meets his chest.

"I was so frightened when I saw that you had been stabbed," I whisper.

He reaches over and lifts my face with his hand and stares deeply into my eyes. The warmth between us is evident. He kisses me gently on the lips and holds me close.

Chapter 19: Proposal

The old iron gas lanterns along the side of the street provide a warm glow to the wet cobblestones. The night air is heavy with the smell of blood as mortals pass by. I try to ignore the aroma as I walk beside William down the street. There are shadows around every corner, shadows of the ones that lived and died on those same streets many years ago. The spirits that continue to roam freely refusing to stay buried with the past. William and I casually meander our way, arm in arm, down Royal Street watching as the spirits drift past intermingled yet eluding the living. Small children perform on the street corners for spare change as I admire the stunning and timeless French Quarter that surrounds us. The lace of the wrought-iron balconies that hover overhead on the historic facades of the buildings that sprawl out in front of us is enchanting to see and the small antique shops that line each side of the street add a certain old-world charm. As we make our way down Royal Street passing St. Peter Street, we turn onto a small alley that runs alongside the St. Louis Cathedral's rear gardens and the Cabildo.

"This is it," he marvels as he looks around taking in all the sights and sounds of the night while facing the narrow alleyway.

"I used to spend some of my time here in this alley. It became known as Pirate's Alley long ago. Come this way I want to show you something," he motions to me as we walk the length of the alley and then turn to face an old building that is painted a bright yellow with white shutters to our left.

"Faulkner House," I say as I read the plaque mounted to the side of the building.

"This is where William Faulkner once lived, the Nobel Prize-winning American author." William states.

"Yes, I know who he is." I peer into the windows of the building.

"It has been turned into a bookstore and I know how much you love bookstores, so I thought you would love this one," he smiles.

"You thought right!" I beam and then see the sign on the door with the hours of operation listed.

"Oh, but it's closed. The sign says that it closed at 5:30 p.m." I look back at him in disappointment but just as the words leave my lips William knocks lightly on the door. A friendly man comes to the window and waves. He opens the door and says,

"Welcome to Faulkner House Books."

I am surprised and turn to face William.

"I made special arrangements to view the store after hours. We have the whole bookstore to ourselves." His eyes are gleaming with exuberance when he sees my face light up.

We step inside the small building and I find myself surrounded by many different books, first editions, and rare classics, only this time I'm not searching for any answers I am just enjoying the experience. We spend nearly an hour of our time looking around at all the small store has to offer. William picks up an antique first edition on poetry and buys it for me. We leave the bookstore, thanking the man who has graciously opened the store for us, and continue back down the alley until we reach the St. Anthony Gardens to the rear of the cathedral. We stroll into the gardens through the wrought-iron gate and I am captivated by my surroundings, taking in all of the wonderful sights of the garden as my skin glows softly in the light of the moon. I remain perfectly still gazing up at the stars in the night sky. The gentle warm summer breeze rustles the leaves in the trees above me. William walks up standing quietly behind me running his fingers through my hair moving it out of the way so that he can kiss me on the back of the neck.

He stops for a moment looking up at the cathedral seemingly drawn back to the past by some distant memory and then whispers in my ear, "Marry me."

"What?" I reply and turn towards him as he is already down on one knee.

"Abigail, I am truly and completely in love with you. You have my heart and my soul; every fiber of my being is in your possession. I love you deeply, more deeply than you will ever know. Abigail Catherine, will you please do me the honor of being my bride?"

He holds in his hand a little black box and inside is the most perfect one-carat diamond solitaire engagement ring. I reach for his hand and he stands up in front of me with his eyes wide with anticipation. I move my body close to his and press my lips to his lips, kissing him softly and then I whisper, "Yes."

It is the second time that he has asked me to spend my life with him eternally and it is the second time that I have accepted. William wraps his arms around me, and we embrace under the light of the full moon. He is the happiest that I have ever seen him, and I share in that happiness. My whole world at this very moment in time is perfect.

"Let's not wait!" He beams with eagerness to his voice.

"What's the rush? We have all the time in the world," I answer in a cavalier tone.

"I have learned that is not always the case, my dear," he manages a small half-smile and I know what he means.

"Would you like to be married here in this cathedral tomorrow night at the stroke of midnight?" He asks.

I feel butterflies in my stomach at the thought of being married in twenty-four hours but there is an excitement inside of me too.

"I would love to," I say with a smile on my face.

I will marry William here tomorrow night in St. Louis Cathedral, only the two of us with God as our witness. I begin to wonder if two vampires such as ourselves can stand before God in a church and vow our undying love for one another, but the more I think about it the more I begin to realize that William didn't have the choice of his fate long ago on that night along the bayou and when I was unknowingly faced with the same fate it was love for him that I chose in the park that night. I know deep down that we are not damned, and it has been told, as truth, that everything on this earth comes to an end eventually, even the earth itself. I know that it is no different for the immortal ones.

"This calls for a toast," William announces while holding me close.

"Let's go find a small lounge that isn't too far from here and I will order us some champagne."

We begin to walk back down the alley and a block over to Bourbon Street. We find a small Jazz bar and proceed inside.

There is a man in the corner behind a baby grand piano playing a soft melody and another man sitting next to him blowing somberly into a trumpet creating the haunting sound of the blues. The atmosphere is mellow and pleasant. There are small tables dressed in linens and spaced liberally throughout the small dark but cozy room. A small candle flickers on each table. The hostess leads us over to a quiet table in the corner across the room from the band. William promptly orders a bottle of their best champagne. The waitress brings it out to us with two flutes.

"To our love," he says holding up the flute as I touch mine to his making a crisp ringing sound with the crystal. We kiss and then listen to the sultry sounds of the band as they play. William reaches across the table and holds my left hand in his gently touching the shiny engagement ring.

We stay until the band stops playing. The night is darker and appears dreary as we step out of the bar. The sky above is a deep black and is now filled with clouds. The moon and the stars are no longer visible. Lightning streaks across the sky in the distance and the rumble of thunder is faint. A thin fog is building, and it rolls through the streets of the French Quarter casting an eerie view to the city. Two tourists turn onto a deserted street ahead. William speaks to me with his eyes and I know what he is saying. I can feel the burn starting inside. We saunter towards the two lonely tourists like cats stalking their prey. The lost couple turns down a dark and damp alleyway and then they stop turning around quickly to see the two of us standing at each of their sides. Immediately, the donors are entranced by our gaze. I step closer to the man who is short enough for me to reach his jugular. I run my fingers through his hair at the back of his head and pull to the side, biting down on the soft flesh of his neck, drinking in his blood slowly. I glance over and see William feeding on the female donor. We feed until completely satisfied and then we leave the mortals in the alley as we walk back to Royal Street. Rounding the corner onto the street it starts to rain. William grabs my hand and we start to run down the street towards the house. The rain is coming down harder now and we splash through the puddles forming on the sidewalk. Pulling the gate open to the courtyard and running up to the front door of the house William hurriedly put the key in the lock and turns the knob, opening the door. Laughing as we scurry inside the house, we stand motionless staring at one another as our wet clothes dripping on the floor.

"You go change; I'll start a fire." He says.

I walk into the guest room and rummage through my suitcase for a nightgown. William bends down next to the fireplace putting a new set of logs on the rack and striking a match. The fire starts slowly but builds up speed and becomes hot, fast. He stands turning towards me, watching now as I pull the wet clothes off my glistening body. I can feel the fire grow hotter as he watches me. I step out of the small room. The light from the fire shines through the thin silky gown that clings to my delicate frame. All my curves are visible to him. I move closer and stand next to the warm fireplace by his side. He touches my face with his cold fingers. The rush from the feed earlier courses through my veins and I am trying hard to control my emotions but the way he looks standing there with his shirt stuck to his wet body is too much for me to take. I wrap my arms around his back and press myself against him feeling the cool wetness of his hard body. He kisses me deep and long. I sigh as I come up for air and then I lean my head back as he picks me up and lays me on the bed in the guest room.

"Abigail, I want you so badly." He moans.

"I want you too," I whisper with my eyes tightly shut enjoying the pleasure of his touch. Suddenly, he stands next to the bed and undresses. I stare up at his beautiful body as he slips into a dry pair of pajama bottoms. He slowly gets into bed next to me placing his arm around my waist. I continue staring at him never taking my eyes off his face. He kisses me again.

"We have to wait," he whispers.

"Tomorrow night, I promise," he says.

His words are like exquisite torture to my ears. I let out a heavy sigh and hold on tight to him. I know better than to protest because he will win, and I can wait one more night.

Chapter 20: Fairytale

"It's a beautifully cloudy day outside," William calls out to me from the living room. I am still resting in bed. He sits down next to me now.

"Good Morning, sweet girl." He leans over and kisses me on the forehead. I roll over onto my side and reach my arms out for him. Placing his arms around my body he pulls me up into a sitting position next to him. I move my face in close to his and kiss him passionately. Then I look at my left ring finger and admire my new diamond engagement ring. He tucks the strands of hair that fall into my face back behind my ear.

"Let me see this for a moment." He takes my finger and begins to slip the ring off.

"William, what are you doing?" I protest slightly and with his eyes, he reassures me that everything is alright. He slips the ring off my finger and says, "Look at the underside."

I take the ring from him and I see an inscription. One tiny perfectly engraved word, *Endless.*

"Endless, Abigail, is my love for you."

He takes the ring and places it back on my finger where it will stay. He leans in closer to me and his eyes gently linger in my gaze. Words aren't needed as he quietly takes me into his arms and kisses me softly on the lips leaving me breathless.

"We have a big day ahead of us." He states through parted lips that still hovered close to mine. His breath is cool against my face as I inhale the sweetness of it. My eyes are slightly open as I peek at him through my long eyelashes while smiling joyfully.

William is already dressed and ready. He coaxes me out of the warm bed and hurries me along to the bathroom where I can change into my clothes.

"I'll be waiting in the kitchen," he says enthusiastically. I shut the door to the bathroom and shower. Changing into my clothes and brushing my hair before I step back out to find him tapping the top of the kitchen table at an impatient pace.

"There you are." He stands up and pushes the chair back in place.

"Are you ready?"

I giggle at him for a minute and then say, "Someone is excited."

He smiles back and shakes his head in agreement. We make our way out the door, across the courtyard, and to his car. We drive down the street and turn right heading towards one of New Orleans' oldest and finest jewelry stores.

"Let's go pick out matching wedding bands." He says as he pulls the car into the parking lot along the side of the building. We enter the store and are greeted almost immediately by a very helpful employee. We pick out his and her gold bands.

"They will need to be sized," the jeweler tells both of us.

William looks at me with a small hint of worry on his face.

"Will they be ready by this afternoon?" He asks the jeweler.

"I don't think I can have them ready by…" the jeweler stops short and stares into William's eyes and changes his mind mid-sentence.

"Yes, I will have them ready by 3:00 p.m."

"Perfect," William says.

I watch the jeweler stand behind the counter with a fixed smile on his face as we turn and leave the store.

"Would you like to look for a wedding gown now?" He asks me as we walk over to the car.

"Yes, I would love to!" I beam.

"Do you need a suit?" I ask.

"I sure do." He pulls the car out of the parking lot.

We drive to a small boutique a couple of blocks away. I sit on a small armchair and watch as he tries on different suits.

"How do you like this one?" He asks as he walks out of the dressing room.

"I like it. It is simple yet elegant."

William stands in front of the full-length mirrors turning and evaluating the suit.

"I like it too. I'll take this one, please."

He summons the ladies that work in the boutique over to where he stands. He speaks with them briefly and then walks back into the fitting room and changes out of it. There is no time for alterations, but it won't be necessary either because the suit fits him well enough.

He walks out of the fitting room holding the suit by its hanger. He hands it to one of the ladies and then turns to me.

"I'll leave you in the hands of these perfectly capable ladies to find the gown of your dreams. I have some other things to take care of before tonight."

He picks up my hand and kisses the top of it, then disappears out of the doors. I am the happiest I have ever been as I try on dress after dress. The two ladies that work in the boutique wait on me hand and foot. One of them is older and of medium height with dark brown long straight hair. She has an exotic accent that I can't place. The other lady is taller and thinner with fiery red curly hair. She has a Yat accent, the most pronounced of the New Orleans accents, almost sounding like she is from New York City but with a Southern drawl which is typical for the area. I don't smell the aroma of blood in this boutique that I have become almost accustomed to in the mortal world. The ladies have ivory white skin and their eyes are the same piercing pale color. I realize now that they are immortal too.

I have tried on four gowns, thus far and none of them are right. The lady with dark brown hair and an exotic accent brings out another gown. The very second, I lay my eyes on it I know it is the one. It is the most elegant wedding gown that I have ever seen.

"This is a gown is from a very notable designer's luxe collection. It is a silk organza strapless mermaid with asymmetrically draped layers." The dark-haired woman holds the gown out for me. I nod to her and then take it with me to try on in the changing area. I walk out into the larger room and pass in front of the mirror catching a glimpse of myself in it, I am speechless. I turn from side to side admiring the gown.

"Oh, my dear, you are breathtaking in this gown." The redhead woman comments as she stands back and watches me.

"Gorgeous," the other one agrees.

I turn around to see the back of the dress in the mirror, feeling like I am a part of a fairy tale.

William steps through the door as I am lounging on the chenille love seat in the front lobby of the boutique speaking with the two immortal ladies.

"There's my beautiful bride-to-be." He flashes his brilliant smile at me and the two ladies swoon.

"Yes, indeed, she is very beautiful and very happy too." The immortal with the exotic accent stands and stares at me.

"Did you find a gown?" He asks as he crosses the small room and takes my hand in his as I slowly rise from my place on the sofa.

"Yes, I found the most magnificent gown."

William takes care of the bill. With suit and gown in garment bags, we leave the boutique as the ladies watch us go.

William places the garment bags in the trunk of the car and we walk down the street to Jackson Square. There are artists sketching charcoals of the scenery and jazz musicians playing their saxophones in front of the cathedral. Mortals walk past enjoying the sights and sounds of the square while William and I linger listening to the music. I can smell the blood of the mortals all around us and it is so enticing. Trying to get it off my mind, I point across the square where I catch a hint of the sweet scent of beignets and coffee from Decatur Street. I know that I will have to feed again soon but until then I will try to ignore it by focusing on something that I miss from my own mortal life.

"I would like to try a beignet and some coffee," I say sheepishly.

"O.k.," he replies understandingly as we cross the street to the outdoor portion of the café remembering when I tried the barbeque chicken at the festival several days ago.

I am excited, hoping that a beignet will taste as good to me now as it did during my mortal life but realizing that it is a long shot. I order one beignet and two coffees. We sit at one of the little tables and I quickly pick up the little donut covered with powdered sugar and take a big bite. I chew it slowly as William watches me closely.

"Is it how you remember?" he asks with a curious look on his face.

"No, not at all, too sweet," I reply as I hold my napkin to my mouth and spit the donut in it. I take a sip of the hot coffee. At least the coffee is bearable.

"Sorry, love. I know you were hoping it would," he frowns but I can tell he thinks it's funny to watch me learn. He sips his coffee.

"It's alright, I'll survive," I poke out my bottom lip for added sympathy from him.

"Come here, you have some powdered sugar... right there," he points and reaches for me, pulling me closer to him and kissing me gently on the mouth.

"I think I've learned my lesson this time. No more food." I grin.

"You don't need anything sweet anyway. You're sweet enough as it is." He laughs.

"I love you, William." She smiled. "Thank you for being so patient with me."

"I love you, too and it's easy being patient with you."

"Alright, there is one more thing I need to take care of before tonight," he says as he gets up from his chair.

"What is it?" I question.

"Follow me," he replies motioning for me to follow.

We walk across Jackson Square and to the front of the beautiful St. Louis Cathedral. William takes my hand and we quickly slip into the cathedral through the side entrance unnoticed. The air inside smells like incense and candle wax. The stained-glass windows cast a rainbow of color across the pews in the middle of the sanctuary. A large crucifix hangs on the wall behind the altar as we pass in front genuflecting for a moment and then making our way over to the confessionals.

"Wait right here, my love."

William pulls the curtain back and steps in as I stand right outside the curtain, listening.

"Father, please, I need to speak with you." I can hear William's voice say.

"Are you here for a confession?" The priest responds and he sounds older with a reverent tone to his voice.

"Not exactly, more like a favor," William replies.

"What is it that you want?" The priest asked.

"I desire to marry my one true love here tonight at midnight. I have waited for her longer than you can know my dear priest. I cannot wait any longer. I love her more than my own life. It will just be the two of us in a private ceremony. We will say our own vows. And you will allow my bride to ready herself here at the cathedral just before the ceremony is to begin."

It is quiet for a few minutes and then William steps out of the confessional.

What happened? Did he agree to let us get married here tonight?" I ask.

"Well, of course, my dear. Mind control has its advantages, the old priest was more than obliging, and with my charm, he wasn't able to resist." He winks at me.

We make our way back out to the square but not before lighting a candle.

This day has been perfect as most days are now since William and I are together. As we meandered through the French Quarter, the warm gentle breeze blows past us and the horse-drawn carriages move slowly down the streets. We make it back to the boutique and into the car.

"I think I am going to call a realtor and put the old Devereux place up for sale," William says on the car ride back to the cottage with a pensive expression on his face.

"Oh, really, why?" I ask, a bit surprised by his statement.

"It is something that I have thought about doing for a long time. It holds some unpleasant memories from the past and I want to look forward to the future now, our future."

He turns the car onto Royal Street and then up the driveway of the home. "Anyway, a house like this one located in the French Quarter would bring in a lot of money for us," he says.

I remain quiet as we get out of the car. William opens the trunk and carefully removes the garment bags carrying them inside the house. I follow closely behind.
The sun is starting to set, and William is constantly pacing around the house. He won't stay still for one single minute as I sit on the couch and watch his every move.

"Are you nervous?" I finally ask him.

He looks up quickly at me, seemingly a little surprised by what I have just asked him.

"Me? No, why would I be nervous?" he smiles crookedly with a slightly tense brow.

I stand up and move over to where he is, taking his hand in mine. He relaxes a little with my touch.

"William, it's alright to be a little nervous. I am."

"You are?" he looks even more relaxed now.

"I know that I shouldn't be, but I have to admit, I am too, just a little bit. But I know why I just want everything to be perfect for you tonight," he admits.

"You're the sweetest man. I feel the same way. I want everything to be perfect too and you know what? It already is."

He pulls me closer to him and we embrace, holding each other while our nerves melt away.

Chapter 21: Completely

The moon is but a sliver in the clear night sky as I watch William walk down the stairs and into the living room of this old house on Royal Street. He adjusts his tie in the mirror and then calls out to me.

"Are you ready yet, sweetheart? It is almost time to go to the cathedral."

I walk into the room from the small foyer with my makeup flawlessly fixed and my hair gathered up in the back with a couple of soft curls hanging freely down by the sides of my face. My gown is draped over my arm in its garment bag. I will get dressed at the cathedral in the bride's room so that William won't see me in it before the ceremony.

"Close your eyes," he says and then I feel him placing a necklace around my neck. I open my eyes to see a strand of pearls next to the diamond heart pendant that my mother and father had given me for my high school graduation. I feel the delicate pearls with my fingers and then walk over closer to the mirror placing the garment bag on the chair next to it.

"They are absolutely beautiful, William."

"They were given to me by my mother before I left France. She told me that one day I would find the woman of my dreams and she wanted me to give them to her on our wedding day," he says as he stands behind me. I admire them for several minutes in the mirror. I turn around and kiss him softly.

"Thank you, for saving me that night in the park, for bringing me to this life with you, and for making all of my dreams come true," I say feeling so much love that I might cry for the first time since my immortal life began.

"I was empty inside without your love, Abigail…now my life is complete," he says in a serious tone. "Now, let's go get hitched." He winks at me and we smile at one another and leave the old cottage. As we step out onto the sidewalk in front of the house there is a black limousine parked out front. The driver opens the rear passenger door for us, and we get in.

I stand in front of the mirror in the bride's room of the cathedral and make a few last-minute adjustments. I smooth my dress down along my hips and turn to see myself better in the mirror. Turning back around and looking at my reflection, I begin to think for a moment about my parents. I touch the small heart pendant around my neck. Behind me, in the reflection, I see a small bouquet of white lilies and light pink roses on a table near the door to the room. I walk over and pick up the bouquet.

Standing in front of the door I breathe in deeply. Then exhaling slowly, I turn the knob and exit the room.

William, handsome as ever, in a crisp black suit waits anxiously at the front of the ornate altar inside the beautiful cathedral. The lights are dim almost to complete darkness and there are candles lit all around the inside illuminating my way as I slowly pace myself down the center aisle towards him. He gazes at me from the far side of the aisle and our eyes meet. I feel like a princess in a simple white gown. The pearls that delicately hang around my neck glisten with the light and the diamond heart next to it sparkles. I find my place beside him. Lost in one another's gaze he holds out his hand and I place my hand in his. In the distance, near the back of the church, the old priest sits and watches in the silence of the shadows, trying hard not to be seen.

William pauses for a moment as his eyes are full of emotion. Then he begins, "I, William Delaflote, take you, Abigail Dubois, to be my wife. I promise to always be true to you, to always protect you, and to always be there for you. I will love and honor you all the days of my life."

He places the delicate gold band on my left ring finger. I smile as tears form in my eyes.

"You came into my life, William, when I needed you the most. The love that you have shown me has been more than I ever knew existed and I will be forever thankful. I, Abigail Dubois, take you, William Delaflote, to be my husband. I promise to be true to you always and forever. I will love and honor you all the days of my life."

I place the gold band on his finger, and we begin to kiss as tears of joy stream down from my eyes. He kisses each one of them as they fall. Then sweeping me off my feet and into his arms he carries me back down the aisle as his wife. As we are leaving out of the double doors of the cathedral the old priest stops us and looks into William's eyes. William puts me down gently.

"I know what you both are." He stares directly at William.

"Your charms did not affect me earlier, today. I allowed this to take place because I saw in your eyes the love of your heart and soul, William, for your young bride. Your marriage is blessed. Go and have a happy life together."

William is stunned by the act of kindness from this man of faith and for once is speechless. He nods and we leave the church. As we step through the doors there in front of us in the dark square is a horse-drawn carriage.

I turn to William and ask, "Did you do this?"

"Yes." He says shaking his head. He helps me into the carriage, and I look back at the priest standing in the doors of the cathedral smiling at us. I see William silently mouth the words *Thank you* back to him. The old priest waves and closes the door behind him. William speaks briefly to the driver and then ascends into the carriage next to me.

"Where are we going?" I inquire as I kiss him on the neck.

"It's a surprise," he answers.

The horse is white, and the carriage is ivory. It is decorated with white roses and little clear twinkling lights all around. The driver steers the horse slowly down the stone street while William holds me close to him. We rode slowly down several city blocks before the carriage comes to a complete stop. William hops down and extends a hand to me as he helps me out of the carriage and to the ground.

"Bienville House, my lady," William says as he motions towards the hotel. It is a beautiful piece of centuries-old history laid out before my eyes. As we enter the French parlor-style lobby, there are hand-painted murals on the walls that surround us and worldly furnishings gracing the entryway. William proceeds to the front desk and speaks for a moment with a man who seems very pleasant and friendly. The man follows him back over to where I stand.

"This is Jack. He is an old friend of mine. We've known each other for a very long time." William says as he looks over at the man.

"It's nice to meet you, miss. William has spoken very highly of you."

Jack takes my hand and kisses it gently. I notice the same pale eyes on his face, and I can't smell the scent of blood coming from him.

"He's going to take a photograph. He's a professional photographer in his spare time and we need a picture of our wedding night."

"You thought of it all, didn't you?"

The man points the camera at us as we stand next to a beautiful floral arrangement on a large exquisitely detailed accent table in the grand lobby. We both give a big smile as the camera flashes.

"One more," William tells him, and he leans in closer to me kissing me on the lips as the camera flashes one more time.

"Thank you," William says as he walks over and shakes his friend's hand.

"You're quite welcome. It is nice meeting you, Abigail. Oh, you can pick them up tomorrow evening at the front desk." He tells William and then walks back to the counter.

"When did you arrange all of this?" I ask, looking around. He smiles but doesn't answer as we step over to the elevators.

"We don't have a change of clothing or any of our things with us," I say as we ride the elevator to our floor.

"Don't you worry about a thing, I have it all taken care of," he replies as he leans in and steals a kiss.

The doors open and we step out onto the second floor of the hotel. Walking a short way down the hall, we arrive at our suite. William opens the door and then lifts me off of my feet once again carrying me over the threshold. He carries me into the bedroom and lays me gently on the bed. There are red rose petals scattered across the ivory silk bedding as he slowly moves towards me pressing his body carefully over the top of mine and kissing my cool milky white shoulder. A bottle of champagne in a bucket with ice and two crystal flutes have been placed beside the bed on the nightstand.

"Would you like a glass of champagne?" He whispers in my ear.

Feeling the chills that he has created in me, I answer, "Yes."

He opens the bottle of champagne and pours it into the flutes.

"I'll be right back," he says. Then he leaves the room momentarily but not before giving me another long, slow kiss.

I quickly take off my wedding dress and place it on the chair next to the bed. He steps back into the bedroom no longer wearing his suit jacket or tie and the top two buttons of his shirt are undone. I am laying on the bed with the silk sheets covering me loosely as some of the delicate rose petals gently cling to my body. I hold my hand out for him and he slowly makes his way over to the bed never taking his eyes off me. Standing before me he starts to unbutton his shirt revealing the muscles that hid beneath. I move towards him easing myself across the silk sheets as it falls away from me bearing my nakedness to him. Then I gently push his hands out of the way as I finish off the last button. I run my fingers up and over his broad shoulders, pulling his shirt back and away from his chest, down his arms, and to the floor below, exposing his cool smooth sculpted skin. I kiss him softly up and around to his neck as my fingers trace the way for my lips to follow. With both of his arms, he gently places his hands behind my back and presses himself against me for warmth. He eases me back down on the top of the bed and kisses me hard and deep. Then moving along the nape of my neck and over to my ear whispering the words, I love you as he undresses the rest of the way. He kisses me again and then holds me for a moment in his arms. I don't want to rush the moment. I want to savor it. I breathe in his fragrance, laying my head firmly to his chest, listening to his heart beating louder as my pulse begins to quicken.

"Abigail…" he stops and looks up at me. His expression is one of concern and desire. He knows that I have never been with a man before this moment.

"William, I need you. I want you, now," I whisper. And with those words he takes me, and I become his, completely.

When we finally rise from the bed, William reaches over for the glasses of champagne. He takes a sip, but it is flat. He pours another glass for the two of us.

"I will go get our robes." He stands up and walks over to the bathroom. I enjoy the view. He comes back with a robe wrapped around himself and one in his hand for me. I stand up and he helps me put it on. I tie it around my waist. The softness of the fabric feels good against my skin but not as good as William's body. We enter the living area and for the first time since we had arrived, and I notice the large size of the suite. It has a full-size kitchen that is connected to a separate living room with a fireplace. There is a balcony that overlooks the courtyard with a heated pool and spa.

"This place is gorgeous, William."

"You need to see the bathroom. It has terrazzo flooring, marble countertops, and a Jacuzzi garden tub." He smiles at me and then gives me a wink.

"Oh, we will have to give that a try, won't we?" I respond.

"Are you hungry?" he asks walking over to the sofa where the telephone is on an end table.

"Famished," I state.

He picks up the receiver to the phone and presses the button for room service.

"Room service, can I help you?" The woman on the other end speaks clearly.

"Yes, we would like some chocolate-covered strawberries and two glasses of your finest champagne."

"We will have that up to you in a moment," she says, and William hangs up the phone.

"Dinner will be here in a minute."

As we wait for room service to arrive, we occupy our time in each other's arms watching some television. After a few moments, there is a knock at the door and William is up and off of the sofa quicker than the eye could see as he heads for the door. I continue to lounge on the sofa. He opens the door and lets the young man of average height and weight into the room. He is carrying a tray with two glasses of sparkling wine and the chocolate-covered strawberries in his hand. As he walks across the room to place the tray onto the bar in the kitchen, I catch him with my stare. He puts the tray down and I motion for him to come closer and sit next to me on the sofa. He does exactly that and William follows and sits across from us in a chair.

"Ladies first," William says as he looks at the young man sitting next to me.

I keep the donor hypnotized with my gaze as I move in and slowly lick my lips. I bite down on his neck and feed with much delight. William comes over and sits next to us. I can sense his hunger is taking over him. As I finish and lean back on the sofa with satisfaction, William begins feeding on the same bite mark on the donor's neck. Between the two of us, we only take a little over a pint from the donor. When we are done with him, William erases his memory, heals the wound on his neck, tips him very well, and sends him on his way. I, in the meantime, find my way back to the bedroom. William walks into the room where I am waiting for him in the bed. Smiling and flexing my finger in a motion that commands him to come to me, he steps eagerly to my side and we make love for the rest of the night.

Chapter 22: Warning

Daylight broke many hours earlier, but I am the first to get out of bed. We spent most of the morning, talking and making love. I walk across the bedroom to where the closet is located wearing nothing but the silk sheet from the bed. I open the closet doors to find a wardrobe of different styles. Each piece of clothing draped over wooden hangers. I glance at all the stylish clothing. There is also a new pair of designer blue jeans and a pale pink short-sleeved couture tee shirt with a large fleur de lis on the front of it made with little clear crystal rhinestones. I reach for the jeans and the shirt.

When I turn around, I see William is now awake.

"How did you arrange all of this without me knowing?" I ask as I hold the clothes in front of me on the wooden hangers.

"I just made a few phone calls. I made the reservations for the suite before we left Lake Charles and the clothes were brought from the boutique in the lobby downstairs. They should fit, you're a size 6, right?" He asks.

I laugh and nod in agreement.

"You're amazing, William Delaflote." I smile and wink at him.

"So are you, Abigail Dubois Delaflote," he says as he winks back at me. I hadn't given it much thought before this moment but when he says it out loud, I know it is true. My name is now Abigail Delaflote. It sounds strange to me at first.

"Abigail Delaflote," I say.

It is perfect, just like my love for him and I am very happy to be his wife. I finally have a family again and it is William. I take the clothes off the hangers and walk into the bathroom to change. When I come out William is already dressed and waiting for me on the sofa in the living area. He is watching the news and getting the latest update on the weather conditions for the day. It will be cloudy with an increased chance of rain in the late afternoon or early evening.

"There you are. You look beautiful as always." He turns off the television.

"Let's go do some more sight-seeing," I announce while walking over to the kitchen. I pour myself a glass of water and drink it in a hurry.

"That sounds like a plan," William says as we leave the room and head towards the elevator.

When the elevator doors open on the lobby level we step out and begin walking towards the front doors of the hotel. Suddenly, everything feels as if it is happening in slow motion. My head is light and there is a tiny hum in my ears. I am quickly transported into a vision of the past. A portrait of an early Nineteenth-Century New Orleans is being painted out in great detail around me. As we both make our way out the doors of the grand hotel and onto the streets of the old French Quarter, I see amazing sights. The streets are different. Instead of cobblestone and pavement, they are mud and dirt. The cars are gone and in their place are horse-drawn carriages and men riding on horseback. The streetlights are now lanterned. All the mortals are dressed in the fashions of the early eighteen-hundreds. I look over at William who walks alongside me and he is dressed differently too. He looks like he did in the painting I saw in his study back at home. He wears a long, narrow cravat tied into a small bow and a knee-length coat that is buttoned down the front. He also wears a waistcoat slightly shorter than the other coat and trousers with boots. I look down at myself and I, too, am now wearing clothing from that period. I am wearing an Empire silhouette gown that is periwinkle blue and extravagantly trimmed with lace. It is short-sleeved, and the low neckline enhances my bosom slightly. My hair is done in a mass of curls around my forehead and ears with the back in a loose Romanesque style bun and of course, I am wearing a bonnet covering my head. Its crown and brim are adorned with ornamentation and feathers. I am wrapped loosely in a cream-colored shawl made from cashmere. White silk gloves cover my arms and hands. My slippers are thin and made of delicate leather. I am holding a fan in one hand to ward off the heat from the warm humid day. Pacing alongside the hotel, I watch the busy dirt street to the side of us and as quickly as it has begun it is over. I am back in the present and the vision of the past has dissipated as we make our way over to Canal Street. We ride one of the streetcars to City Park.

The light this afternoon is softer than the usual light of midday. The clouds above filter the sun's rays and create a soft natural opaque hue around us as we walk through the park. The green grass under our feet crunch ever so lightly and the birds fly by in the air singing the tunes of nature. Now and then the sun will peek out between the small openings of the clouds casting its rays onto the landscape below.

"Angel-rays," William comments looking out into the distance.

"What?" I ask.

"When the sun's rays cross the sky from heaven above and touch the earth, they are called angel rays. It means that the angels are watching."

I stare up at the sky feeling the brief and sudden sunlight upon my face. The warmth feels good only for a moment though. Then I instinctively shy away from it bringing my face back down to gaze at the ground beneath me.

"That's beautiful. I've never heard of that before." I say looking over at him.

"I remember my mother telling me that as a child. It's one of the few things I do remember. I guess it left an impression on me."

He kicks the acorns that are lying on the ground in the patch of bare earth that we now walk across.

"I wish I could've met them." My tone is low.

"That goes for me too, about your parents I mean."

I stare down at the ground in silence.

"I'm sorry. That was a dumb thing to say." He is remorseful.

"No, it wasn't. I know you would have loved them." I smile over at him and he holds my hand. We come to a bridge and walk up to it, stopping near the middle and looking out across the water in silence for a few minutes.

"When we get back home, we need to make plans for a honeymoon," William says as he turns and leans back against the side of the bridge watching several mortals pass us by.

"O.K., where will we go?" I ask, excitedly.

"I don't know. Is there any place in the whole world that you would love to see?" He questions.

"Oh, yes, there are many. Let me think for a minute. I would love to go to Paris, France."

"Then that is where we will go." He wraps his arms around me, and we kiss.

"When was the last time you went home, to Bordeaux, I mean?" I ask him while resting my head on his chest.

"The last time I was there was for my parent's funerals. My father died first. I stayed with my mother for as long as I could, but my visa expired, and I had to return. By the time I was able to make it back she had already passed away, so I ended up going for her funeral instead."

"I'm sorry," I whisper.

"No, they both lived a very long and happy life." He squeezes me tight.

"What were their names?" I ask as I hold onto him peering across the open park.

"Francois Jacque Delaflote and Marie Elise Abney Delaflote," he answers in a low tone and seems distant as he speaks their names, thinking of his childhood home, I would assume.

"I still own our family's chateau over there in Bordeaux. I have a house-sitting service that I hired to watch over it for me.

They keep me updated on the condition of the property and any repairs that might need to be done. They are a good group. They are immortals too. You would like them. I received word the other day before we left Lake Charles that everything is fine with the property."

Then I remembered the letter that he had kept out of the pile of junk that he had thrown into the trash.

"Maybe when we are in Paris for our official honeymoon, we can visit Bordeaux. I would love to show you where I grew up and bring you to my family's chateau. You're a part of the family now too." He smiles with what seems like pride welling up inside of him as he looks down at me. I love the feeling of being in his arms and thinking of myself as belonging to a family again.

"Do you have any relatives left in Bordeaux?" I ask eagerly.

"I have some, but they are so distant, and they don't even realize that we are related. It is better that way, though. You know what I mean, right?" He mutters and I shake my head. We continue walking down the other side of the bridge and onto the pathway that leads to the amusement park. I watch as the carousel moves around in circles as we stroll past towards the large oaks in the distance. Magnificent in their beauty and grandeur, the branches reach out and upward to the sky. The darkness of the bark calls out to all that pass beneath. The coolness of the shade that the majestic beauties provide is a gift to the nature that surrounds them. I pause underneath one such tree and read aloud the plaque posted about its history.

"This site, history tells us, was a favorite location for many duels fought by hot-blooded young blades in the Antebellum era of the South, here mostly young French and Spanish gentlemen settled their differences with swords and pistols. This was the field of satisfaction for wounded pride and honor."

Turning to William and facing him now, I know. I know that this is where he had dueled Lawrence.

"Is this…" I start to ask the question anyway and he nods at the same time I speak. I extend my hand to him and he approaches me, taking my hand in his, the coolness of our skin feeling warm as we touch. I stare deep into his eyes for a moment, searching in amazement by his long life.

We continue to wander through the park making our way into the Botanical Gardens and admiring the sculptures and artwork in the museum. On the ride back in the streetcar, we sit in silence, enjoying our time with one another and the beautiful overcast day. We get off the streetcar at our stop and walk down the sidewalk back to our hotel.

"Do you want to go down to the pool when we get back?" William asks.

"Yes, that sounds good," I reply.

When we get back to the suite, we change into bathing suits. We make our way down to the pool and spa located in the courtyard area. We relax in the warmth of the waters of the jetted spa as it bubbles and swirls around our bodies. William and I sit side by side in the spa staring up at the cloudy sky and enjoying the day. I lift my hand out of the water and admire my new wedding ring as William takes my hand and kisses the ring while looking at me and then kisses me on the lips gently saying, "You've made me the happiest immortal man in the history of the world."

I smile and say, "I love you, Will."

He kisses me again.

"What would you like to do tonight?" I ask him as he rests his head against the edge of the spa closing his eyes to shield them from the momentary break in the clouds as the sun slightly shines through and then disappears again behind a thick blanket of white and gray.

"What do you want to do?" He reverses the question.

"Anything as long as we're together," I reply relaxing in the warm bubbling water. We lounge in silence for a few moments. Drops of cool rain begin to fall one by one as William sits up holding his hand in the air to catch them. He looks over at me as I rest with my eyes slightly closed but still able to see.

"It's beginning to rain, Abigail," he says.

"I know isn't it delightful?" I open my eyes wide and filled with contentment. The rain begins to fall harder and that is when I sit up and move closer to William. We face each other now only inches from one another as the rain falls on us and the lightning cracks like a whip in the sky.

"Let's go up to the room now," I say, and we step out of the spa and wrap ourselves in towels running to the doors of the hotel. Dripping wet as we make our way to the elevators, the chill from the air conditioning inside the lobby sends shivers up and down me. To warm ourselves, we cling to one another and wait for the doors to open as we start kissing, lost in the moment. When the doors to the elevator open, we make our way in clumsily never letting go of each other's grasp as I pull him close to me against the inside. William quickly presses the button to our floor. The doors open as William reaches for the key card to our suite, pulling it out of his pocket. He picks me up and carries me down the hallway to the room. He unlocks the door, continuing to kiss me as he carries me over to the bed, closing the bedroom door behind us.

I rest while William takes a shower. When he comes out of the bathroom he is dressed in jeans and a black long-sleeved button-down shirt. The scent of his cologne fills the room as he stands next to the bed. His hair is wet and disheveled as he ran his fingers through it, smoothing it out slightly. His pale blue eyes sting me into motion as I lift my body to the edge of the bed to be near him.

"Your eyes still entreat me in some unspoken language, William," I say as I reach up and caress the side of his face with the back of my hand.

"You will always have that power over me."

"Do you mind it?" He asks me in a seductive whisper.

"Not at all," I whisper back. "It's my turn."

He looks at me with a confused expression on his face.

"To take a shower," I state, and then I hop off the bed.

"Look in the closet. I had another outfit sent to the room for you. I'm going down to the lobby to get our pictures from Jack while you take a shower."

"Okay," I answer and walk over to the closet to find a black dress on a hanger and a pair of black open-toe high heels on the floor below. The dress is simple but elegant with spaghetti straps. I hold it up and look at it in the mirror. It is short, hitting me probably mid-thigh. I hang it back in the closet and enter the bathroom, shutting the door behind me.

I exit the bedroom wearing the dress and heels. William is sitting in the living area watching television. I walk over and sit next to him on the sofa.

"Where are the pictures?" I ask.

"Right here," he points at a manila envelope lying on top of the coffee table in front of them. Quickly, I reach for it.

"Did you look at them already?" I hold the envelope in my hands anxiously awaiting to open it.

"No, I wanted to wait for you," he replies.

I open the envelope with excitement and pull out the two pictures of us on our wedding night in the lobby of the hotel.

"We look so happy." I gaze at the photographs.

"That's because we are," he says and kisses me on the side of the head, lingering for a moment and breathing in deeply to smell the floral scent of my hair.

"I spoke with Jack about the best bars to go to tonight and he recommended this place down on Toulouse Street. The bartenders there are immortal. He told me that they serve special drinks that appeal to our taste buds. Do you want to check it out?"

"Sure."

I place the pictures back in the manila envelope.

"Oh, he gave me the pictures on a disk too. We can print out more if we want to."

He gets up and walks over to the bar. The disk is lying next to his wallet which he grabs and stuffs into his back pocket. I pick up my purse and we head out the door.

"I arranged for a car to take us around the city tonight. I didn't want you to have to walk around in high heels."

"Thank you. That was very thoughtful."

The driver of the black town car stands by the side of the rear door holding it open for us. We arrive at the bar a few minutes later. The outside of the bar is painted in a dark red and the door is jet black. When we enter through the door, we find ourselves walking down a narrow alleyway. The inside of the bar looks like an old dungeon. Red lights are illuminating the room with an open bar. There are cages and skulls. A coffin hangs from the ceiling. A true vampire novelty. Mortals are walking around the bar seemingly unaware of the undead presence around them. The pulsating music beats loudly from upstairs. William walks up to the bar and orders two drinks. The bartender's eyes are familiar. When he delivers the drinks to William, they are ruby red. Turning away from the bar he hands one to me.

"Cheers," he says and then takes a sip.

"How is it?" I ask.

"Quite good it's a mixture of Merlot and blood. The Merlot keeps the blood from coagulating." William seems to be savoring its taste. Then I take a sip and swallow. The drink is at room temperature.

"Um, delightful," I swoon.

"It's still better when it comes directly from the veins of a donor." I smile slyly and William agrees.

We find a place to sit and drink, sipping slowly, enjoying the bloody concoction.

"Can I get you anything else?" A waitress walks up to the table and asks.

"Two more, please." William motions to the drink in front of him.

The waitress leaves our table and heads over to the bar. The bartender looks in William's direction and prepares the drinks.

"Where do they get the blood," I ask as I sip my drink.

"Jack told me that they get their supply from dealers," William answers.

"Dealers, what do you mean, dealers? I don't know what you mean."

"There are certain immortals that work for blood banks and they deal blood to various customers," he states.

"You already knew about this sort of thing?" I ask in a surprised tone.

"Yes." He sips on the drink casually.

"Do the mortals willing give the blood or are they mesmerized into it?"

"Sometimes both," he answers and then looks over at me.

"Are you alright? I sometimes forget that you are still getting used to this new way of life."

"Yeah, I'm just a little surprised that's all."

I watch the bartender as he works. I know that there is so much that I don't know about this life. It unnerves me for a minute but then I stare down at the drink in my hand and I take another sip. It tastes so good to me that it seems inconsequential where or how the blood is received.

As I glance over at the entrance into the bar, I can't help but notice a strange old woman staring at me. I turn my head in the other direction and watch the waitress walk back to our table with two more drinks on her tray. She places them in front of both me and William then leaves quickly. I finish off the first drink and start sipping on the second one more slowly this time, savoring the taste. I peer back over at the door, but the old woman is no longer there. Then I notice that she has moved closer to the center of the room and is pacing herself slowly in my direction. She stops in front of our table starring right at me. The old woman is tawny skinned with wild black eyes and her hair is in knots, tied up in a handkerchief on top of her head. She is wearing old tattered clothing and smells like the earth. She reaches across the table and touches me on the hand. I flinch but the woman grabs hold of me tighter.

"Take your hands off of her at once," William barks in a threatening tone and stands suddenly next to the old woman but she ignores him. She stares deep into my eyes seeing into my very soul it seems and giving out a warning.

291

"Girl, you are in grave danger. I see two of you. The one from the past will be your downfall in the future."

"That's enough, let go of her hand this instant!" William insists as I sit frozen with fear from the words she has just spoken and the look that possesses the old woman's eyes. William motions to the bartender. Then the woman lets go of my hand as the bouncer pulls her away from the table and escorts her out of the building. William sits back down.

"Abigail…" he says in a tense voice.

I am silent and don't mutter one single word. The smell still lingers from the old woman and it assaults my senses. Quickly there is a vision flashing before my eyes. I see the freshly dug earth and I can smell the wet dirt. I feel as though I am suffocating under the ground. The black heaviness oppresses me and holds me down. Panic-stricken fear takes over my expression and my eyes are wide, frozen. William begins to shake my arm.

"Abigail, please speak to me! Are you alright? He pleads, aghast by my reaction.

Then I snap out of it while shaking my head slowly, "Yes…no…I mean I don't know. What just happened?"

"Is everything alright over here?" The bartender stands before us.

"Yes, I'm okay," I tell him but I'm not very convincing. I am still shaken by the vision.

"I'm sorry for that. She has been in here before bothering our patrons. She's just some crazy old woman. Don't pay any attention to her." He tells me. "I'll send two more drinks over, on the house."

He walks back to the bar.

"Are you sure you're alright?" William leans over closer to me placing an arm around my back for added comfort. I take another sip of my drink and shake my head. I want to tell him about the vision, but I decide against it. I don't want to think about it anymore. The waitress brings two more drinks to the table. I finish my third drink quickly and the rush I feel coursing through my body is reinvigorating. The music upstairs is calling out to me.

"Let's go dance," I say and take William by the hand leading him upstairs.

The dance floor is crowded. Mortals and immortals alike share the space, shifting their bodies with the beat. William quickly finishes his drink and places the empty glass on a deserted table before meeting me in the center of the dance floor where I am already in motion. We move effortlessly in time with the music. We dance through a few songs and then decide to go up to the third floor.

There is another bar here on the third floor with skulls along the walls. There is a cage in the corner with a mortal woman dancing inside of it. I stand next to William while he orders another round of drinks. I watch as the woman in the cage dances erotically. Then the mortal woman's eyes become fixed on something across the room. She climbs down methodically from the cage as another mortal takes her place. An immortal man is standing in the far-right corner waiting for her. She stands in front of him as he places his arms around her and bites down on her neck, feeding on her. William hands me a drink and I follow him to a table keeping my eyes on the immortal man as he feeds. We sit at the table and drink.

After we finish our drink, we decide it is time to leave the bar.

"We should get some of our things and bring them back with us to the suite. We can get the car too." He tells me.

William asks the driver to drop us off at the old Devereux house.

When we arrive at the house, the driver opens the door to the car for us, and William tips him. We go into the house and light a fire to remove the cool dampness inside. I sit down on the sofa and watch him.

"Oh, you know what? I need to go to the convenience store around the corner real quick," he says slightly annoyed.

"I just need a few things. Do you want to come?"

"No, I'll stay. You just got the fire going."

"Okay, I won't stay long. Lock the door behind me."

He kisses me on the forehead and leaves the house.

Chapter 23: Visions

William has only been gone a few minutes and I am sitting here alone on the sofa in front of the fireplace, staring up at the painting above the mantel. Suddenly I feel an inner force tugging at me towards the bedroom upstairs, Elizabeth's bedroom. I am trying my best to ignore it but it starts to grow stronger. Reluctantly, I start to walk over to the staircase and pause for a moment looking up the dimly lit stairs. I slowly begin to climb up onto the first few steps. Stopping briefly as I contemplate going back to the sofa and forgetting about venturing into Elizabeth's bedroom. I can see to the top of the staircase from where I stand, and the curiosity is just too great to fight off any longer. As I continue my ascent into the unknown at a quicker pace now, I find myself standing in front of the bedroom door. I stop for a few seconds deciding whether it is a good idea to enter the room. I begin to think about William and what he will say if he finds out that I am going into the forbidden bedroom but it is as though I can hear Elizabeth's voice calling to me from beyond the grave inviting me into the last moments of her life on this earth. Turning the old knob on the door, it creaks as I open it.

I hesitantly step into the dark dusty room and back into time. Nothing seems to have changed and it must have looked this way that same fateful night over a hundred years earlier. The bed is small, and the sheets are old, yellowed, and tattered with age. There are cobwebs in the upper corners of the room and a thick layer of dust covers all the furniture. Melted candle wax clings to a small table with a sketch of Elizabeth sandwiched in between. Suddenly and without warning, as I stand in the middle of the bedroom, I start to have a memory lurch. A dull hum begins ringing in my ears and I feel like I am being transported through time. The room around me begins to spin and it slowly transforms back to that night on October 12, 1814.

I see Elizabeth sitting at the small desk in the corner of the room. I see her turn toward the sound of a knock coming from the bedroom door. I turn also as I follow her with my eyes as she walks quickly to open the door. I can feel what Elizabeth is feeling and I know that Elizabeth thinks it is William behind the door. He has come back from his voyage at sea. Her love has returned to her once again from his long journey. I feel overwhelmed with the emotions surging through Elizabeth. I am reliving the vivid memory, seeing it play out before me in the small room as if it is happening all over again. Elizabeth opens the door with excitement but in front of her stands another man, one

297

that I have never seen before in any of my previous memories, but I know who he is. Elizabeth's mood changes into one of disappointment and I feel it in the center of my soul. Lawrence tells her that William isn't coming back. That he will never be coming back because he is dead. Lies, all lies.

"I don't believe you," Elizabeth cries out in the memory.

"Why would I lie?" Lawrence says as he hands her William's belongings from the ship. He stands silently staring at Elizabeth and then reaches out to offer comfort, but she pulls away and orders him to leave immediately.

"I will leave you for now, but I will be back. Elizabeth, look at the bright side, I will always be there for you. It's a new beginning for us," he says and then shuts the door behind him. She throws a vase from the top of her desk at the door and then falls to her knees onto the hardwood floor clutching William's clothes in her arms, burying her face into them trying to capture a hint of his cologne one last time as tears streamed down her face. I can smell the faint scent of William's cologne as Elizabeth cries. She cries out in agony, but she doesn't give up immediately and holds onto hope for the rest of the night. Hoping and praying for William to return to her not wanting to believe the news that Lawrence has delivered but as dawn approaches and William doesn't return, terrible sinking grief sets into her soul and she knows that she has

lost him forever. She can feel that he is dead just as she had been told. She senses it in the pit of her stomach.

Her parents offer her support and comfort from behind the closed bedroom door, pleading furiously for her to open it, but nothing can console her from this loss. I feel her pain as it rips through her. Elizabeth stumbles over to the small desk, taking out a pen and paper, tears running down her cheeks staining it as she writes:

To my beloved Mother and Father,
I cannot go on in this world without William. I would never be able to endure the torture of a life lived without him. My love for him will never die.
-Elizabeth

Elizabeth takes a small gun out of the desk drawer that she has always kept close by as a means of protection. But this time it will provide for her the protection from a life filled with the despair and pain of losing her one true love as she pulls the trigger her lifeless body falls at my feet.

"Elizabeth?" A voice suddenly jolts me out of the memory lapse. I turn to see where the voice has come from and there behind me stands a strange man in the doorway to the bedroom.

"No," I answer not being able to see his face at first but as he moves closer towards me the light from outside of the room reveals him to me, but I did not recognize him. Coming from downstairs I can hear William calling out to me as he comes rushing up the staircase to the bedroom.

"Why are you here, Lawrence?" He directs the question at the man as he pushes past him and steps quickly to my side taking me in his arms.

"Are you alright, Abigail?" William asks with concern in his voice for my safety.

"Yes," I reply holding him close.

"I was passing by and saw the light on inside. I thought I would check it out. I didn't know you were in town. Long time no see, little brother," Lawrence answers William's earlier question.

I stand silent and in shock. This is William's brother, Lawrence, the man that lied to Elizabeth and caused her death. There are some physical similarities between the two brothers, but they aren't striking. The major differences in their looks are that Lawrence is shorter and blonde as opposed to William's height and dark hair. Lawrence has the same pale blue eyes that William has but they are bloodshot and don't have the same life to them that

I am accustomed to seeing in William's eyes. His appearance is haggard, dirty, and unshaven. His teeth are yellowed, and he smells like a combination of cigarette smoke and cheap bourbon. He is slurring his words as he speaks and I feel very fearful with him in the room as he stares at me with a look on his face that I don't quite understand, it's as though he is studying everything about me from head to toe. A feeling of dread washes over me as I look into his eyes and I must turn away quickly from his gaze because it repulses me.

"Can we, please, go back downstairs?" William asks in utter annoyance from what I imagine is since Lawrence is in Elizabeth's bedroom.

"Are you sure you're alright, Abigail?" He helps me down the stairs slowly.

"I've been better…I'm sorry…William. I know I shouldn't have."

"Please don't apologize, this is your house too."

He places his arm around my lower back. He sits me down on one of the kitchen table chairs then he turns to his brother with a glare that is colder than ice.

"Well, this is interesting, a family reunion of sorts," Lawrence says as he steps out into the living area from the staircase.

"Get out," William barks loudly and points at the front door.

"That's no way to treat your brother and after all this time, I thought you might have missed me," Lawrence snickers and flashes a devilish grin at William.

"You're drunk. Now leave this house or else," William growls.

"Oh really, or else what, little brother what will you do?" Lawrence questions as he moves closer to William with a threatening look on his face.

William stiffens ready for the confrontation, but I step in between them pushing back on William's chest gently trying to keep them from starting a fight.

"Stop, please, William," I beg and continue to push William back slightly while sandwiched in between the two brothers, fear crosses my face as my eyes meet William's. He reacts to me realizing the fear that I am feeling and lets his stance soften a bit but doesn't turn away from Lawrence completely.

"You're not going to introduce me to your pretty little lady friend, William? She seems so familiar to me already." Lawrence chuckles. "She looks a little like someone we used to know, doesn't she, dear brother?"

He turns and stares at the painting over the fireplace mantel. I look directly at Elizabeth's face in the painting. I had noticed a resemblance before but now it is undeniable. I glance over at William as he looks in the same direction. His expression is blank and hard to read.

"You're not worth introducing her to," William says with a look of disgust on his face as he turns his stare to his brother.

"Oh, I'm sorry… it looks like congratulations are in order."

Lawrence moves closer to me reaching for the rings on my finger and then gazing at the one on William's hand.

William steps in front of me blocking Lawrence from touching me. I am pretty sure it is because he knows Lawrence will be able to detect my ability for seeing into the past. This would be something he wouldn't want Lawrence to know. I am now standing behind William gaping at what is happening around me and becoming more fearful by the moment. I can sense that Lawrence wants to know more about me, by the way, he looks at me with his bloodshot eyes and it scares me more than anything else.

"Well, you need to work on your manners, little brother. I'll go for now. I know when I'm not welcomed. Abigail, some other time then," he says and like a flash, he is out the front door and onto the dark streets of the French Quarter. William quickly follows behind him locking the door.

"I'm so sorry," I say as I rush to William's waiting arms. I am trembling as he holds me trying to calm me down. "I should have made sure the door was locked when you left to go to the store."

"It's alright. I should have locked it, instead." His tone is low and soothing. It makes me feel better.

"Don't worry about him, Abigail. He's just an old drunk now," he says as he rubs my back gently.

"Why did you go into Elizabeth's old room?"

The concern in his voice is apparent.

"I don't know why I did it. I shouldn't have but the curiosity got the best of me, I felt drawn to it," I confess as I tremble again.

"I saw everything that happened that night as if I were reliving it. It was horrible, William, so horrible!" I begin to sob burying my head in his chest.

He lifts my face to meet his and wipes away my tears saying, "I'm sorry, Abigail. I shouldn't have left you alone tonight and I should have never brought you here to this house in the first place."

"No, I wanted to come, remember? I wanted to see for myself and to remember the past." I kiss him on the cheek for reassurance.

"We have to leave the city now that Lawrence knows we are here, it's not a good idea to stay," he says as he starts to gather our things and pack them in the suitcases.

"Please, William, I don't want to leave New Orleans just yet," I plead, still trembling slightly. "We were having such a good time please don't let him ruin it. Let's just go back to the suite and forget this even happened."

William looks at me uneasily and then reluctantly agrees. We continue to pack up all of our belongings, locking the house and placing our luggage in the trunk of the car, we drive back to the hotel. When we arrive, William valet parks and summons the bellhop to bring our luggage up to the suite. Once inside the room, he sits down on the sofa and starts searching on his cell phone, and then places a call.

"Who are you calling?" I ask, standing in the doorway to the bedroom.

"A realtor that I know here in town," he replies.

"Yes, this is William Delaflote. I would like to talk to you as soon as possible about selling the house on Royal Street. You can call me back at this number," he proceeds to leave the message for the realtor. I turn and walk slowly into the bedroom shutting the door behind me, leaving it ajar just a tiny bit. I lay down on the comfortable bed while William remains in the other room. I am feeling weak and don't understand. I had received enough nutrition from the drinks earlier at the bar to last me until tomorrow night. If it gets any worse, I will have William call for room service again. That is always the easiest option. As I lay here, I suddenly begin to feel even weaker and very dizzy all at the same time. I struggle to get out of bed. Fearful of what is happening to me, I want to be by William's side. I have never felt like this before. I feel like I am being held down by invisible hands, stuck to the bed not able to move, and then it begins, the humming in my ears. A very powerful vision starts.

A ship is docked along the seawall. The clouds are building, and it looks as though a storm is brewing out over the Gulf. Lawrence steps off the ship and makes his way along the dimly lit streets of New Orleans. There is a rotten stench in the air that night as he wanders into one of the bars on Bourbon Street. It is filled with his shipmates from the long voyage home. Ladies of the evening are entertaining the men as they lounge on wooden bar stools and at tables drinking their fill of whiskey. Lawrence is looking for a good time, a drink in one hand and a loose woman in the other. He walks up to the bartender and calls out his order which he has in front of him in a matter of minutes. He turns and looks out across the room for a good-looking potential when he spots a tall voluptuous redhead. Her eyes meet his gaze and he seem to be pulled in her direction by a seductive force. She smiles at him with bedroom eyes as he swaggers over to where she stands next to the staircase that leads to the second floor.

"Are you looking for a good time, sailor?" She inquires.

"I've been gone for over a month, woman, what do you think?" He replies in a slightly annoyed tone.

"It's going to cost you. Are you good for it?" She mutters, looking around her.

He nods and up the staircase, they ascend to an empty bedroom waiting to be occupied. He pushes her into the room, spilling his drink onto the floor, and starts fumbling with the woman's corset as he maneuvers her towards the bed.

"Hold up, payment first, then the fun can begin," she says staring directly at him, deep into his eyes. Lawrence can't resist her hypnotic gaze and her eyes are an intoxicatingly pale green. He stands motionless and dumb as he stares into her eyes entranced by their beauty.

Then the woman whispers in his ear, "I don't take cash. Payment is only by blood."

She pushes him to the bed, jumping on top of and straddling him. Then biting him hard on the neck, she sucks the blood out of his body. She is in a frenzy as she tears open his shirt and begins biting him all over his chest and arms. Blood oozes out of every mark slowly as he lay dying underneath her. She hops off him and crosses the room feeling the rush of satisfaction. Lawrence lay on the tired little bed burning inside, deep inside. The pain rips through him like whips peeling off his flesh, leaving open wounds in its place.

"Please...help me..." he mumbles as he falls in and out of consciousness. The woman sits across the room on a chair rocking back and forth as she seems to enjoy the torment that she has caused him. Toying with him as he lay there begging for relief.

"Isn't this fun?" She replies, maliciously, to his cries. "Why haven't you died yet?"

"Please" he cries.

"Oh, don't be such a baby, here, since you don't seem to want to die tonight, I'll give you a reason to live."

She gets up from the chair and sits beside him on the bed, biting her wrist she lets the blood trickle into his anxiously awaiting mouth. He flails around the bed as she teases him with her blood but then he finds the strength somewhere deep inside and he grabs her by the arm and latched his mouth around her wrist like a leach. He drains her dry and leaves her dead in his place on that little worn-out bed. He stands up peering down at her frozen face. The wounds on his chest heal immediately. Flinging the door wide open, he descends the same staircase that brought him to the depths of hell that night feeling strong and satisfied as walks out onto the dark streets of New Orleans with an insatiable thirst for blood.

I sit up straight in the bed and call out for William who comes running immediately into the bedroom.

"What is it? Are you alright?" He asks looking at me with worry in his expression as he touches the side of my face.

"I had another vision. Do you know how Lawrence was turned?" I ask staring straight at him with wide frozen eyes.

"No, he never talked about it, and I didn't see him much after Elizabeth died. Why? Did you have a vision about Lawrence?" He asks.

"Yes. He met a woman at a bar one night. She was a vampire. She drained him but it must not have been enough because he didn't die. She offered her blood to him," I break my speech and pause for a moment.

"Go on, what happened?" William asks leaning in closer to me and placing his arm around my waist.

"He took her wrist into his mouth and drained all of the blood from her. He left her there to die. His face and his eyes," I hesitate. "I felt as though I were looking at pure evil."

Chapter 24: Out for Blood

As the sun comes up in the morning sky, William lays in the bed still resting when I decide to go down to the pool again and take another relaxing swim. I get up and walk over to the balcony of our suite to look down at the courtyard where the pool is located. No one is there and the sky is cloudy appearing as though it might rain again. I hope that it will remain this way so I can have some time alone to unwind my tight muscles from our late night on the town. I have no reason to fear being alone at the pool because there is no way Lawrence knows where we are. I will be safe. I make my way into the bathroom and put on my bathing suit along with some waterproof sunscreen. I pull a black terry cloth cover-up on over my bathing suit and then I leave the room with my key card in hand. The elevator ride down is slow. I walk across the courtyard to the small pool that is inviting me in. The water is clear and smooth, and it looks like a mirror. I slip off my cover-up revealing a black string bikini underneath and place it on a lounge chair beside me. I grab a fresh warm towel off the towel cart. I kick off my flip-flops and step into the heated pool slowly lowering myself down the alabaster steps. When the water is even with my waist I dive in, swimming the whole length of the pool and back. The water is warm, and it feels good against my always cool skin. The courtyard is filled with tropical plants and tall palms that provide shade from the infrequent sunlight peering from behind the clouds. Little sparrows fly back and forth from the trees above and I begin to think back at the time when William told her about his capability for communicating with nature. I am starting to wonder if I possess the same inside of me. It is a rare ability for an immortal. I decide that it will be alright if I don't find the magic inside of me because since I met William, I have found enough magic to last forever.

I continue to enjoy the warmth of the water as I relax on the steps with my head resting against the side of the pool, my body is immersed completely from the neck down. I close my eyes and think about my wedding night. I picture myself walking down the aisle of the St. Louis Cathedral to where William stood at the front waiting for me with loving anticipation in his beautiful pale blue eyes. As I daydream, I feel a hand touch me on the shoulder and it is cool like William's. Keeping my eyes shut, I hear a voice that isn't anything like William's.

"What a touching memory, you played it out so well for me in your mind since I wasn't invited."

I quickly sit up. I'm startled and move away from the hand that is touching me. I turn to see who it is. He is crouched over me at the edge of the pool, looking directly at me with bloodshot blue eyes. It is Lawrence. I begin to feel a familiar fear and dread wash over me again as soon as I lock eyes with his.

"Don't be frightened of me, Abigail. I don't know what you think you remember about me, but I can tell you it is probably false. I don't mean you any harm. I'm just a little misunderstood that's all. I can be a nice guy," he mutters in a slight raspy Southern drawl.

The smell of cigarettes and bourbon waft in the air as he speaks, and it makes me feel sick to my stomach. He stands up gaping down at me and I start to feel very vulnerable in the large open water of the pool, wrapping my hands around my chest to conceal myself from his prying eyes. He walks over to my lounge chair, picks up the towel, and brings it over to the edge of the pool. He unfolds it and holds it out for me between his open arms.

"Come, you should get out of the pool and sit next to me over there on the lounge chair so we can get to know each other better. We are family now, you know."

He winks at me and chuckles. It makes me feel very uneasy.

I slowly and hesitantly make my way up the steps of the pool keeping my gaze on him the whole time as he looks my body over with a lust in his eyes that is apparent as I move closer to him. I stand in front of him for a moment as the water drips off my wet bathing suit. My pale skin glistens in the brief sunlight. I stare into his desire-filled eyes. He lowers the towel and stares deeply back into mine. Then I reach out and take the towel from him hastily wrapping it around my body in one quick motion. I walk over to the chair and sit down, not knowing why I am staying and feeling like I should go back to the suite instead. I am strangely curious about him though and I want to know more. He follows me and sits too close for my comfort as he reaches out with his hand and places his fingers on the side of my face. I move away from his touch. I don't feel the warmth behind it like I do when William touches me.

"You remind me so much of her," he says with an emptiness to his tone.

"Elizabeth, you mean," I say quietly but with a hint of defiance in my voice.

"Yes, you are just as beautiful as she was. It is striking."

He looks as if he can see straight through me into the past. I am silent as I turn my face away from his glare.

"Oh, I'm sure my little brother has told you all about how much you remind him of her. I'm sure that is what attracted him to you in the first place. Too bad he found you first," he says as he tries to touch me on the arm, but I pull away.

"William loves me, for me. It doesn't have anything to do with her."

My tone has a sharp edge to it as I stare directly into his eyes.

"I'm sure that is what he has told you, even convinced you but…"

"But nothing…he loves me and only me." I interrupt.

"Do you remember Elizabeth being in love with me at one time?" He is smiling to himself as he looks up at the trees.

I think for a moment and feel like what he is saying is true, but I don't remember it.

"No," I reply, feeling very confused.

I try to tell myself not to believe anything that he says but it is hard as doubt is beginning to seep into my mind.

"Well, she was in love with me until she met my little brother. He took her from me, you know." His eyes have a hard stare in them as he looks up at the balcony to the suite where we are staying.

As I shift in the chair to move further from him my towel falls slightly from around my chest exposing the wet bikini top that clings to me. I pull it up quickly but not quickly enough, Lawrence has that look in his eyes again and it repulses me.

He then says, "Well I never saw as much of Elizabeth as I have seen of you today. William is one lucky man to have a woman as beautiful as you. I'm almost a little jealous of that brother of mine. Where is William anyway, he seems to leave you alone an awful lot."

"How did you find us here?" I ask while standing up.

"Oh, I have my connections here in New Orleans, you know."

His tone is shifty and esoteric.

"You mean spies," I say with even more disgust now by his presence.

"Something like that I guess you could say. I know you don't like me much, Eliza...I mean Abigail but that could all change one day soon...real soon."

I don't answer him. He frightens me and he knows it. As I am putting my flip-flops back on my feet, I hear William's voice from across the courtyard.

"Abigail, I didn't know where you had gone."

William's expression explains the fear that he feels.

I turn to look where Lawrence is sitting, and he is no longer there. William walks up to me and puts his loving arms around me saying, "Please, don't scare me like that again."

I nod and we head back up to the suite hand in hand. I don't tell him that Lawrence was at the pool with me and I know it is wrong of me to do. I feel that it might be something that I will come to regret later. The morning newspaper has been delivered to the suite and it is on the floor in the hallway in front of the door.

William picks it up and tucks it under his arm as he opens the door. We step into the room and he places the paper on the bar in the kitchen. He pours himself a glass of water and then turns to see the print in big bold black type across the front of the newspaper. It reads:

Woman found dead in an alleyway, drained of all blood, no wound found.

This is the second victim found in less than a week.

William and I look at one another.

"Do you think it could be…," I stop and quietly walk over to the window and look out at the courtyard below.

"What?" He asks standing near the door to the bedroom now.

"Lawrence," I say looking down at the pool and remembering my earlier encounter with him.

"Oh, no, I don't think so."

He shrugs at the thought.

"He's not a nice guy that's for sure but I don't think he has gone rogue."

"Don't you remember the vision that I had?" I ask, reminding him, turning around to face him now. My expression is one of distrust and disbelief.

316

William stares at me and seems confused by my reaction.

"I know that it is unusual for a newborn to kill his maker but even, so I don't think that Lawrence has anything to do with the two murders," he says.

"Can we leave today and go back home, please?" I ask and turn back around to face the window.

"Sure, if that is what you want."

He stood motionless in the doorway.

"Yes, it is. I will pack my things now."

I walk past him and into the bedroom shutting the door behind me. I know he doesn't understand the sudden change in my mood. I don't even understand my reaction and the only explanation I can come up with is that it has something to do with the headline on the newspaper not to mention the stress from seeing Lawrence earlier. William leaves me alone to pack and I turn on the television to watch the news. Local reporters are swarming around the scene of the mysterious crime. The news channel replays footage of the woman's body being carried away on a gurney in a body bag. The coroner's office says that there isn't any blood found in the victim's body and no apparent wounds. The police don't have any leads and are baffled by the way the woman was murdered. I turn off the television and start to think back at the vision I had about the night Lawrence was turned.

Chapter 25: Doubt

The car slowly rolls up the long driveway to our house on Shell Beach Drive and I feel a sense of relief to be home after our time in New Orleans. My thoughts linger on the warning that the old woman in the bar had given me. I can't quite shake the feeling that something bad is going to happen to me and I also can't shake the doubt that Lawrence has planted in my mind about William's love for me. I know in my heart that it feels right, at least to me, but how does he feel, I wonder. Am I just a replacement for the one true love he lost long ago?

"It's good to be back at home, isn't it?" He parks the car next to the house and turns to look at me. I gaze out the window at the house that I have grown to love and agree with him.

"You've been very quiet the whole way home. Is everything o.k.?" He asks reaching over and brushing my dark blonde hair away from my face.

"Yes, everything is alright."

My tone is flat and unconvincing.

I open the passenger side door and step out of the car leaving William sitting in the driver's seat. I walk up the path to the front porch and wait for him. He unloads the luggage out of the trunk and then meets me by the front door. He unlocks the door and I step into the house. Making my way up the stairs not saying another word, I turn to look at him as I walk into the master bedroom. He is peering up at me from where he stands, and I shut the bedroom door behind me. I know he is worried about me because it shows on his face and he knows that I am upset about the old homeless woman that we had encountered in New Orleans. He must also know that I am shaken up about seeing Lawrence too.

After a few minutes, I notice how quiet the house is and it is unsettling. I proceed back down the staircase to see where William has gone. The luggage has been left at the front door and I peer out the window that looks out onto the front porch. He must have called for Ghost because the bird sits perched on the banister of the porch railing and blinks his large round yellow eyes. William is stroking the back of the owl's head, seeming to communicate silently with him. I open the door and walk over beside him. William snaps back to reality and looks over at me.

"Do you remember when you told me that I saved you in the park that night?" He asks.

"Yes," I say.

"Well, it felt like it was the other way around. You saved me. I am now complete."

He continues to stroke the feathers on Ghost's back and stares out into the darkness of the night. Through the breaks in the thick pine trees, I can see the stars shining in the sky above. Lost in thought, I realize that William is now sitting down on one of the rocking chairs. He holds the owl as he smooths the feathers on its breast, looking up at me. I scan the large lot with my eyes and then fix them on the owl.

"It's a beautiful night," I say as I listen to the crickets chirping in the background. William leans back on the rocking chair and gazes out into the night.

"You look deep in thought. What were you thinking about?" I inquire.

"I was thinking about all of the many years that I spent alone in this life. I remember all the nights I would sit here on this porch feeling as though I had somehow been cursed and not knowing why or for what. There were so many nights that I wished that Lawrence had just let me die on the bayou that night. I felt trapped in some sort of limbo between heaven and hell. My soul was crying out for death with every breath that I took. A real death that would free me from the life that I was forced to live." He pauses.

"I felt the same way about my mortal life," I say as my eyes meet his and I smile faintly.

"I confronted Lawrence one night about what he had told Elizabeth. He claimed that he hadn't any idea what I was talking about. That it wasn't him that had told her about me dying. I knew it was a lie and I continued to press him on the issue until he finally admitted it. He said that he had done it because I had stolen her from him, and he wanted her back."

I sit quietly now on the porch swing, listening and looking down at the old wooden slates on the floor. The doubt hasn't left me and now it is creeping back into my brain, invading my every thought.

"The anger inside of him started to grow after Elizabeth died. It consumed him and I hated him after I found out what he had done. I could have killed him with my bare hands that night but something somewhere inside of me couldn't do it. I think it was because I had more than just a brotherly bond with him. He was my maker and I couldn't find the strength to kill my maker. I left New Orleans and never wanted to see him again. It had been a long time too until the other night at the old Bernard home. I didn't even know if he still existed and I didn't care either," he states plainly as he looks out into the darkness.

"Why do you love me, William?"

I turn to meet his pale blue eyes with my question. My demeanor is cold towards him as I shift into a more rigid position on the swing.

He pauses for a moment, surprised by what I have just asked him.

"I've told you why I love you, Abigail, why are you asking me this?"

"Just answer the question!" I yell, becoming increasingly upset.

He just sits motionless, stunned by my sudden emotional outburst, and seemingly not knowing how to react. He doesn't answer.

"Are you still in love with Elizabeth? Or are you in love with me? Which is it?"

I stand up next to the swing and glare at him.

"Where is all of this coming from? Why are you, suddenly, doubting my feelings for you?"

I can feel that he is hurt, and the pain can be heard in his voice. I am frozen in place with my arms folded tightly around my body not answering him.

"Are you only with me now because of her, because I remind you of her?"

Tears start to well up in my eyes.

William is silent and just stares at me and it's obvious to me that he does not know what to do or say. I turn quickly and walk back into the house, slamming the screen door behind me. I grab my purse off the foyer table and make my way back out the front door. William rushes over to me and takes me by the arm trying to stop me.

"Please Abigail…you know I love you," he pleads with me.

I pull away from him and continue out across the front lawn. He runs after me trying to make me listen, to understand, but he should be able to see in my eyes that I don't want to hear anything that he has to say to me.

"Did Lawrence do this? Did he plant this seed of doubt in you?" He asks as he walks beside me quickly to keep up with my pace, but I don't answer him.

"Where are you going?"

He stops as I walk forward further away from him.

"I'm going back where I belong, my house!" I yell back at him.

"But your car isn't here?"

"I'll walk it isn't that far!" I cry out as tears stream down my face. As I look back, I can see William motionless with a dumb-founded expression not knowing what to do only knowing that I don't want him near me, not at this very moment anyway.

The agony I feel as I walk away takes over my whole body. It feels like my soul is being ripped out of me. I hear him call out to Ghost.

"Go and keep a watch over her for me. Come back and let me know when she has made it home alright. Go," he says.

The owl flew fast and follows me as I walk down the road and into the park. I stomp furiously along the gravel pathway passing the small bench where I had sat the night, I wanted my mortal life to end. I slow down as I notice ahead of me the exact spot where William had taken me in his strong arms and saved me. As the tears start to flow down my face, I think back to the first night I saw him in the bookstore. His beautiful face occupies my every thought now and I don't know if I have the strength to continue walking away from him. I am so confused. My heart tells me to run back to his open arms, but my mind tells me to push on forward. I continue to walk at a much faster pace now, the separation from him tearing through me like jagged blades. I exit the park and run down the street to the front lawn of my old house. Fumbling for my house keys, I hear a rustling in the tree next to the porch and see Ghost perched on the branch above.

"I made it home alright, Ghost. You can go back and tell him now."

I unlock the door and go inside. Throwing myself down on the sofa and burying my face into the pillows I begin to cry as my mind spins with confusion and doubt.

"I knew this was all too good to be true," I mumble to myself into the damp spot on the pillow caused by my tears. I lay here in the dark empty house that I had gladly forgotten about since I had been in the happiness of William's home.

Daylight streams into the small living room and fills it with a soft glow. The light gently coaxes my eyes to open. I feel dazed as I stare out across the room. Then I remember where I am and why. My head is pounding but my heart feels very still. I close my eyes again and see his face staring back at me. I am a part of him and that will never change. My head starts to pound harder, as my mind is calling out for him. I can feel that he is near. I look out the window from where I sit on the sofa. It is a sunny day. Once again, the day is inappropriate to the way I feel. Then I walk over to the blinds pulling one of the slats up so that I can see more clearly out the window. William's black sports car sits in my driveway. I quickly let the slat fall back into place and stagger across the room to get a drink of water in the kitchen. Then suddenly there is a knock at the door, and I freeze perfectly still not moving one single inch.

"Abigail, please let me in. We need to talk."

William knocks at the door again, but I don't answer him.

"Please listen to me, Abigail. I know Lawrence did this to you. He is a master at mind control and persuasion. Please don't let him come between us like this. He's just jealous that we have one another."

Then there is silence as I expect he is waiting for an answer, but I remain as quiet as I possibly can. He knows I am here. I am sure of it. I continue to stand in the middle of the kitchen, listening.

"Before you came into my life, I had nothing. It was just a mere existence. You brought love back into my heart, Abigail, and you brought life back to me. Abigail, please."

Then silence again for several minutes as I walk closer to the door. I press my hand and my cheek against the wood. William starts to speak.

"I love the way you smile. The way your face lights up when you discover something new. I love the way your hair falls softly across your face when you are lying in my arms. I love the way your forehead crinkles into tiny little lines when you are thinking. I love the way your eyes sparkle when you investigate mine. I could list all the things that I love most about you and it would take me into the night or maybe into forever. All I know, Abigail, is that I love you and only you, and wherever you are, that is where I want to be."

I stare at the door feeling him on the other side but there is nothing, I say not a single word in reply. I wait for a moment and then I peer out of the window to see that he has walked back to his car. I quickly open the front door. He turns to see me and then rushes over to my side.

"Abigail."

I stop him by placing my finger on his lips and then I smile. He takes me into his arms, and we kiss.

"I'm sorry I ever doubted our love. I don't know what came over me," I say between frantic kisses.

"It was Lawrence. I would be willing to bet. What exactly did he say to you when you saw him in Elizabeth's old room that night?" William asks me.

"Not much, he called me by her name when he saw me. I had my back to him as he walked into the room and it was dark. You came home right after that."

I feel guilty because I am hiding information from him.

"He didn't say anything else to you?" He questions with a curious look on his face.

I lead him into the house and over to the dining room table where we both sit down. "What is it? Is there something you're not telling me?" He asks.

"Yes."

I stare at him, shaking my head up and down in agreement.

"What? Abigail, what happened?"

"I know I should have told you sooner, but do you remember the morning you found me at the pool alone and you were worried because you didn't know where I was at?"

"Yes." He answers.

"Well, I wasn't alone the whole time," I say.

"Lawrence was with you…how did he know where we were?"

William stands up suddenly and starts to pace back and forth alongside the table.

"He told me that he has connections in New Orleans and that found out through some other immortals that he knew," I answer.

William is still and stares out into space. Then he sits back down on one of the dining room chairs, leaning he places both of his elbows on the top of the table with his hands folded together in front of his face. He doesn't say a word.

"William, don't worry, it's alright. He's just an old drunk. He's harmless, right?"

"Did he touch you?" He asks looking up at me now.

"No, I don't know what you mean, inappropriately?"

I am confused by his question.

"No, but now that you mention it, did he?"

His eyes become slightly enraged.

"No, he didn't. He disgusted me by the way he looked at me though."

I tremble for a moment at the memory.

"Alright, you're sure then that he didn't touch you in any way," he asks one more time.

I think about it for a minute as I pause and look down at the floor. William is very still as he watches me, and it must become apparent by my body language that he had. It is then that I see William's temper begin to rise.

"Yes, he did touch me on the shoulder. He saw the memory that I was having about our wedding."

William stands up again and begins to pace some more, shaking his head.

"I don't understand, what…what is wrong with that?" I ask.

"I thought it was strange that he could see what I was thinking just by touching me. Is that one of his capabilities?"

"He knows," he comments with a look of defeat.

"Knows what?" I question.

"William, tell me, what does he know?"

"He knows that you can see into the past!"

He raises his voice slightly, which he has never done. I can see in his eyes that he is unusually upset but I don't understand why.

"What is wrong with that and how does he know? I was only having a memory about us and not anything else."

I am becoming even more confused now.

"Well, first, he can tell just by touching you. He can touch an immortal and be able to know what they can do. Secondly, I just don't like it. I have a very bad feeling about it."

"You told me that he was harmless, just an old drunk. Now you're telling me that he is dangerous."

My tone is a mixture of annoyance and fear.

"Why do you have a bad feeling about it? What could he possibly do?" I ask.

"I don't know. I'm probably just being paranoid," he says trying to convince himself of it.

"The only thing that worries me about it is that he used to be very obsessed with finding the lost treasures along the bayou. After I came to settle here, he would try to come to my house with the other crew members. He only tried to stay at my house once, but I refused him and threw him off my property. He never came back, but my old crewmates would tell me stories about how he would talk all of the time about the buried treasure and that he would spend his spare time searching for it."

"He was searching for the treasure that you were accused of stealing?" I ask him.

"Yes, and I now worry that you are in danger because he knows about your capability."

We stare at one another for a long time and then I speak.

"He wouldn't do that William," I say trying to sound convinced and I can see it in his eyes that he can't believe what I just said to him.

"How can you say that? After everything you know about him."

"I don't know. I just feel like he won't do anything like that. It happened so long ago. He can't possibly think that the treasure is still out there and even if it is there must not be much left to it all."

"You're probably right," he says as he leans over and kisses me on the lips.

"Everything will be fine, I'm not worried," I whisper and then stand up from the table to walk over into the kitchen.

"Would you like to go somewhere nice for dinner tonight?" He asks as he follows me and leans against the doorway. I open the refrigerator and start tossing the food into the garbage can.

"That sounds good, I am hungry."

"Are you ready to go back now?" He asks as he smiles at me.

"Yes, I am ready."

I smile back at him.

Chapter 26: Prized Possession

When we arrive back at his house William picks me up and carries me over the threshold.

"I didn't get a chance to do this last night."

He smiles as he carries me into the house. I wrap my arms around his neck and kiss him deeply. He kicks the door shut behind him and carries me up the stairs to the bedroom. He lays me on the bed and then he lays down next to me.

"Please don't ever leave me again, Abigail, you don't know the pain it caused me to see you walk away last night," he whispers as he gazes into my pale amber eyes.

"I promise," I reply and then I kiss him softly on the lips. He kisses me back more deeply and longer. Then we make love slowly, taking the time to explore one another in ways that we hadn't before done.

The night air is thin and breezy not thick and humid like most summer nights in Louisiana. The casino is busy with mortals gambling their money away and the aroma in the room is a mixture of cigarettes and blood. William and I walk across the casino floor to the other side where the lounge is located. We are greeted by a hostess who seats us in a nice quiet spot in the corner of the dimly lit room. William pulls the chair out for me and I sit down.

"I'll be right back. Are you going to be alright here by yourself?" He questions with concern in his tone.

"Yes, of course," I answer.

He kisses me and walks over to the hostess. I watch as she points him in a direction outside of the lounge. I wonder where he is going. As I follow him with my eyes I am distracted by the mortals on the casino floor gambling and drinking. I cast my gaze to the interior of the lounge and scan it for potential donors. A man and woman are sitting at the bar drinking and laughing. There is a group of people sitting at one of the larger tables in the middle of the room, talking loudly. Then I notice a promising prospect sitting at a table across from where I sit, a small woman who appears to be alone. I will keep an eye on this one. Dinner time can't come too soon. As I wait at the table, a waitress comes over and hands me a white note card folded in half.

"This is for you it is from your gentleman friend," says the waitress as she then turns and walks away. I open the note and read it silently to myself.

Meet me in Room 313 for the surprise of your life. -W

I smile, looking out across the casino floor at the elevators then quickly leave the table. I wonder what he has planned for us this time. He is always so romantic and full of little surprises. I cross the casino floor and then wait impatiently for the elevator to come. The doors open and I step inside pressing the button to the third floor. The ride in the elevator seems slow to me and I realize that it would have been faster to take the stairs. I anxiously anticipate the surprise rendezvous with William. Maybe he has arranged a private dinner for the two of us. He knows how much I relish the thought of not hunting for my food and I am feeling very hungry, almost weak. I turn towards the mirrored elevator walls to appraise my appearance, wanting to look my best for him. Pulling the lipstick out of my small handbag and freshening up my lips in the blood-red color that he loves so much, I hear the soft ring of a bell as the elevator reaches its destination on the third floor. The doors open wide and I step out into the hallway. I look both ways and then I see a sign on the wall in front of me pointing left for rooms 300 – 320. I turn to my left and head down the burgundy-carpeted hall until I come to room 313. The door to the room is cracked open slightly and I enter cautiously.

"William," I call out in a low uncertain tone as I walk further into the room. Then I notice that he isn't here and quickly I start to feel the uneasiness of the situation. Suddenly the door slams shut behind me and I turn immediately to see who it is, praying the whole time that it will be William. Instead, Lawrence is standing directly in front of me with a threatening look on his face and a low guttural growl coming from inside his chest. Then, as if, from out of nowhere, I am hit by something hard and I fall to the floor. It is his fist. He grabs me by one arm and pulls me up, throwing me across the room onto the bed. I try to scramble to my feet, but he is on top of me in a flash pinning me down.

"Surprise," he whispers in my ear.

I struggle beneath him and begin to feel as though I will win my freedom but then he swiftly raises his head and with his canines bearing down towards me, he bites me hard on the neck and begins drinking in my blood, draining half of the life out of my body. I am too weak to fight him anymore. He rolls onto his side next to me, stroking my cheek with the top side of his hand.

"You look much paler than usual, Elizabeth, are you thirsty?" He taunts.

The burn is beginning in the pit of my core, but this burn is much more intense than the one I feel from hunger. It is the same burn that I felt the night William made me immortal. Only this time I don't have the safety of his arms to see me through it. This time it means an end and not a beginning.

"This should do it," he says as he stands up and places a note for William on the desk near the window.

"Would you like to know what it says, my dear?" He asks.

I can't respond. I only writhe in pain.

"Oh, you're not talking to me now. Are you mad at me?"

He grins devilishly at me.

"Well, get over it," he says as he picks me up in his arms holding me over his shoulder and running down the hall to the stairwell. Leaving a trail of my blood behind him, he disappears with me into the pitch-black moonless night.

"William should be wondering where you are right about now. I can see him asking around if anyone has seen you and finding out that a message was left for you to meet him in room 313. He goes up to the room to find the blood and then the note that I have left for him. Oh, this is good. I wish I could see the fire in his eyes when he realizes what I have done."

He chuckles with a deep rasp in his throat.

I can't respond because I am too weak and having difficulty breathing. The massive loss of blood is slowly taking its toll on me. I feel as though I am having an out-of-body experience, watching as this all happens in slow motion around me. He throws me onto the back seat of an old rusted car. It smells putrid and I feel like gagging as I lay on top of smelly dirty clothes and trash. Slamming the back door, he jumps into the driver's seat and drives fast, peeling out in the parking lot and speeding away from the casino. I watch through blurry vision as the streetlights in the back window above me flash past one at a time in constant intervals.

Through the pain, I begin to imagine William stepping out of the men's room and quickly walking back into the lounge. From across the room, he can see that I am not at the table anymore. He sits down and waits, thinking that maybe I have gone into the ladies' room for a moment. Several minutes pass by and I haven't returned. He begins to get a little nervous.

"Miss, could you please tell me if you know where the young lady that was sitting at this table went?" He asks the waitress as she passes in front of the table.

She stops, shrugs her shoulders, and says, "I'm sorry, I don't know." Then she walks back to the bar. He stands up, walking out of the lounge and into the casino. He sees a young woman standing near the restroom area.

"Excuse me, I'm sorry to bother you but could you check and see if there is a young lady by the name of Abigail in the restroom. She has dark blonde shoulder-length hair and she is wearing a blue dress."

"Sure," she says, and then she enters the small restroom. She comes back out almost immediately.

"There's no one in there."

"Thank you for your help."

He smiles nervously at her. He moves around the casino floor looking across the smoke-filled room. When he doesn't see me, he walks back to the lounge hoping that maybe I am back at the table. As he enters the dimly lit lounge, he sees that I still am not there. He walks over to the table and sits back down. Looking down at the table he notices a small white folded note card. The one that Lawrence had sent to me. He picks it up and opens it. He reads what is written inside. Hatred smolders in his eyes intermingled with terror as he crumbles the note card and throws it down on the table. He jumps up and takes off, running across the casino floor, pushing several people out of his way. He makes it to the elevators and then realizes that the stairs will be much faster. He is frantic and he fears the worst. Reaching the third floor he runs down the long hallway looking at every door for the room number. He stops almost immediately when he sees blood on the floor in front of him. He can smell that it is mine. Turning towards the door with the number 313 marked neatly on the front of it, he busts it in with one swift motion and then enters the room to find it empty. He can see that there has been a struggle as he walks into the middle of the room and there is fresh blood on the bed near the windows. He looks around the room for any evidence that will lead him to me when he sees the other note. He picks it up with shaky hands and reads it.

She is mine now, little brother. – Lawrence

With a fury stronger than anything he has ever felt before he lands his fist into the center of the desk smashing it into pieces.

I feel like we have been driving for about ten or fifteen minutes from what I can tell when Lawrence finally stops the car. The motion is making me dizzy and extremely disoriented. I see him get out of the car and then he slams the door behind him, and I can hear his footsteps on the gravel beneath his feet. I lay here in the dark car looking out into the space in front of me, trying as hard as I can to maintain consciousness. My eyes are heavy in my head and I have trouble keeping them open. I can hear the faint sound of glass breaking in the distance. Struggling to lift my arm to open the car door, I attempt to move my body closer to reach the handle, but I am too weak. I just lay staring up into the tall trees outside the car window, I see a large bird fly past, and then it flies past again. Hearing it call out softly as it soars through the night air, I realize it is Ghost. Knowing now that Lawrence has brought me to William's house I slip in and out of unconsciousness.

I hear Lawrence walking back with a pair of keys and I see through the car window that he holds a shovel in his hand. He walks around to the back of the car and throws the shovel into the trunk. Then he returns to the driver's seat. He backs down the long gravel driveway, turning the car and crossing the road pulling up in front of the pier where the yacht is docked. Jumping out of the car he walks over and opens the trunk of the old car taking the shovel out. Leaning it against the side of the car, he opens the back door grabbing me by my arms. Pulling my limp body out of the backseat, he holds me close to his chest and buries his face in my hair, taking a long deep breath, savoring my scent.

"You smell so good, Elizabeth, I can't wait to get you alone," he whispers in my ear.

Flinging me over his shoulder, he grabs the shovel and heads toward the pier. I am very still and fall unconscious for the moment but as he walks with me down the long pier, I wake up momentarily. Not knowing where we are, I look around and see the yacht. I recognize it through my blurry vision. As we get closer, I see the name, my name, on the side of the yacht near the front. Lawrence lifts me over the railing that runs along the side of the yacht and drops me onto the deck below. I hit it hard. I try to lift my body as I pull my dead weight with my hands clenching the side of the railing. It is of no use though because I am still too weak. I fall back down, out of breath, and in more pain. Lawrence unties the yacht from the pier and jumps inside of it. Picking me up with one arm, he carries me down to the cabin below and lays me on the bed. He rushes back up the stairs and I begin to feel the yacht speed down the lake towards the ship channel. I feel the yacht turn right and then it slows down before coming to a complete stop. He kills the engine and I can hear him docking it.

He descends the stairs into the cabin where I lay on the bed with two bottles of wine in his hands.

"What a nice boat. My little brother sure did well for himself. You know he never once invited me over to his house during all these years. I tried to visit him, but he kicked me out. He's never had very good manners. I honestly don't know what you see in him." He looks over at me as if waiting for a reply, but I remain silent.

"Oh, so you're still not talking to me, huh?"

He opens one of the bottles of wine and takes a swig out of it.

"You know, now that I see all of the good fortunes that he has had while I have barely scrapped by day after day, year after year in this God-forsaken immortal life, it is just beginning to piss me off. I don't think I'll mind one bit separating you two permanently after all. He's just had too much good luck for his good, Elizabeth."

"I'm not Elizabeth. Don't call me by her name." I muster up the strength to rebuke what he has just said.

"Well, you know what missy?" He says as he pulls my hair to his face and sniffs it.

"*All* I see when I look at you is *her* face staring back at me."

He leans in closer and kisses me on the lips. His touch is revolting, and I spit at him but he only laughs loudly in response.

"Rejecting me all over again for that brother of mine, huh, well, he won't get his happy ending after all. I'll make sure of that," he says as he wipes the spit off his face and stands above me by the side of the bed looking down into my defiant eyes.

"Now the only thing I ask of you is to be a good girl for me and remember... remember where that treasure is buried. As soon as I find it, I'll be rich, richer than my dear brother, and then maybe you will be interested in me. You do like money, don't you?" He inquires as he walks over to the other side of the cabin and pours himself a glass of red wine from the bottle.

"Everyone is for sale at the right price. Isn't that true, Elizabeth?"

He sips on the wine and stares at me.

"Stop calling me that. I will never love you. There is no amount of money on earth that will make me yours. I belong to William and he belongs to me."

Lawrence suddenly jumps across the small room and pins me to the bed, slapping me across the face.

"Shut up! You're making me sick, just hearing your voice right now is turning my stomach!" He shouts in my face.

I am in more pain now and too weak from the loss of blood to fight him off. I lay on the bed staring up at him in fear as his face glazes over with an expression that I don't understand. His eyes seem to hold certain remorse for what he has just done to me.

"I'm sorry, Elizabeth, I didn't mean to hurt you. Please forgive me," he pleads.

I turn my face away from his and begin to cry softly. He kisses me on the cheek and leaves me alone. He then walks back up to the deck of the boat.

I start to stir ever so slightly, and I slowly begin to open my eyes. My vision of William is still blurry, and I feel extremely dizzy. My head pounds and the burn is still intense. I feel a presence next to me on the bed. Lawrence is watching me closely as he holds my hand in his, hoping to see any memory that might lead him to the treasure while I slip in and out of consciousness.

"William..." I say in a low muffle.

"Well, hello, there. Are you ready to remember now?" He asks me.

"What? Where am I?" I bellow as I try to focus on the face in front of me. Then the realization of my surroundings hit me. I roll over onto my side with my back to him.

"Where's the treasure buried?" He probes becoming increasingly impatient.

"You mean the treasure that William was accused of stealing, you're crazy if you think it's still out there."

I start to laugh, mocking him and then the laugh turns into a hoarse cough.

"Oh, but my dear, I'm not after the treasure William was accused of stealing because you're right it's not there anymore," he says with a grin.

"What do you mean? How do you know…," I murmur as I roll back over, facing him now to see the expression on his face. His eyes tell the story and I know what he means.

"You… You were the one? You stole the treasure and hid it. But why, why did you frame your brother for it?"

"Oh, you don't know anything, do you? Sure, I was the one who stole the treasure, but I didn't directly rat out my brother. Someone else did that. I may have just…oh… I don't know… maybe put the little birdie in someone else's ear. Those shipmates of ours never liked William very much anyway and you know some pirates just like a good fight. They were so hungry to find the missing treasure for Lafitte in hopes of a reward, that they would have believed anything you told them. Speaking of hungry…" He saunters towards me and latches onto my wrist sucking the life right out of me little by little.

When he is finished, I am weaker than I had been before. I am losing my immortal life slowly and the fire inside of me begins to burn hotter. The pain is excruciating and almost unbearable. Struggling to find my voice I ask in a shaky tone, "What happened to the treasure then? Why are you so destitute?"

"Destitute? What do you mean?" He asks as he wipes the blood off his lips.

"Down and out, why are you so down and out?" I mumble, doubling over in pain.

"Oh, my dear Elizabeth, that was nearly two hundred years ago. That money is long gone now."

"Why did you save William that night on the bayou after the others had left him for dead?"

I twist in the bed and turn to see his face more clearly.

"I couldn't just stand there and let my little brother die right in front of me. What do I look like, a monster? Don't answer that."

His laughter is abrasive as the sound comes from deep inside his throat, but my eyes betray my thoughts of agreement with his question as he stares directly at me.

"Why, Elizabeth, that's hurtful." He continues to laugh.

"Now where are my cigarettes?" He pushes himself up off the bed, feeling around in his pockets and then he walks over to the cabinet where he left them. He lights one and blows the smoke in my face. He picks up the bottle of red wine and takes a swig.

"Ah, that's good. My little brother buys the expensive stuff," he says as he wipes his mouth.

"Well, to answer your earlier question about why I didn't just let William die, I guess it was because I just wasn't ready for the competition to end," he says with a smirk.

"You mean your competition for Elizabeth's love," I respond in a flat tone tinged with pain.

He shakes his head in agreement and then he staggers over to the bed. He sits down next to me and smooths my hair back away from my face.

"I honestly didn't know that she would kill herself that night. I thought I could turn her and make her mine before William came back. And I didn't know if he would ever come back either. I loved her so much, Abigail. I never wanted her to die."

His expression is one of sheer agony as he caresses the side of my face.

"Do you feel sorry for me now?" He asks with a wicked look in his eyes.

"You're sick," I mutter.

"You never really loved her. You just wanted her for her money, you thought of her as a prized possession."

He laughs and then starts to cough cigarette smoke from his lungs as he beats his chest with his fist in the process.

"You're right, Abigail. You know so much, don't you? I bet you never lost anything or anyone close to you before."

He walks over to the tinted glass door of the cabin and then turns around and faces me.

"I just didn't want William to have her," he says.

"I just have one question to ask you. Did you kill the women in the news back in New Orleans?" I question.

"Well, let's see, should I answer your question truthfully? Um, I can tell you all about the night after I left you and my brother at Elizabeth's old house on Royal Street. I walked along the streets of the French Quarter and the fog slowly started to roll in around me as I made my way to Bourbon Street for the only solace I truly know and the only one that comes in my favorite form, a whiskey bottle. With my daily wage shoved deep into my pants pocket from working the docks during the day, I walked along the crowded streets full of mortal tourists. I entered my regular nightly refuge and sat down at the bar motioning to the bartender. He asked me what I wanted, and I told him whiskey, straight up, of course. A band played loudly in the far corner and I stared down into my glass of whiskey. My thoughts always seem to bring me back to another place that was much simpler, warmer, and kinder. I stared at the whiskey for several minutes before drinking it, as my heart ached within my chest, longing for a time that now only feels like a distant dream to me. The warmth began to chill as I stared at my reflection in the mirrored wall behind the bar. Lines crease my face now and my eyes are dead, void of any life. That night I was out for blood. I was angry over my brother's good fortune and I wanted to take it out on someone. Seeing William with you had brought back a lot of unwanted memories and the demons inside of me were feeling restless. My anger began to simmer. Slowly the bar filled up with more mortals as I watched them walk in from where I sat hunched over my whiskey. I was feeling very thirsty and the drink in my hand wasn't going to quench it. I wanted blood but most of all, I wanted revenge.

The door swung open and then slammed shut, catching my attention. The stale night air flooded the room with the swinging motion of the door. A group of young women walked over to the table closest to where I sat. There were four of them. The first three I didn't notice but the one that trailed behind made me pay closer attention. She was of average height and well-built. She had deep reddish auburn hair about shoulder length. She reminded me of my maker. She would do, I thought as I stared at the pretty young mortal. I watched as she sat down at the table. I followed her every move with my eyes. A waitress walked over and took the group's order and then left the table. She came back shortly with two pitchers of beer. I watched as the young woman drank and laughed. I was taken by her beauty, just like the night I met my maker. I licked my lips thinking about what I had in store for her.

As I watched out of the corner of my eye, a man walked up to the table. He began talking to the women. Then his attention became focused on the pretty red head. He spoke with her for a few moments as I watched in disgust, my anger turning into a jealous rage. I signaled the bartender to bring me another drink. The young woman got up and followed the man over to the pool tables as I followed them with my glare. I watched the man closely, sizing him up but of course, no mere mortal was any match for my powers. Then my rage turned into envy. I began to long for the simplicity of being mortal again and the warm touch of a woman with love in her eyes for me, not revulsion. In case you haven't noticed, Abigail, I am no longer physically attractive. Those days ended after Elizabeth died, it seemed as though a part of me died with her that night. Maybe it was the guilt that had eaten away at me through the years or maybe it was the hatred for my brother, William. It doesn't matter either way because when I see a woman that I want, I just take her. She is defenseless.

Well, the couple continued playing pool well into the night as I patiently watched and waited. It was the early hours of the morning when they finished. The young woman waved goodbye to her friends, grabbed her purse from the table, and left out the door with the man by her side. I quickly paid for my tab and followed them out into the hazy night. The streets were less crowded as I paced slowly a short distance behind them. Music filled the air

349

from the open doors of the bars that lined the sides of the street. I began to control the woman's thoughts with my mind as we walked further into the darkness. I placed fear and doubt in her head. I forced her to tell her companion to leave her alone, without even saying one word to her. I filled the man's mind with anger, and he didn't question the young woman's motives. He spoke a few choice words to her and then abruptly turned around leaving her alone by the side of an old building.

I watched as the man walked away. I continued to pursue the woman guiding her every move with my thoughts. Shepherding her down a dark narrow alley, I then closed in on her suddenly. She turned and stood frozen, hypnotized by my stare. I took her into my arms caressing the smooth silkiness of her skin. Then kissing her softly on the lips and taking in her arousing aroma with one long deep breath. I ran my hands through the back of her reddish-brown hair combing her long locks with my fingers. Leaning in ever-so-slightly, I placed my ear against her heaving chest and felt the warmth of her bosom with the side of his face. I listened to the melodic rhythm of the heart beating inside. The sound drummed in my mind like a symphony, awaking my very soul.

Slowly raising my face upward and tracing her silhouette with my lips I reached her neck, the tan of her bare skin, intrigued me. The pulse moving in time with her heart at the base of her long delicate neck excited me. The sensuality of it was nearly too much for me to take and I wished she was Elizabeth. I lingered, enjoying the moment almost feeling human again. Then I was abruptly reminded of my carnal lust, not the lust for flesh but the blood lust. The smell of her twisted my insides into knots and the burn began to rise through my body. So, did my anger for what I had become. It had simmered into a boil now as my lips neared her throat. I bit down on the woman, drinking in her blood and taking her life. I drained her dry and dropped her to the cold damp stone street beneath." Lawrence stares deep into my wide-open eyes.

"Now I have a question for you, Abigail. Do you believe what I have just told you?"

He turns and leaves the room as he scales up the stairs to the top of the yacht. My eyes roll back into my head and I lose consciousness again. I am awakened to something cold and wet on my face. Lawrence stands over me holding an empty cup.

"Wake up. You'll have plenty of time to sleep when I'm done with you."

He leans over and wipes my face off with his dirty fingers.

"Now, come on, tell me where the treasure is?" He prods.

"What treasure?" I question.

"Stop playing stupid, Abigail! Napolean's treasure!" He yells as he stumbles closer to me intoxicated by the bottles of wine he has ingested.

I remember what William told me when we were talking about the legend of the buried treasure. He mentioned that Lafitte had his men bury some of Napolean's wealth along the bayou.

"I'm too weak to remember, Lawrence. You've drained me of too much blood. Please, I need to feed!" I plead with him, but it does not affect him. He only stares at me in amusement.

"You're a pretty good actress, Abigail, but I'm sorry you're just going to have to do your best remembering what little energy you have. I can't risk you gaining your strength back."

"What happened? Why aren't you referring to me as Elizabeth anymore?" I inquire.

"Oh, I decided that you're nothing like her. She was a much better woman than you'll ever be."

He stares coldly at me. Then I hear the cry of an owl from outside of the yacht in the far distance.

Chapter 27. Buried Treasure

As I slip into unconsciousness again, I see in my mind that Lawrence is now sitting on the deck of the yacht staring out at the dark murky water of the ship channel and the moon is but a sliver in the clear night sky and the stars shine brightly above. I can feel him wishing that his life had turned out differently. He throws his used-up cigarette into the water and he stands up and stretches. Then he descends the stairs down to where I am lying on the bed.

My eyes pop open and I begin to yell.

"What is it?" He scolds.

"I remember," I say hastily.

"You're not trying to fool me, are you?"

He looks at me with skepticism written across his face.

"No…no, I remember. I see it in my mind. It's not far from where William was left for dead that night on Contraband Bayou. It's in the same spot."

I try to maneuver myself over to the edge of the bed but can't budge my weight.

"I don't believe you. That's too coincidental. You're making it all up."

He turns to walk back up the steps.

"No, I'm not. Do you remember when the other shipmates placed a small white cross in memorial to William because they thought he was dead?" I ask.

"Yes, go on…" he turns and walks over to the side of the bed.

"Well, it is also to mark the same spot
where Napolean's treasures are buried, so they wouldn't forget," I say breathlessly.

"Oh, yeah, x marks the spot," Lawrence responds while scratching his head and then sits down next to me.

"Only in this case, a cross marks the spot," I say as I look up at him, hoping he will believe me.

"Good work, Abigail."

He jumps and runs up the stairs to the deck of the boat. I can feel the boat drifting a little as it begins to move from the shore of the island. I hear the boat motors start-up and can sense that the boat is moving. I suddenly feel a surge of fear take over me because I am bluffing. I didn't remember anything about the buried treasure, and I will pay dearly when he finds out that it is all a lie. I can only hope that William will find me in time. I begin to cry at the thought of him searching for me. I close my eyes and picture his face. I can see his beautiful pale blue eyes in my mind gazing at me warmly. I can feel his strong arms wrapped around me providing comfort from the searing pain. It feels so real that I try to convince myself that he is lying next to me but then as the yacht takes a hard left turn I am rocked back to reality. I open my eyes and wonder if I will ever see him again. Tears stream down my face.

We seem to have traveled about a mile or two down the ship channel and I know that we are getting closer. Then the motors are quiet as we drift on the water for a few seconds and then I feel a jolt as the boat seems to have hit the shore, stopping completely.

"Let's go. Get up!" Lawrence commands as he makes his way back down the stairs and stands at the foot of the bed looking at me expectantly. He laughs loudly because he knows that I am too weak to move.

"Do I have to do everything?" He asks as he rolls his eyes and moves closer to me, pulling me up by my arms and hanging me over his shoulder again. Carrying me back up to the deck of the boat he walks over to the edge and carefully jumps down onto the marshy ground. There is no need for flashlights because of our capability for night vision. I can see the little yellow eyes of alligators reflecting off my vision as they pop up and then descend back under the black water.

"It's over there," I say as I point him in the right direction. He lumbers through the tall grass for several minutes before stopping in front of the small white cross under the big oak tree. He places me down on the soft ground near the tree. I begin to think about the significance of the small white cross to William. He told me that it symbolizes one life ending and another life beginning. I can't help but feel like my immortal life is now ending although it had only newly begun.

"I'm going to get the shovel. Don't go anywhere," Lawrence says and laughs loudly then runs back to the yacht. He comes back quickly and starts digging in front of the cross. I watch him as he curses the ground in which he digs, stopping for a minute to catch his breath. It comes to my attention that vampires are usually extremely physically fit but that he must be the exception to the rule because he doesn't appear to be. I remember William telling me that Lawrence had been consumed with hatred for so many years. As I drift in and out of consciousness, Lawrence continues to dig for the treasure. I dream about William, my guardian angel. I see him standing over the small white cross crying. He is grieving a loss. Then I see the name on the cross and it reads, Abigail. Suddenly, a voice wakes me from the dream, and it is a hoarse-sounding devilish voice. Lawrence is standing over me.

"I've been digging and digging! I don't see any treasure!" He glares at me with fire in his bloodshot eyes.

"I don't know, Lawrence. That is what I saw in my memory."

I feel sick because I know what is coming next. I can see it in his eyes, and I can feel it in the pit of my stomach.

"You're lying to me."

He reaches out and touches me on the arm.

"I knew it, nothing. There is no memory. There never was…only lies."

He descends upon me, biting me hard on the neck again only this time he doesn't stop. He drains me of all blood. I am barely clinging to life. I can still see with blurry vision and hear faintly. Pulling away from me with blood running down his chin, he licks his lips. He stands beside my body and kicks me into the shallow hole that he has just dug. Taking the shovel in his hands, he begins to cover me with fresh dirt when I hear a voice coming from behind him.

"Where is Abigail?"

A deep growl fills the air around us. I see Lawrence turn around and William is standing there.

"I don't know, little brother, she's your wife. You should take better care of your loved ones you know."

Lawrence turns back to finish filling the hole with dirt. William jumps from where he is standing and tackles Lawrence to the ground. Lawrence pushes him up and off across the clearing.

Quickly he has William backed up against a tree. They growl deeply at one another as William takes the upper hand and knocks Lawrence back away from him. Lawrence goes straight for William with canines exposed as William jumps through the air and slams him against a tree next to the grave where I lie. Lawrence hits the tree with extreme force and a jagged branch impaled him through the chest. It punctures his heart and his limp body hangs from the tree.

"Brother, you can't kill me. We're family."

I can hear Lawrence plead for his life.

"Abigail is my family now! Tell me where she is!" William yells.

"But I am your maker. What about the unbreakable bond between us?" Lawrence asks with eyes that are cold and emotionless even when faced with immortal death.

"My bond is with Abigail now, nothing else matters to me. Now tell me where she is!"

"It's too late, William, I'm sorry. Once again, you're too late. She is gone. She's dead."

Lawrence glares at William one last time. Then William grabs the shovel that lay beside his feet and rams it into Lawrence's neck severing his head from his body.

William looks down at the freshly dug hole in front of the cross. He sees me exposed through the dirt. Jumping down from the tree gently but swiftly, he starts to brush the dirt away from my body.

"Abigail. Oh my God. Abigail," he cries, pulling me out from underneath the dirt and cradling my lifeless body in his arms.

"Abigail, please baby, don't go. Don't leave me, not now. You have to come back."

My body remains motionless and he quickly bites his wrist letting the blood from his body flow into my mouth. I can feel myself slipping away. He waits but there is nothing, I remain lifeless.

"Don't leave me, baby, please, I know you are still in there," he whispers in my ear.

"Oh, God, please," he cries out in agony. He holds me tight against his chest rocking with me back and forth. Still nothing. As he holds me, he slowly begins to sing the words to the song from our first dance.

"Darling, Je Vous Aime Beaucoup…You know you've completely stolen my heart…I love you, yes I do," his voice is low and shaky. He silently sits with me cradled to his chest as tears begin to stream down his face. One of them falls and lands on my cheek rolling onto my parted lips. He continues to hold me close, placing his face against mine and kissing me softly on the mouth. His tears fall onto my skin as he moves his ear to my chest hoping to hear the beat of my heart but there is nothing. He continues to lay there for some time with me in his arms and his head presses against my chest, listening to the empty hollow inside. Then suddenly my heart starts to beat faintly. He leans in closer to my mouth and he feels my cool breath on his cheek. I am barely hanging on to life. He picks me up gently and places me on the ground beside the hole. Picking up a can of gasoline that sits near the tree, he douses Lawrence's dead body with it and lights a match tossing it in the same direction. The tree that impales him goes up in flames. William then bends down and picks me up carrying me back to the yacht. He lays me down on the bed and covers me with a blanket. Steering the boat away from the land he turns it around and heads for home.

Chapter 28: Home Sweet Home

William carries me up the stairs to the bedroom and places me on the bed. He washes the dirt off my badly bruised body and changes me into a nightgown. He lays next to me and listens to my heart faintly beating. It is getting stronger by the moment. My eyes start to flutter, and I open them into little slivers testing out space around me. William's face is the first thing I see. I manage a tiny smile but can't talk. Then I shut my eyes again, lying perfectly still.

He offers me his wrist placing it next to my lips as the blood seeps into my mouth. As I slowly drink in some of his blood carefully, he begins to grow tired and weak too. He closes his eyes and rests with me through the early morning hours until the afternoon. He awakes to see my eyes open, watching him.

"Abigail," he whispers and kisses me softly on the lips. I smile at him.

"What happened?"

My voice is shaky and weak.

"Don't worry about that now. You need your rest," he answers.

"Everything is alright. Lawrence will never hurt you again."

I close my eyes as he places his hand on my cheek, caressing my soft ivory skin.

"I don't know what I would have done if I had lost you," he whispers in my ear.

Several days have passed now and William finds different reasons for mortals to occupy the home. He must feed more since he is sharing with me to build up my strength. He won't leave me alone in the house for even a second. He calls the maid service to come out to the house a couple of times and he feeds off them. He then offers some of the blood to me through his veins but as I regain more strength, I can feed on a donor on my own.

Standing in the doorway to the bedroom, he watches me as I rest. He walks over and climbs into bed with me as I turn to face him.

"You're looking much better," he says quietly.

"Thank you, I feel much better," I replied holding my hand out for his. He holds my hand gently, kissing the top of it.

"What happened, William? I don't remember everything."

I cast my gaze on his pale blue eyes, waiting for an answer.

"Lawrence left you a note at the casino to meet him in one of the rooms. You thought it was from me. Once I realized that you had been tricked by Lawrence, I rushed to the hotel room, but it was empty and I saw signs of a struggle. I ran back down the stairwell to the casino floor. Pushing past the mortals on my way out to the parking lot, I jumped into my car and sped away. I raced across town until made it to the house. I thought you might be home and I was calling out to you. I searched all the rooms, but nothing had been touched or was out of place. I bolted back down the stairs and into the living area and then I turned toward the back of the house. I spotted the back door hanging ajar and the broken glass on the floor. I readied myself for an attack but still, there wasn't any sign of Lawrence or you. I slowly and cautiously made my way around the kitchen to see if anything had been stolen. The keys to the yacht were gone. I rummaged through the cabinet drawer where I always leave the keys to the yacht, but they weren't there. Then I ran back through the house and out the front door, across the lawn, down the driveway, and out to the edge of the road. I could see the pier across the road and the yacht was missing. So, I ran out onto the pier and scanned the water's surface, but I couldn't see the yacht anywhere. I summoned Ghost to my side. I waited for several seconds but he didn't come. Suddenly Ghost came soaring through the air from the west side of the lake. I could see my old friend heading straight for me. He lands swiftly and safely onto my outstretched hand. I stroked his feathers and told him that he was a good boy. I ask him if he saw where you and Lawrence went and after listening carefully to the bird's thoughts I know exactly where Lawrence had taken you. I felt the fury building inside of me." Then he kisses me on the forehead.

"I remember the note and seeing him in the hotel room. I remember being in the car as he drove to the house and I remember being on the yacht. But I don't remember what happened after I led him to the clearing."

William hesitates for a minute not wanting to recall that terrible night, but he knows that I need to know what happened.

"Well, he drained you and buried you in the hole that he had dug while searching for the treasure. I walked up on him and we fought. He was impaled by a broken tree branch and when he wouldn't tell me where you were, I killed him."

"How did you find me?" I ask as I place my head on his chest.

"I saw your hand sticking out of the dirt. The gold from your wedding ring caught the light and signaled me to you." He presses his face on the top of my head and breathes in deeply.

"I remember seeing and hearing Ghost during the time that Lawrence had me. You sent him to find where he had taken me?" I ask as I play with the buttons on his shirt.

"Yes."

I can feel his cool breath in my hair, and it sends welcomed shivers through my body.

"How did you get to me without the yacht?" I shift my body and look up at him.

"I took the Jet Ski."

"I didn't know you had a Jet Ski," I say and smile.

"It's a good thing."

"Yes, it's a very good thing." He smiles back at me and then we kissed on the lips.

"What has been all of the commotions on the outside of the house for the past couple of days?" I ask as I sit upright in the bed.

"Oh, nothing, I'm just having some maintenance done around the house." He pats my hand and kisses me on the cheek.

"Are you feeling strong enough to walk now?" He asks.

"Yes, please let me out of this bed already, Dr. Delaflote. You have been wonderful to me, but I need to get up and stretch my legs." I smile and wink at him.

"Your color is better and your eyes have that piercing sparkle that I love so much. Alright, I'll let you out on one condition." He holds his hand out to stop me from bounding out of the bed.

"What?" I ask with a cautious tone to my voice and an edge of impatience.

"You have to come outside with me in the front for a moment. I have something that I want to show you."

He has that mischievous look in his eyes again that I have become accustomed to seeing. He helps me out of the bed and I hold onto him until I am sure of my footing. When I realize that I am strong enough to stand on my own I take the first step. I walk out of the bedroom and down the staircase. He opens the door for me, and I step outside onto the front porch. We walk hand in hand down the steps and onto the front lawn. As I turn around, looking up at the house, tears fill my eyes. The house is painted in a fresh coat of antique white and the shutters are painted a brilliant black. It looks new again and it is beautiful.

William whispers, "Welcome home, Abigail. Welcome home."

Made in the USA
Monee, IL
19 February 2022

91498136R00203